Moth to a Flame

Michael Omer

Moth to a Flame Copyright © 2015 by Michael Omer
All rights reserved.

Cover art Copyright © 2015 by Shahar Kober
All rights reserved.

For Yael

Author's Note

Moth to a Flame is part of a series about a town called Narrowdale. This is not a real town, and will not be found on any map.
Which is probably a good thing.
There are several links in this book. These links are actual live links to Amy's blog. Though they are not crucial for the story, Amy is awesome and her blog is fun to read. It's worth mentioning that no one was hurt during the production of this blog. Why? Oh, no reason (author walks away, whistling innocently).
Amy is also fictional, as are the rest of the characters in this book.

Chapter One

The thing that the principal refuses to understand is that Ron Hammond, the missing history teacher, cannot be replaced. Everyone agrees about that. Well… all the girls agree about that. The boys in the class couldn't care less. Ron Hammond, with his well-developed body, his tight-fitting shirts, his amazing hair. His "please, call me Ron," accompanied by a devilish smile, full of perfect white teeth. Who can replace *that*? No one, that's who.

And yet, a replacement there is, teaching us about the four freedoms.

Is there anything more important than freedom? The human race has always strived for freedom. Freedom from oppression, freedom from ignorance, freedom from persecution. How we long to soar on the wings of freedom. Specifically, how I would love to soar on the wings of freedom out of this lesson about the four freedoms in Roosevelt's State of the Union speech in 1941.

It's quite impressive how dull freedom can become in the hands of a boring teacher.

"Can anyone name the four freedoms in Roosevelt's speech? Anyone? Anyone? Freedom one: speech and expression…"

I'm sure that back in 1941, President Roosevelt's speech was all the rage. People probably talked about nothing else. They would be like, "Hey, Sam, have you heard the State of the Union speech?" and

Sam would reply, "Have I? Why, I've listened to it three times today. It's my favorite State of the Union speech. I have a poster of it in my room!" But I'm not sure I can relate to it the way they did. Definitely not when the content of the speech is being dismantled by Mrs. Fletcher, the replacement history teacher.

"Freedom four: freedom from fear…"

I'm pretty sure that once you assign numbers to freedoms, they begin to lose their meaning. I sigh and glance at Coral. She is sitting, her entire body alert, drinking in each and every word that leaves Mrs. Fletcher's mouth, her long auburn hair tucked carefully behind her ears. How can someone concentrate so hard on anything? Perhaps she's sleeping with her eyes open? Or dead? I poke Coral with my finger. She slowly turns her head and looks at me. Her eyes are full of uncomprehending irritation. Who are you and why are you bothering me, her dark brown eyes seem to ask me. She turns back to the teacher. Perhaps this is not Coral. Perhaps it's just her body, her brain snatched by aliens. Only in Narrowdale do aliens, uh… snatch the brains of students…?

I guess not.

Okay, Amy, stop mucking about. This lesson is important. I open my notebook, leave a few empty lines to fill in the missing details and begin summarizing Mrs. Fletcher's wise words.

When the president says beware the eagle of America he lists his dreams with world stage

I stare at the sentence I just wrote. I might have missed a few words there. I definitely spaced out for a moment, and she probably said something important that I didn't write down. Either that, or President Roosevelt was a pretty strange guy. I sigh and put my pen down. I can't really listen in class. That's something that other people do. I'm more of a "not listening in class" kind of girl.

I look at the time. That's impossible! Twenty-three minutes left? We've already been in this class for five days. Has time really stopped altogether?

"What are the president's thoughts about those who do not support what he's asking? Anyone? Anyone? He thinks that…"

Mrs. Fletcher should receive an award for the way she says "anyone." She says it as if it is merely a cough, or a sneeze, something that punctuates her lifeless monologue. By no means is it a word that implies that she is interested in having someone say, "Yes! I know the answer to that!"

I idly wonder if Mrs. Fletcher will stay. She's been teaching us for almost four weeks already. It is by far the longest a replacement has stayed ever since Ron Hammond, the previous history teacher, disappeared a month and a half ago.

The first replacement was Mrs. Thompson, a young, energetic teacher who immediately acquired the unhappy nickname "The Brain." She started out by mispronouncing half of the names in the class and followed by trying to get us to introduce ourselves by stating our name and favorite animal. That tactic blew up in her face almost instantly. It took her ten minutes to get everyone to calm down after a cat/reproductive organ pun. Later she accidentally said that Boston was a state (at least I assume it was an accident–no way to be sure), and when she wrote the word *Amendment* on the board she spelled it "Amedment," then argued with one of the students for five minutes, claiming that is how the word was spelled. Finally she was reduced to tears, left in the middle of a lesson, and never returned.

I check the time again. Seventeen minutes more. Impossible. I draw seventeen squares in my notebook, preparing to check every minute until the end of the lesson. Pathetic, no doubt, but one has to survive in this climate of utter boredom. One minute down already, hurray!

The second replacement was Mr. Roumanis. He had some interesting, though not exactly desirable, traits. It was generally agreed upon that he showered only once a year, between July and August. After all, when it rained there was no point in showering. One could simply stand on the street and wash. And the winter was too cold to get wet. The front row quickly retreated to whatever empty seats were available in the back, escaping the noxious odors he brought with him. The second row wished to retreat as well… but no empty seats left.

Mr. Roumanis also managed to say several strange things. When Tiffany had asked to go to the bathroom during the lesson, he'd replied, "Yes, go ahead. Maybe you'll manage to produce something wiser while there." And when Bill ate a snack during class, Mr. Roumanis told him, "I don't allow eating during my lessons, and I think that in your case it is an especially bad idea." While it's true that Tiffany is not the brightest bulb in the electricity shed, and Bill is a bit overweight, those remarks were frowned upon. Mr. Roumanis was quickly fired.

I tick three more minutes in my notebook. I think about Peter. Last time I met him, we had a nice, short conversation about the weather. I couldn't think of anything better to talk about. I should prepare a list of topics for next time. I doodle in my notebook, try to draw Peter, to catch his cute smile, his dark eyes, his short cropped hair, his… I stare at the page. This is not Peter. This is Charlie Brown, after he fell into the hazardous waste container. There is a reason I never draw. Then I let myself get lost in images of Peter, his uniform sitting snugly on his wide shoulders, Peter walking with me in a sunlit meadow, Peter smiling at me in a restaurant, Peter emerging from the swimming pool, his torso wet…

Is it getting warm in here? Two more minutes pass by.

And then we got Mrs. Fletcher. The woman who can dry an ocean simply by talking. Who can make a rainbow seem dull and gray. Who can suck the life force out of a person with nothing more than a string of words delivered in an incredibly monotone voice. The only mildly interesting thing about her is her mustache, which immediately sparked a discussion in class. Why doesn't she do something about it? Doesn't she know it's there? How many hairs does the mustache have? Students tried repeatedly to count, but Mrs. Fletcher insists on talking while she's in the class, making the mustache move.

But can anyone compare their determination to mine? Or their boredom? I start counting. One, two three…

Finally the last minute is ticked, the bell rings and Coral and I join the throng of students walking towards the cafeteria.

"Seventeen," I report to Coral. "Eleven on the left side, six on the right. Isn't that strange? You'd think a mustache would be symmetrical. Maybe she started plucking it off and gave up in the middle? What do you think?"

"I have no idea what you're talking about," Coral says.

We enter the cafeteria and I'm momentarily blinded by the neon light. Why do they make it so bright? Do they really want us to see the food better? Coral and I locate an empty table and sit down.

"Mrs. Fletcher's mustache. I managed to count the hairs. Seventeen, eleven on the left…"

"Mrs. Fletcher has a mustache?"

"Haven't you noticed?" I ask, dumbfounded. "It's like… the first thing you see when she walks in the room. Seriously, first her mustache comes in, then she follows. You never spotted it? You're really weird."

"Right, I'm the weird one. Not you, with your mustaches."

"Haven't you been paying attention? It's Mrs. Fletcher's mustache, not mine."

"Whatever." We sit down at an empty table. "Did you start studying for the math test?"

"There's a test tomorrow?" I panic.

"Tomorrow?" She looks surprised. "No, next Tuesday."

"Next Tuesday… like… a week from now?"

"It's a very important test."

"I didn't know there was a test," I say, getting my sandwich from my lunch bag. "How did you find out about it?"

"How did I…? I looked at the test date sheet, of course."

"Oh, right!" I lost my date sheet, and haven't bothered printing a new one. Maybe I should study with Coral. It couldn't hurt. "When are you planning on studying?"

"I started two days ago."

"Two days ago?" I nearly shout. Is she seriously studying more than a week in advance to a math test?

"It's a very important test. This year's grades are taken into consideration for our college applications…"

"College? Which college looks at your ninth grade scores?"

"All of them," she says, her eyes haunted. "You seriously should start studying."

Shane sits down next to me, plopping a cafeteria tray on the table. "What's up?" he asks. I glance at his tray, nearly losing my appetite. I tend to avoid the cafeteria food in school, but Shane eats it every day. Somehow, he manages to stay in perfect health. His plate holds peas swimming in green ooze, rice that seems to have been both overcooked and undercooked, and question mark meat (the question mark being the animal this meat belongs to).

"This," I say, "is one of the longest days ever. Do you guys feel it? The dimension of time stretching to infinity?"

"Isn't time already infinite?" Coral asks, quirking her eyebrow.

"Well... more infinity, then. Infinity times twenty."

"Only in Narrowdale..." Shane starts. I half smile at him. I can almost see the cogs in his brain spinning, trying to concoct a weird story. Does a brain have cogs? A brain should definitely have cogs.

"Only in Narrowdale does a bus go around the town at midnight, completely empty."

"Does it have a driver?" Coral asks.

"It does, but no one can see his face. The bus doesn't stop at any bus stop, its windows are dark and it has no license plate."

"Its engine makes no sound," I suggest. I take a bite from my sandwich.

"And the air becomes colder when it passes through," Coral adds.

"Right" Shane says. "And when it completes its route, it stops near the mall for five minutes. No one gets on, no one gets off."

"Are you done?" I ask.

"I guess," he shrugs.

"Only in Narrowdale..." I say, my sandwich momentarily forgotten. "Only in Narrowdale are there teachers with asymmetrical mustaches. Eleven hairs on the left side, six on the right. How is that even possible?"

Chapter Two

The school day finally ends. I feel like I should get an award for surviving it. Coral and I leave together. Dozens of students fill the corridor, trying desperately to escape this prison of force-fed knowledge. But tomorrow we will all be back.

As we get closer to the school bus, I slow down.

"I think I'll walk home today," I say.

"What?" Coral looks at me in surprise. "Why?"

"Well..." Why, Amy? Seriously, think of a reasonable answer. "Fresh... air?"

"Suit yourself." She shrugs. "I'm going on the bus."

"Okay."

"It'll give me more time to study for the test."

"The test that's a week from now?" I ask, a bit snidely.

"It's a very impo—"

"Okay, okay, I get it," I interrupt her.

"Anyway, I don't have so much time on the weekend," she says. "So I should really cram in as much studying time as I can before that."

"You're right," I say. "There will be no studying time this weekend. And you know why?"

"Let me guess," she says, smiling. "Maybe it's my friend's birthday, and we're going out?"

"That's right," I say. "It's your wonderful friend's birthday. That would be me. There is no studying on my birthday."

"Absolutely," she says. "Did you invite Shane?"

"Well, I kinda wanted this to be a girls' night out," I say "Nicole and the Jennifers are coming over for the weekend. Why, do you think he'll mind?"

"I don't know, it's hard to know with Shane." She shrugs. "I suppose it's okay. It'll give him food for thought. He'll probably imagine us wearing shortie pajamas and having a pillow fight."

"Wearing... I... what?"

"You know, shortie pajamas, pillow fight. The standard male fantasy for a girls' sleepover party."

"Seriously?" I raise my eyebrows. "Why a pillow fight?"

"I don't know," she says. "It's a mystery."

"Should I tell the girls to bring their shortie pajamas?"

"There's really no need."

"Okay. Your bus is about to leave," I say, pointing at the bus.

"Right, bye!"

She quickly runs towards the bus. I turn around and start walking home.

Why are you walking home, Amy? Why is fresh air so important all of a sudden? Could it be that fresh air is not the real reason for this midday walk? Is it possible that, in fact, there is a completely different reason? Perhaps you've managed to memorize a certain security guy's shift schedule, and you're pretty sure that he's patrolling right now? Is it even possible that you've also managed to plot the route of his daily patrol, and happily enough, it could intersect with your route on your way home? Is there a remote possibility that all this was orchestrated for a chance encounter with said security guy? No, that would be ridiculous! Ha ha, the very thought, ha ha ha. Ha. Ahem.

Fine, maybe it's possible.

But seriously, fresh air is really important, right? I mean, I stay inside the stuffy school all day long, breathing in the sweat and stench of boys who have not yet discovered that deodorant is a thing. Could you really blame me for wanting some fresh air on my way home?

I reach a small junction. If I continue straight, to Jefferson Street, I'll get home faster. I turn right towards Fairfax Street. The air is fresher in that direction. And, yeah okay, Peter's route always goes through Fairfax Street.

The sky is bright blue, and although it's a bit chilly, the sun casts warm rays upon the street as I walk. Noon in Narrowdale is a sleepy time of day, though frankly, when isn't? There's that musky, pleasant smell in the air that is frequent after rainfall. I would have thoroughly enjoyed all that… except I've reached the end of the street, with no Peter in sight. Where is he? Maybe he started earlier, and has already passed through? Or perhaps he's late, and is only about to reach the street now? In that case, I could turn around and walk the other way to hopefully meet him. But how would I explain the fact that I'm walking towards school? And let's be frank. There's a point at which all this semi-stalking is no longer even remotely cute, and instead becomes a bit disturbing and incredibly pathetic.

Fine, fine. Sadly I carry on towards my house, resigned to the fact that all I got from this trip is fresh air. Stupid fresh air. My feet hurt. There's really nothing wrong with the school bus and its stale air. Seriously, from this day on, I intend to reach places only via vehicles. That's why man invented wheels. So that his feet won't hurt.

A police car drives by me and turns onto a small street I never noticed before. Lake Street. That's odd. Usually there are no police cars in Narrowdale. That's why we have private security. If a police car is present, it means something pretty serious is happening. And that, among other things, might explain where Peter is. He is at the serious thing place. Which is probably on Lake Street. I mull over this as I walk onward. What could have happened? Well, that's a stupid question. This is Narrowdale, so pretty much anything could have happened. I begin to feel curious.

I stop and turn around, heading back to Lake Street. At least now I can say that meeting Peter is just a bonus. I am mostly just curious. What could have warranted a police car in Narrowdale?

Three police cars, in fact. They are all parked around a small, shabby-looking house. One of the officers is in the process of tying a police tape around the premise. Three more officers, two men and a woman, are standing on the sidewalk, talking with each other.

"Hello," I say in my naive and innocent voice. My voices come in many tastes. Naive and innocent is a popular one, but I also have charming and full of humor, melancholy and deep, submissive and chaste (my mother's favorite), and the new freshly developed one – tantalizing and mysterious. (Still working on that one. I think it currently has a bit of hysteria and desperation in it.)

"There's nothing to see here," says one of the policemen. He reminds me of my old Mr. Potato Head. A big, potato-shaped body, hardly any neck, short limbs and mismatched ears. I take another look at the house. Without the crime scene tape it would be one of those small old homes, in which old men and women live, sitting all day on the porch, talking about the good old days when young people had manners. However, a crime scene tape makes everything seem more ominous.

"What happened here?" I ask.

"Little girl, you can't be here," says the woman officer. She has sharp features, especially her nose, which brings to mind an angry woodpecker. I don't like her at all. Little girl? What little girl?

"I'm just walking home," I say, the very example of innocence.

"Where is your home?" asks Mr. Potato.

Ah. Interesting question. Home, in fact, is back the way I came, but I don't know if that would be a good answer. I do however, have a perfect answer, in Anthony language.

Anthony language is a rarely known language that Anthony, my brother, claims to have invented. The thing with Anthony language is, you connect several syllables together in a way that sounds as if they should make sense… except they don't. And you mumble a bit. For some reason people expect teens to mumble, so they don't find it odd. In such a way, you can answer any question and carry on as if nothing happened.

"Oh, I live on Bagrfeph Street," I say, motioning with my hand in a way that pretty much encompasses half of Narrowdale. I can see the officer frowning, trying to decipher my answer, but the entire point of Anthony language is to avoid giving him the time to do that. "Where's Narrowdale's private security? I thought they're supposed to be the first responders in any–"

"Amy?"

Bonus time!

"Peter!" I say, smiling at him as he exits the house. He looks at me, his eyes full of concern. I look back, engraving the image in my mind, for later use. As always, he looks striking in his uniform. I wonder if he had it tailored to fit him so well, or if it was pure luck. His face is different somehow. Sad and... shocked?

"Amy, what are you doing here?" he asks.

"Is everything okay?" I ask, ignoring the question.

"I... Yes. No. Not everything is okay. You can't be here."

"What's wrong? Why are the police here?"

"Little girl," the potato cop starts to say, but Peter is already at my side, his hand on my shoulder, gently leading me away. I try to concentrate on being coherent despite the hand-on-shoulder situation. "The policeman said this is a crime scene. What crime?"

"Something happened to the lady that lives here, and–"

"What happened? Is she dead?" I ask.

"What?" His eyes widen, and I realize that I'm right. "No, of course not... I just... Amy, don't you need to go home?"

"Not really."

"Okay, but I do have to get back there and, uh... Look, please go home, okay? It was really nice to see you." His hand leaves my shoulder and he turns and walks away.

Who lives in this house? Is she really dead? What did Peter mean when he said it was nice to see me? Why three squad cars? Is it possible that the woman was murdered? Was Peter really glad to see me?

Chapter Three

I finally get home, take the key from my bag and open the door. Ever since Mom started working in Narrowdale's library, the house is empty when I get back from school. I drop the school bag in the middle of the living room and march to the refrigerator. There's a note in Mom's handwriting tacked to it. I scan it quickly.

'Hey, sweetie. There's broccoli and lasagna in plastic containers in the fridge. Don't heat them in the container, it isn't healthy, put them on a plate. And please eat at least a bit of the wholesome food I made before you start consuming the usual trash. If I find your school bag on the living room floor when I get back, I will burn it, and dance happily around the fire. Love, Mom.'

I open the fridge, move the plastic containers aside and locate some chocolate pudding. I open it and lick the lid. It is a scientific fact that the pudding on the lid is somehow much tastier than the pudding in the cup. Then I take my phone out of my pocket and dial Coral.

"Hello?"

"Hey, Coral, how're things?"

"Fine." She does not sound fine. She sounds on the verge of hysteria.

"Coral, you won't believe what happened today."

"I already know what happened. You walked home instead of

taking the school bus, because you're weird. I really don't believe it, yet somehow it's true."

"That's right. And I saw three police cars outside a house on Lake Street."

"Listen, I'm in the middle of studying–"

"I met Peter, and he told me that the lady that lived there is dead!"

There is a moment of silence. "He told you that?" she finally asks, astonished.

"Well, not exactly..."

"Amy, I have to study."

"But he didn't say otherwise! And the cops were really acting weird, and–"

"Bye, Amy." She hangs up.

Well, to be fair, I didn't have any expectations. I call Shane.

"Amy!" he says.

"That's me."

"What's up?"

"You know Lake Street?"

"No. What's on Lake Street?"

"Well, currently there are three police cars there. A woman who lived there died!"

"Really?" Shane asks. There's a pause while he considers this information. "How do you know?"

"Well... Peter was there, and he didn't exactly deny it."

"He... didn't deny it?"

"Didn't exactly deny it."

"So let me get this straight. You went over to Peter and said, 'Hey, Peter, is the woman living here dead?' and he answered... 'I can't exactly deny it'?"

"It wasn't like that. And in fact, he said she didn't die, but you know how sometimes people lie and you can sort of feel it?"

"Amy, what's going on?"

"It just looked kind of suspicious."

"Yeah, you can count on the police to turn up when things get suspicious," he says. "Amy, what exactly are you looking for?"

I think a bit. "What do you mean?" I ask.

"I mean Tom Ellis was just sentenced to life two weeks ago, right?"

I wince. For a moment I'm back there. Tied in the darkness. The foul taste of the gag in my mouth. Tom Ellis whistling above me. Then I recall the way he looked at me in the courtroom. The way he *smiled*. I shake my head, banishing the images back where they came from.

"What's Tom Ellis got to do with anything?" I snap.

"Well, you gave your testimony in court, you were in a couple of police interviews, and suddenly it's over. He's in prison."

"Yeah?"

"Never mind," he says, and sighs.

"Well, I think I need to study now," I say, irritated.

"That sounds like a good idea."

"Bye." I hang up. I feel frustrated. Shane and his cheap psychology analysis. I've got a real psychologist to analyze me, thank you very much.

I have some homework in Spanish (and there's a very important math test next week!). I sit down on the couch and turn on the TV. I'll do the homework in a bit.

When Mom gets home I'm still slouching in front of the TV.

"Hey, sweetie," she says, then adds in a chilly tone. "Your bag is on the floor."

"I'll pick it up in a moment," I say distractedly.

"Now."

"Okay, okay." I turn off the TV, pick up my school bag and take it to my room. I walk back downstairs.

"Did you eat?" Mom asks, opening the fridge.

"Yeah..." I suddenly recall the two containers she prepared. "I ate something."

"Why didn't you eat what I made?" she asks, sighing.

I consider all the possible lies, and decide that truth is the best policy. "I don't know."

"Well, did you at least eat something healthy?"

"Sure. Very healthy." Truth be damned.

"Okay." She looks at me. "Don't forget you have a session tomorrow with Dr. Greenshpein."

"Tomorrow?" My mood plummets.

"Four o'clock. And this time don't dare even think about canceling. I'm writing him a check. Please remember to hand it to him."

"Yeah, okay," I say in my tortured and suffering voice (forgot to mention that one before. It's a classic).

I trudge back up to my room and close the door. I take out my Spanish notebook and sit in front of the computer. I watch a few video clips, chat with Nicole and Jennifer Scott a bit, post a blog post, play a stupid pattern-matching game.

When I go to sleep the notebook is in the same place, unopened.

http://amy.strangerealm.com/haiku.html

Chapter Four

"So what's the plan for the weekend?" I ask Coral as we're walking her dog.

"You're the birthday girl. What do you want to do?" she says, smiling at me.

"I don't know." I shrug. "What about chess?"

"Chess?" she asks.

"We'll dress up in sexy pajamas and play chess," I say.

"That sounds great." She nods enthusiastically. "Shane would love that."

"I'm sure he would. Hey, where's your dog?" I suddenly notice that her leash is empty.

"What dog?" She looks at me, surprised. "I don't have a dog."

"Oh, right," I say.

"It's a shame that they've angered it," Coral says sadly.

"Who?"

"The predator," she answers. "Now it's out of control. It's a real shame."

I stop and stare at her. "Coral, what are you talking about?"

"Oh, you know what," she tells me, playing with her pajama. "Fill its body with heavy stones. That's the only way to beat it."

"What?"

"They really shouldn't have woken it," she says once more. "It's

Moth to a Flame

angry. And it doesn't like it when its prey escapes."

I hold my breath, and suddenly I can hear a low growl behind me.

I open my eyes as my alarm buzzes happily beside me. I quickly turn it off. Ugh. What a weird dream.

Never mind. I shake the dream off, wash my face, get dressed, get ready for school. Because that's the kind of girl I am. The kind of girl that wakes up and gets ready quickly. I leave home early, so that I'll have time to spare to get to the bus stop. You know why? Because that's the kind of girl I am. The kind of girl who responsibly gets to the bus stop on time, because she takes her studies seriously, and needs to do her Spanish homework on the bus.

My Spanish homework. In my Spanish notebook. Which I left at home. Because that's the kind of girl I am. The kind of girl who messes up.

I run home, cursing myself. I bang open the front door, ignoring my mom's questions, run up to my room, and grab my notebook from the desk. I sprint back outside, running as fast as I can to avoid being late for the bus. I fall down, scratching my elbow, tears of pain bursting from my eyes. I get up, carry on running, and get to the school bus just in time.

Jasmine and Carley look at me with distaste as I sit down in front of them. I don't know what their problem is (well, apart from Carley's slightly bushy eyebrows and mustache, and Jasmine's weird spaghetti-like arms). I think we started off on the wrong foot, them and I. And there have been many additional wrong feet since. Carley makes a weird snorting noise, which I guess is intended to offend me. I ignore her, wipe my eyes with my sleeve, and check out my elbow. It has a long, ugly scratch, which will fit nicely with my upcoming long, ugly day. What a crappy morning. I brace myself for Jasmine and Carley's inevitable remarks about the way I look, but surprisingly they are too busy discussing something else.

"So what did your brother say?" Jasmine asks.

"He just said she was dead," Carley answers. My ears tune in. Carley's brother is Peter. "He said that he can't talk about it."

"Well, my mom says that the entire room was drenched with blood," Jasmine says. "The neighbor who found her threw up six times!"

"Yeah, my dad says he went by the house last night and it was surrounded by cops," Carley says. "So weird. I wonder why she was killed."

I can't contain myself. I turn around. "Who was killed?" I ask. "What happened?"

They both look at me haughtily. However, it's clear that they're both dying to tell me, because after less than two seconds Carley says, "An old woman died on Lake Street. Her body was found yesterday. They think she was murdered!"

"Who found her?" I ask.

"Her neighbor. He said there was some sort of bad smell, so he went over to check it out and—"

"She was ripped apart," Jasmine interrupts. "There was blood on the floor and the walls, and… and the ceiling… There were body parts missing!"

"That's right." Carley nods. "The police are hushing it up, because it's directly connected to the Mafia…"

"Well… Not exactly." Jasmine smiles mysteriously. "I know from a very reliable source, which I can't expose, that she was connected to a very large FBI investigation, and…"

I nod, my attention elsewhere. It is clear that neither of them have any idea what happened, but that won't prevent them both from discussing every little detail about the life and death of the old woman on Lake Street.

Happily, Coral gets on the school bus at the next stop. Usually, Coral's mom drops her at school. However, when she needs to go to work early for some reason, Coral rides with us, the common people. She sits down next to me. It's easy to spot the dark circles under her eyes.

"Did you even sleep last night?" I ask, "You look exhausted."

"I slept," she replies. "I'm fine."

"Did you do the Spanish assignment?" I ask. The question, of course, is merely formal. On the day that Coral won't do her assignment, hell will freeze over, birds will fly backwards, and an acceptable mall will be opened in Narrowdale.

"Sure. Do you want to copy?"

It's nice to have friends that know you so well. I nod and she gets her notebook out of her school bag and hands it over.

"I think I'll copy the assignment during lunch break," I say. "Spanish class is right after lunch, right?"

"Yes." She puts her notebook back in her bag.

"If the CIA had killed her, they wouldn't have done such a messy job!" I hear Carley tell Jasmine.

"That's what they want you to think," Jasmine replies. "My dad said…"

The bus arrives at school, and the noise of the students getting up and jostling each other on their way out drowns out the wise things that Jasmine's dad said, which is really fine by me. Coral and I wait a bit for the chaos to settle, then get off ourselves.

"Did you hear?" I tell Coral. "I was right. An old woman died on Lake Street. They found her body yesterday."

"Really? How do you know?"

"Jasmine and Carley said so."

"Then it must be true."

"You're no fun at all."

"I'm sorry that I'm not ecstatic to pronounce the death of a poor old woman that neither of us is familiar with."

We walk into English class. Coral turns to me. "Amy, listen. I want to pay attention today, because we have an English test three weeks from now, and the lesson today is crucial. I promise that I'll listen to your strange conspiracy theories about dead women during lunch, okay?"

"Okay, okay," I mutter. Mrs. Parker, the English teacher, briskly walks into class, wearing a depressing tweed skirt, a sensible boring shirt, and her everlasting frown. She quickly begins to verbally assault us with a poem. I think there should be a slow acceleration if you want to talk about a poem. You can't just go, "Good morning, class—BAM, poem!" No. It should involve some small milestones along the way. For instance, maybe she could talk about her morning. Then describe her breakfast, which would lead inevitably to a discussion about food, which at some point she might use to reference a cereal advertisement on TV. Then she could say, "Oh, and you know what that jingle reminds me of? This poem I just read yesterday!" At which point it would be a natural part of the conversation.

Anyway, this is not what happens, and I glumly sit, trying to absorb whatever I can, which is not much.

There are more classes, because that's what school is all about. I occasionally hear a partial whisper, a fragment of a conversation about the old woman. "…The guy who found her is currently hospitalized. He's in shock and won't talk to…", "…Isn't dead at all, she simply disappeared without a trace…", "…A lot of cabbage. It really does wonders…"

It is possible that the thing about cabbage is not directly related.

Eventually we sit down around a table in the cafeteria. Coral pulls out her Spanish notebook, which I gratefully take from her hands. I get my sandwich and notebook from my bag and begin to diligently copy the assignment while munching.

"You were right," Shane says, sitting down. "An old woman was killed on Lake Street."

"Really?" Coral says, sounding weary. "Did Jasmine and Carley tell you all about it?"

Shane looks at her in confusion. "Who? No. Everyone in school is talking about it."

"Everyone but Coral," I complain. "She refuses to talk about anything except the upcoming math test." A sandwich crumble falls on Coral's notebook. She makes a small upset choking sound. I quickly remove the offensive crumble. "Sorry," I say, mouth full.

"I can talk about other things besides math," she says. "I just don't like all this gruesome excitement about death."

"So what did you hear?" I ask, flipping a page in Coral's notebook.

"All kinds of nonsense. One person said she was found burned. Another said she hanged herself. I heard someone say she actually drowned…"

"What? In her bathtub?"

"Well… The general consensus was she was found in her bedroom."

"So she drowned in her bed?" I ask.

"It's just stuff people are saying. No need to pay attention to it."

"I heard she was connected to the Mafia," I say. "And that there was an FBI investigation…"

"See?" Coral snaps. "That's why I hate all this. It's just stupid rumors about a woman who died. I had enough death when the year started, with Kimberly White. I'd be happy to avoid additional murders for the rest of my life."

"Do you know what we need to do?" I say. "We need to investigate this."

Coral stares at me. "Did you listen to a word I just said?"

"Think about it," I carry on, getting excited. "We're a great team—we've already demonstrated that with Kimberly's murder. Why shouldn't we investigate this case as well?"

"There's no case!" Coral says.

"Well… this rumor, then."

"Let's see why." She begins to number the reasons on her fingers. "One—we're not the police. Two, we almost got killed last time, especially you. Three, we're just high school students. Four, this has nothing to do with us…"

"This is not a game," Shane tells me. "And you're not Veronica Mars. We got really lucky with Tom Ellis. You're talking nonsense."

I give Coral her notebook back. "I don't think I'm Veronica Mars. I just think it could be interesting, and—"

"Enough!" Coral shakes her head. "Amy, cut it out. We need to focus on our tests. As far as we know there wasn't even a murder. Maybe she had a heart attack. Maybe she killed herself. Maybe she's still alive! Even if she was murdered, the police are already investigating it, and maybe they even know who did it! And even if they don't, they most certainly don't need our help!" She gets up and stomps away.

"Hysterical much?" I say. "What's her pro—"

"She's right," he says. "Did you already forget what a hard time you had, with your nightmares? What about the concussion you got? Why do you keep trying to get yourself into more trouble?"

"Okay, okay," I quickly silence him. "I didn't really mean that we should find the killer. I just thought we should look around a bit—I don't know."

"Well… let's not," Shane suggests.

"Okay," I agree unhappily, then a thought comes to mind. "Hang on! What about a documentary?"

"A documentary?" Shane asks suspiciously.

"Weren't you just telling me the other day how you'd love to film a documentary?"

"Yeah…"

"Well, think about it! It can be an 'another death in Narrowdale' video. We go over to that house. Film it a bit, try to interview one of the cops, maybe do a background segment about the woman."

"We could also interview students here," Shane says thoughtfully. "Like… do a collection of short interviews where they all say what they've heard. And then compare it to the actual story."

"Right! That's a great idea!" I say, excited. "So what do you think?"

He mulls it over. I'm practically vibrating with energy. This is the best idea I had since that time I invented the "spicy-dried peas-cream-cheese-cucumber-potato chips" snack.

"Yeah, okay," he finally says. "But if I see that this is something else, I'm splitting."

"Awesome. We'll meet today at four thirty…" I suddenly recall my appointment. "Damn, no good. Make that five thirty. Near the entrance to Lake Street. It's a one-way street, you'll see."

"Okay."

"It's going to be great, don't worry."

"I'm sure," he mutters. He doesn't look sure at all.

Chapter Five

Cell phones have replaced the need for clocks, and watches. Why would anyone need a clock or a wristwatch? You have a cell phone in your pocket, and it tells the time. However—and that's a big "however"—you need to take the cell phone out of your pocket and glance at it to know the time. And when you do it repeatedly every couple of minutes, it might seem impolite. A person might get the feeling that you don't want to talk to him.

I am wondering if enough time has passed since I last glanced at my cell phone. Probably not.

"How's your sleep?" asks Doctor Greenshpein.

"It's great."

"Really? No more nightmares?"

"No…" I think about last night. "Well… no, not really."

"I see."

He sees. He always sees. It gets frustrating sometimes. As does this couch.

"Your couch is really uncomfortable," I complain as I shift to my side. It feels as if I'm sitting on a crooked wooden chair.

"Is it? My wife chose it. She thought it matched the decor."

Then maybe his wife should sit on it. I shift again, trying to find a reasonable position. Then I stare at the top of his head. He is entirely bald, but there are six or seven hairs that didn't get the memo. They sit innocently on his head, clearly wondering when the other guests will show up and get the party started.

"What are you thinking about?" he asks.

"About school," I quickly lie.

"How's school?"

"It's fine, I guess."

"Really?" His eyebrows shoot up, as they inevitably do. He has hairy eyebrows. Maybe to compensate for his baldness. His eyebrows are very prominent on his face, despite the fact that he wears glasses.

"Yeah. The Spanish teacher was sick or something, so she didn't come in today. It was a bit annoying, because I bothered to copy the homework assignment during lunch, and in retrospect I didn't need to."

"You *bothered* to copy homework?" he asks, raising his eyebrows once more.

"Yeah." I become a bit defensive. "Look, it's not that easy to copy an assignment for Spanish class. There are all those weird punctuation marks, and you have to pay attention when you copy them, because they're really important. And I did it during lunch, so I had to eat while working, which is really bad for the digestion."

"Aha." He stays quiet for a moment. "How are your grades?"

"Not that great."

"Oh? You told me last time you were doing better."

"Better doesn't necessarily mean good," I say. "I'm having a hard time catching up with the days I lost."

"I see."

He sees. Do shrinks always see?

A few weeks after Tom Ellis tried to kill me, Mom announced that I was going to see a psychotherapist. Apparently I was traumatized and had to get professional help to get over it. My claims that I was just fine, it was no big deal—who doesn't almost get murdered every once in a while?—were completely ignored. I found myself in Doctor Greenshpein's small clinic, talking about dreams and murderous psychos. Which was somehow supposed to help me get better.

"Back in LA, were you a good student?" he asks.

"I was fine," I say tersely. "But you know how it is. Someone tried to kill me, I got a concussion, didn't go to school for a while. Same old story, right?"

We sit in silence for a while. Doctor Greenshpein loves silence. I look around the familiar room. There's a large bookcase with hundreds of books. I started reading their titles once, got bored after a dozen. They all seem to be professional books. How many psychology books does one need? The carpet on the floor has a pattern that always mesmerizes me. I find myself slowly following the circular threads, trying to figure out where they begin and where they end. I wonder if he intentionally put in a carpet that might confuse the patients. Maybe he gets them talking by distracting them. Two landscape pictures, boring as hell. A green, flowerless plant in a pot.

"My friend mentioned Tom Ellis on the phone yesterday," I say. "He said I... well... Anyway, he made me remember Tom Ellis."

"And how did that make you feel?"

"I don't like thinking about him, if that's what you mean." I shrug. "But I didn't, like, tear at my hair and run screaming into the closet."

"I heard Tom Ellis got life without parole," Greenshpein says.

"Yup."

"What do you feel about his sentence?"

"I feel great. People like him shouldn't walk around freely. I hope he suffers every day there."

"Why do you need him to suffer?"

"I don't need him to do anything," I say, irritated. "I simply said—"

"Is it because of what he did to you, or is it related to the death of Kimberly White, whom you had dreams about..."

"I was confused. I couldn't have dreamed about someone who died nine years ago, right? That wouldn't make sense."

"Wouldn't it?"

"Did you hear that a woman was killed on Lake Street?" I ask, desperate to change the topic.

"No, I didn't," he says, surprised. "Was it in the paper?"

"Not exactly," I say. "But I heard... some people talking." Better not mention my visit to her house. Shrinks become strangely obsessive about small details like that.

"What people?"

"People at school."

"Okay. And how do you feel about that?"

"I don't think I feel anything."

"So why even mention it?"

"Well, it's interesting, isn't it? That another woman was killed?"

"Another woman? What do you mean by 'another'?"

"I don't mean anything."

"You mean another woman, just as Kimberly was killed?"

"Look, you're twisting my words. It doesn't mean anything."

"I see."

He sees. I don't see. What is there to see? I don't think he sees at all. There's nothing to see here, folks, move along.

"So why are you interested in that woman?" he asks.

It definitely feels like a good time to glance at the cell phone. I pull it out. "Oh, my, look at the time! Nearly five! Man, does time fly when you're having fun." I locate the check Mom wrote for him. "Here you go. For this appointment, and the two before. You've been an amazing help, thanks, Doctor." I get up.

"Amy," he says as I turn to leave.

"Yeah?"

"Before next time, I'd be happy if you figured out why you're so interested in a murder. Especially since you mentioned yourself that you don't know it actually happened."

"Fine. Thanks. Have a lovely evening."

"You too."

I leave, closing the door behind me, feeling immensely relieved.

Chapter Six

I make it to Lake Street on time, but Shane is nowhere to be seen. I check the time—five twenty-seven. Fine, he still has a few minutes.

It's unusually cold today. The air is becoming chilly as the sun slowly sets. As always, once the temperature drops, my ears begin to hurt, and my nose feels as if it's dripping. I have a really warm wool hat, and a wonderful scarf that Mom bought me… but I left both of them at home, and so I'm left only with the feeling of longing for warmer clothes. I begin to do the tribal dance of standing in the cold—left foot, right foot, left foot, right foot, rub hands, breathe on cupped hands to warm numb nose. Left foot, right foot…

Five thirty-one. I call Shane.

"Hey!" he says, answering quickly.

"Where are you?" I ask, my voice a bit harsh.

"I'm on my way."

"On your way? You should be here by now!"

"What are you stressing about? I'll be there in five minutes. Sheesh."

"Just get here already," I say, irritated, and hang up. What's he late for? What if it rained? I would be waiting for him in the rain! I look furiously at the sky. Completely cloudless. Well, it's mid-February. It could have rained!

Left foot, right foot, rub hands… It's getting dark pretty fast. It's probably only my imagination, but Lake Street becomes very foreboding as the darkness sets in. The shadows become oppressive, almost hostile. The houses on the street all seem as if they could hide all manner of potential violent killers. One of the streetlights is flickering, its light pale and hazy. All in all, not a very inviting place to stand in.

Finally Shane arrives. I look at him reproachfully. "It's nice of you to finally show up," I say, trying to control my anger.

"You sound like a teacher," he says. "I'm only five minutes late."

Six minutes. He's six minutes late, but mentioning that will only make me seem petty, which… well, I am. Something inside me knows that it isn't Shane's fault that I'm angry, it's Doctor Greenshpein's fault. Though to be fair, he is actually paid to irritate me.

"My nose is cold," I say. "And my ears."

"You should get a beanie," Shane says, pointing at his own warm-looking black beanie. "It really helps."

"Well, thanks. I'll take that under consideration."

"What's with you today?" he asks as we begin walking down the street.

"Nothing, forget it."

As we approach the house, I can see that only one police car is parked in front of it, a cop sitting inside. As we get closer he opens the door and gets out. It's the potato cop from the day before.

"Can I help you?" he asks.

"Hello again," I say.

He peers at me. "Oh, you're that girl from yesterday, right? Look, I told you, you can't be here."

"Oh, I just thought that we'd drop by," I say, searching for a reason. "We're… writing a report for our school newspaper. About whatever happened here."

He notices Shane's video camera. "Really? Well, this is not school material. You'll hear all about it in this evening's local news report."

"And what will they report?"

"They'll report about what happened here." He looks guardedly at me.

When in doubt, nag them till they break. "But what—"

"Look, little girl, I can't talk about it."

"But you do know what happened, right?"

"Of course I know what happened. Hell, I was the first officer on the scene. It isn't going to be something I'll forget anytime soon, let me tell you that. But I'm not allowed to talk about it."

Something in the way he says that reminds me of Jasmine and Carley. That tone of voice hides a person who is dying to tell every little detail… and once he's out of real details, he'll start inventing new details just to keep talking, to be the one who *knows*.

"It must have been terrible to be the first man on the scene," I say, my tone full of reverence.

"You bet it was," he answers. "In my thirteen years on the force I've never seen anything like it."

"I heard there was a lot of blood," I gamble.

"A lot," he verifies, then asks suspiciously, "Who told you that?"

"My"—I hesitate for a moment—"brother is on the force. So he told me."

"Oh. He shouldn't have said anything," he says, clearly irritated. He's not upset about my imaginary cop brother breaking the rules; he's upset because his moment to shine was taken from him.

"But he was very hazy with the details," I quickly add. "He said he thinks she was cut…"

"Cut?" The policeman snorts. "That's what he was told? I wish she was cut."

I shut up, my eyes full of admiration.

"So what happened?" Shane blurts, his camera pointed at the cop. I want to kill him. Potato cop nearly told us, but now he'll never do it.

"Turn off the camera," the policeman says.

Shane lowers the camera, but I notice that the red light that indicates that he's recording is still on.

"I'll tell you what happened," he grunts. "But it's not something you can write about in your school paper. You two got that?"

We both nod.

"Her entire body was covered with scratches. Not cuts!" He looks at me significantly. "More like… jagged gashes. And her neck... I've never seen anything like it. And I've been a cop for thirteen years. Thirteen! I don't know who could have done such a thing. I—"

The police radio suddenly comes to life, a metallic voice saying something unintelligible. The cop raises a finger, motioning for us to wait. He then gets into the car and starts talking on the radio.

"Did you get that?" I whisper.

"Yeah, but the headlights were in my face," he answers. "I don't think the video will turn out so good."

That's disappointing. We should try and get some additional footage. I look towards the officer. He's talking intently into his radio.

"Come on," I tell Shane, walking quickly towards the house.

"Amy!" He walks after me. "Where are you going?"

"Don't you want to film the house?"

"Yeah, sure but..."

I look backwards towards the cop. He seems as if he's forgotten about us entirely.

"It's going to be a great video," I tell Shane. "You'll see." I lay my hand on the doorknob.

"It'll be locked," he says, his voice hesitant.

I turn it. The door opens.

"Just film it all," I say almost silently, walking inside, ignoring Shane's frantic whispers.

Chapter Seven

For a moment I simply stand in the unlit room, the door still open behind me. My instincts kick in, a bit late as usual, and I fight the desire to walk back, shut the door. My hand fumbles along the wall. A light switch. There must be a light switch somewhere.

"Amy," Shane whispers. "Get out, come on. You can't be here."

I feel the cold plastic touch of the switch. I flick it, and the light turns on. Shane becomes silent. I turn towards him.

"Get in, quickly," I say. "Before the cop sees the light."

And he's about to walk away, leave me there alone. I know he is, and he's right. Even I don't know what I'm doing, and it'd be crazy to join me.

To my surprise, he walks inside. I shut the door. We turn to look at the room.

It's a living room, and it gives a very clear vibe. Old and sad.

The sofa is worn, even torn in a few places, its pattern reminding me of things I saw in my grandparents' house. A half-empty bookcase with an empty vase on top, a few dusty wooden chairs, chipped and worn. There are no pictures. A coffee table with a thin layer of dust all over it. One couch, its corners eaten by rodents. There's an unpleasant smell in the air. Someone died here recently, and I assume the smell is mostly the smell of death, but there's also an old, faint smell of neglect. This place wasn't cleaned frequently, and I can almost feel the mold in the walls, the small bits of food that were left to rot under the couch.

There's a small kitchen connected to the living room, and an entrance to a hallway. There's also a closed door on the opposite side of the room. I feel strangely drawn to it.

"Amy, you promised we wouldn't do anything stupid," Shane says, his voice strained. "And this is stupid. Come on, let's go."

"Two minutes," I say. "Then we leave. I promise."

"Fine. Two minutes."

I begin crossing the room to the other side, when suddenly I hear a strange creaking noise.

"What was that?" asks Shane.

"Probably nothing," I say, unconvinced. "It's an old house. It creaks."

I reach the other side of the living room and open the door. Another dark room. I turn on the light and stare.

Well, this is... different.

The room is nearly empty, but for one thing. In the middle of it stands a huge cage. It's as tall as I am, and occupies almost the entire floor. Inside the cage lies one dirty blanket. The door to the cage is open.

"What the hell did she have here?" Shane whispers.

"Some sort of animal?" I suggest.

"Yeah, but what?"

"I don't know," I answer, getting closer. The cage's floor is wooden, and I can see dozens... hundreds of scratch marks.

"Amy, let's go."

"In a second."

"I'm leaving," Shane says, his voice tense.

I grasp the cage's door, moving it. It swings freely, squeaking as it moves. I kneel and stare at it.

"Check this out." I say. "The door's lock. It's completely bent. I think whatever was here broke out."

He doesn't answer. I turn around. Shane's gone.

"Shane?" I call. My voice echoes unnervingly in the room. There's a moment of silence. Then, from somewhere else in the house, there's another creak. I don't want to be here anymore. This place is... wrong. Just wrong.

I turn around towards the living room and freeze. The room is completely dark. For a second I feel furious. Shane turned off the light! What a nasty thing to do!

"Come on, Shane, that's not funny!"

Silence. I almost call him again, but then I hesitate. Shane would never have done this. He doesn't like practical jokes, and anyway, he was scared. No, the bulb probably burned out.

Either that, or someone else turned off the light.

I shake my head, banishing the thought from my mind. No point in scaring myself. Time to get out. I begin crossing the room, the light behind me illuminating the space enough to get by.

After I take three steps, the light behind me turns off as well. The blackness surrounds me as I freeze in my place. Another bulb burned out? Not likely.

Someone's here.

"Shane?" I say, my voice quivering in fright. I feel completely disoriented. I turned around when the light went out, and now I'm unsure where the front door is. I recall fragments of our conversation with the cop.

Her entire body was covered with scratches... Jagged gashes... I've never seen anything like it

And I know whatever killed that woman is here. With me.

I let out a whimper and stumble forward, trying to feel my way. My hand hits something—I can feel it moving, and then I hear a crash. I freeze once more, holding my breath.

It begins low, almost difficult to hear, but it gets louder and angrier. A menacing, vicious growl. Suddenly, from within the blackness, I can see something move.

I bolt. I don't even know where I'm going. I run into something... the coffee table? Fall down, get up, breathing heavily, short frantic breaths, and limp on. Behind me I hear a snarl. It feels closer, almost on top of me now. My hand meets something wooden. A door. I quickly locate the doorknob, twist it. It opens, and I slip inside and shut the door behind me, leaning against it.

Something crashes into the door, and it vibrates. I pray for the door to hold as I fumble, trying to locate the light switch.

Another growl, much louder, angrier.

I find the light switch and flip it. The light turns on, illuminating the room, and for a second I wonder what all those brown stains on the walls and the floor are. Then I realize that it's dried blood.

The woman's bedroom is completely trashed. The bed is lying on its side against the wall, as if someone picked it up and threw it there. Broken furniture pieces lie everywhere, beyond recognition. Perhaps once the pieces belonged to a chair? No way to tell. The blood… is everywhere. I can see the imprint of a hand in one of the stains on the wall. And the stain on the floor is huge, and there's a strange smearing outline in it, and I know this is where her body was, but I try to push the thought away, because if I start thinking about a dead body lying here…

I realize that I'm repeatedly blubbering, "Oh god, oh god, oh god…"

The door handle suddenly begins moving. I watch it, feeling the terror fill my body as it twists. I throw my entire weight against the door. Someone pushes from the other side, but I manage to keep it closed…

Then something powerful hits it, and I'm thrown backwards as the door flings open.

The cop is staring furiously at me, Shane behind him, pale and worried.

"What the hell are you doing here?" he screams.

Chapter Eight

"This is a crime scene! You shouldn't be here!" the cop keeps yelling.

"I'm... I'm sorry. I just wanted to... I mean..." My brain struggles to find a way to explain this. It completely fails. "I was on my way out..."

"You bet you were," the cop says, grabbing my hand. He grabs Shane as well and pulls us roughly towards the front door. My arm twists a bit and I cry in pain, but he ignores me, yanking us both, his face red with rage.

"Do you know that what you did was illegal?" he asks as we're crossing the living room. I notice the vase shattered on the floor, probably my doing.

"Do you want to be sent to juvie?" he carries on. "Is that what you want?"

"No," I say, my voice strained in pain and fear. "I'm really sorry."

"Sorry. What good does it do me that you're sorry?" he says. The front door is already open and he half pushes, half throws us outside.

"I don't want to see either of you here again, you got that?"

We both nod. I realize that I'm shaking.

"Especially not you, girl," the cop hisses at me. "And if I see one picture from this place in your damn school newspaper, I'll have you both arrested. Now get the hell out of here!"

The last sentence is so loud, I find myself flinching. Shane and I turn and run away.

We run out of Lake Street. We keep running until we get to an intersection. Shane's house is one way, mine the other. We stop, breathless. I struggle to calm myself, a bitter taste in my mouth. My side hurts from the effort, my lungs are burning with the cold air, my leg hurts where I hit the table, my arm hurts where the cop grabbed me... I've been better.

"What happened in there?" Shane asks me.

"I don't know," I answer, catching my breath. "There was someone... something there, with me. It felt like it wanted to kill me."

"Something? What do you mean, something?"

"There was a growl," I say, shivering at the memory. "I don't know. It turned off the lights."

"There was something that growled... and turned off the lights?" Shane frowns. "Amy, that doesn't make sense."

"Well, I don't know what it was, okay Shane? But it wanted to hurt me. Why the hell did you call the cop?"

"Call him? Are you nuts? He noticed me as I was leaving. And then we heard something crash from inside, and we heard you scream."

"I screamed?" I hadn't even noticed. "Yeah, I guess it was when the thing growled at me... I don't know."

"Well, you don't know, and I don't care." Shane looks at me in anger. "It was stupid to come with you. I should have known better. I don't know what the hell is wrong with you, what makes you keep flinging yourself head-on into dangerous places, but you're not taking me with you."

Tears spring from my eyes. "I'm sorry, I just wanted to do something exciting. And I was really thrilled about the documentary idea. I didn't know it would turn out so badly!"

"Well, no," he hisses at me. "You didn't. But you could have guessed. Who breaks into a murder scene? Seriously, Amy!"

"Look, I'm sorry, I didn't mean for this to get so out of hand—"

"I don't care what you meant, Amy, I'm done with this story.

Coral was right. Let the police handle this." He turns around and stomps away.

I remain behind sniffing, feeling guilty. I've put my friend in danger, again. For absolutely no good reason. I wait for a moment, letting my heartbeat slow down, massaging the place where I hurt my leg. I check out the time. It's only a quarter to seven. Weird, it feels like the middle of the night. Finally, I wipe my eyes and begin limping back home.

It's really chilly now, and I stick my hands deep inside my pockets, losing myself in the image of a warm house, of a hot shower. It'd be wonderful to thaw my frozen face. My ears are practically falling off by now. My strides are short and fast, as they always are when I'm cold. I'll be home in ten minutes. Only ten. Maybe even a bit less if I walk fast enough. Just a little bit...

Something snaps behind me. It sounds like a small twig. Then I hear some leaves rustling. I turn around and scan the street. It's empty, but not far away from me there's a patch of shrubs, and I realize the sounds probably came from there. Must be a small bird, or a cat, but deep inside I know it's something much more threatening. It's the creature that I saw in the old woman's house. The one that killed the woman, tore out her throat, mauled her body over and over again. It has followed me here.

My feet start moving again. It's nothing, it must be nothing, I just need to keep going. I'll get home soon; there's no reason to be afraid. I glance back, unable to help myself. The patch of shrubs is almost invisible in the dark, but it remains still. And then I notice something. Two blue dots within the leaves. Cold eyes, watching me. I turn around and begin running, and I can hear a snarl behind me, the shrubs rustling noisily as the creature bursts out from within and chases me. I run, already out of breath once more, hearing heavy panting behind me. I run into the road, hoping, praying that it won't follow me, knowing that it will, that it'll never stop, that...

"Good evening!" someone calls from the other side of the street. I almost burst out crying in relief as I run towards Alex, our neighbor. I look behind me... there's nothing there.

"You shouldn't cross the street like that. You could get hit," Alex tells me reproachfully. He is holding his dog, Moka, by a leash.

"I know," I say. "I just thought I saw…" I look back once more, into the shrubs. Did I only imagine it? Suddenly I'm not sure I heard or saw anything. "I don't know. I got scared."

He nods. "I get scared too, at night, sometimes. That's why I have Moka to protect me."

"Yeah."

"Well, have a lovely evening," he says and begins to walk away. I look at him, feeling desperate. What if I did hear something? What if once he's gone, the creature will return?

"You know what?" he says, turning around. "I think Moka and I were just done with our little walk. I think we should go back home now, right, Moka?"

The dog wags her tail.

"Would you mind if we join you?" he asks, walking back towards me.

"Mind? No, I don't mind at all," I say, trying to keep the immense relief from my voice.

We walk down the dark street in silence.

"It's cold, isn't it?" he says.

I look at him. He doesn't look cold at all. He's wearing a thin shirt, and no coat. He has no gloves, nor a hat. "Yeah," I say. "It's very cold."

"It's the middle of February." He nods. "Cold time of the year."

"I guess."

"Back in Russia it was colder."

"You're from Russia?" I ask. I suddenly realize that he does have a trace of accent when he speaks.

"I grew up in Russia," he says. "I came here… long ago."

"Oh. Do you miss Russia?"

"Not really."

He doesn't seem to want to talk about it, and I let it go.

"These days…" he says. "They're not very good. Are they?"

"I… you mean the cold?" I ask.

"No. I mean everything else." He looks at me. "You know what I mean."

I have no idea. "I don't think I do," I say slowly.

"Oh, you know. You can feel it." He nods to himself. "I can see you do. These are evil days."

What does he mean? Is he talking about politics? I don't recall things going haywire more than usual. I struggle to make sense of it. "Alex, what do you—"

"Here we are," he says, interrupting me. We've reached our respective homes. "Thank you for escorting us." He winks at me with a small smile and opens the gate to his yard.

"Good night, Alex," I say.

"Good night, Amy."

I open the door and walk inside. Mom and Dad are in the living room, watching TV.

"Hi, sweetie," Mom says. "I'm making beef casserole for dinner." She glances at me. "Go take a warm shower. You look completely frozen."

"Good idea, Mom," I say and walk upstairs. I take off my clothes. There's a black bruise on my shin, and another smaller bruise on my arm, where the cop grabbed me. I enter the shower and turn on the hot water, washing the pain, cold, and fear away.

Chapter Nine

It's the middle of the night, twenty minutes past one, and I can't fall asleep. I toss and turn in bed, trying to make sense of the past afternoon. That cage that we saw, its door open, the lock bent. The creature that chased me, growling and snarling. The bloody room. The blue eyes in the street. Were there really eyes there? Or did I simply imagine it? My brain keep churning with the day's events, and I shiver every time I recall that low, menacing growl. I haven't felt like this since the nights when I dreamed of Kimberly's kidnapping.

What if I do manage to fall asleep? Will I have nightmares about the woman on Lake Street, or about the creature that chased me? Wake up screaming once more? Why did I start this? I knew it was a bad idea, knew there was something wrong the moment I saw the first police car turning onto Lake Street. Still, there's something in me that wishes to assemble the puzzle, figure it out, keep trying to shuffle the pieces—a dead, mauled woman, a huge blood stain, an open cage, a growling creature… This all seems pretty clear. But… the light switches? And to be fair, if the creature had wanted to kill me in that house, it could have done it without any problem. I wasn't exactly the most clever and elusive prey. It just doesn't fit. I am trying to assemble a puzzle with many missing pieces. Yet… something in me doesn't want to give up.

I sit up in bed. The floor is freezing cold. I put on my slippers and get up. I wonder if I should go and crank up the thermostat. Typically, this results in an argument with my dad later on, so I decide against it. I approach the window and stare outside. There's a light on in Alex's house, and I can see him through the window. He seems to be packing, tossing clothes into a large duffel bag. Moka is on the floor by the bed, looking at him, an expression of extreme boredom on her face. He turns to his night table, picking up a dark object from it. I squint, trying to figure out what it is… but he tosses it carelessly into his duffel bag as well. He zips it up, and I decide that spying on your neighbor is not a very polite thing to do. I go back to bed, wrapping myself in my blanket, intent on going back to sleep.

What was Alex talking about today? He said these days were evil. Well, if you watch the news, every day is evil, but I don't recall anyone talking about a specific terrible event… except for the Lake Street murder, of course. Could that be what he was talking about? When he talked, he sounded almost as if it was… personal. Something that he and I shared somehow, but I have no idea how that could be.

I suddenly recall the dream I had last night.

"It's a shame that they've angered it."

"Who?"

"The predator… It's angry. And it doesn't like it when its prey escapes."

I shiver in my bed. Was there anything else Coral said in my dream? I try to remember, but nothing comes to mind.

I have to go to sleep soon. If I don't, I'll be half a zombie tomorrow. Sleep! I try to command myself. I empty my thoughts, trying to push the dead woman, Alex, and the dream from my mind. I close my eyes, relaxing my breath. I just need to sleep. Forget about the creature, growling in the darkness, two cold blue eyes gazing at me malevolently as it plans to pounce on me, scratch me with its claws, snap my neck with rows of sharp, long teeth…

I struggle with those thoughts, but they come at me from all sides, tormenting me, and I know the creature is there. It might be lurking outside right now, just waiting for an opportunity to get me.

My blanket suddenly feels heavy, suffocating. I try to throw it off but it coils, twisting around my legs, my arms, my neck, covering my mouth and my nose, smothering me, and all I can think of is Alex's voice saying, "These are evil days… Evil days… You know what I mean… Evil days…" I can't get free. I want to scream but my mouth is blocked. I push at it again and again and it tightens like some sort of predatory snake… "The predator, it's angry…"

Eventually I fall off the bed.

I scramble up, switch on the light. I stare at the evil blanket, which doesn't seem evil at all. Just a blanket. Have I fallen asleep? Probably.

Though it didn't feel as if I was asleep.

These are evil days. I knew it since the first moment I found out that someone had died on Lake Street. Just like I knew it the first time I heard Tom Ellis's strange whistling outside my window. Something wicked this way comes, and it's coming to Narrowdale. And my instincts scream at me to stay away, to escape it as fast as I can… But there's something else in me, and it pushes me towards the danger instead.

Like a moth to the flame, isn't that the phrase? I always thought that this was some silly mistake made by God. He was so busy what with all the creation of the earth and the beasts, and man, and handling Adam and Eve's shenanigans, that he hadn't noticed he created a creature that's attracted to the thing that kills it. Or, if we're trying to be more scientific, why isn't there a moth that doesn't fly into flames? Shouldn't evolution have taken care of that?

And now I am the moth, and I know how it feels. I simply can't tear my eyes away. I have to push and prod at this, over and over, until I figure it out. And even though I suspect I almost died today… I still can't shake the feeling that I need to investigate this further.

I sit down by my table, turn on my laptop. The usual messages, video clips and time wasters all wink at me, trying to sell their services. This time I am stronger, logging in to my blog instead, writing a new blog post. I publish it and turn the laptop off. Sleep can be postponed even longer, but should it be?

I look at my bed. My warm, evil blanket waits for me. Well… maybe not evil. Me and this blanket have gone through a lot of cold nights together. We had a long and lovely relationship. What's one murder attempt between such good friends? I lie back in bed, huddling under the blanket, which does not try to strangle me again.

And eventually, with the light on, I fall asleep.

http://amy.strangerealm.com/crimeScene.html

Chapter Ten

I stir the cereal in my bowl tiredly. It does not look appetizing. Then again, I let it soak in its milk for a few minutes while I stared at the bowl, nodding off occasionally, so I can blame only myself. I shovel some soft, spongy cereal up with my spoon, and aim it towards my mouth. Though it seems like a simple procedure, I find great difficulty with it. My mouth is not nearly wide enough, and some of the milk ends up dribbling down my chin. This is a pathetic display of eating skills that would better match a four-year-old. I sigh, wipe my chin and try again. This time the spongy mess makes it into my mouth in its entirety. Let's hear it for Amy. Hip hip hurray. I'm so tired.

The doorbell rings, making me flinch and causing my spoon-holding hand to jolt. A splotch of milk ends up on my right pant leg. A normal human being would try and clean it with a wet towel, maybe even change her pants. I, however, feel satisfied with brushing it with my hand and letting the milk find a new home within the fabric of my pants, where it will definitely add an interesting fragrance. My, my, Amy, is that a new perfume you're wearing today? Why, yes, it's called eau de la yogurt, I can't recommend it highly enough.

The doorbell rings once more. I do the expected, which is yell, "Mom! Someone's at the door!" and then ignore it, hoping it will go away.

"Can you see who it is, sweetie? I'm in the middle of something here!"

In the middle? In the middle of doing what? What could be so important that it can take precedence over opening the door and letting me eat my sludge in peace? I sigh, drop my half-full bowl in the sink and walk to the front door.

It takes me a second to get to the door, and meanwhile, the doorbell rings once more. Now that I'm near the door, its shrill buzz threatens to drill a hole in my delicate, sleep-deprived brain. "Fine, fine, hang on," I say, my voice much harsher than it was supposed to be. I unlock the door and open it.

"Alex!" I say in surprise.

"Good morning, Amy," he says.

"My mom is in the middle of something," I say. "Hang on, I'll call her."

"No need," he quickly replies. "I came here to talk to you."

"Me?"

"Yes. I am going away for a few days, and I need someone to take care of Moka for me. Could you please do that?"

"A few... I mean... take care? What...?" My mental facilities are not up to the task of struggling with this.

"She just needs to be taken for a walk twice a day, and to be fed after her walk. Oh, and you should make sure she has enough water."

"I'm not sure I'm the right person for this..."

"Of course you are! Moka really likes you. And I would really appreciate it. I will pay for this service as well, of course. Ten dollars a day. That's a good rate for dog walking, isn't it?"

I don't have the dog walking price chart with me. "Maybe you should get a professional dog walker... I'm sure there's a lot of those in Narrowdale."

"Oh, I just thought... you know. What with all you two have gone through together..."

"What we've gone through together?" This conversation is taking a weird turn. "What are you talking about?"

"Well, someone saved your life from that evil man, right?"

I cross my arms and fix my stare at him. "You said you didn't know anything about that."

"About what?"

"About the animal that attacked Tom Ellis."

"I don't. But it sounds like you were very lucky," he says. "Why, if someone saved my life, I would be thrilled at the opportunity to repay—"

"Okay, okay, I'll do it." I crack under the passive aggressive assault.

"Good! Her food is by the door, and you can fill the water from the hose in the yard. Oh, and her leash is hanging from a nail on the wall. Just for a couple of days. No more than a week."

"A week?"

"Oh, and when you walk her, don't let her eat cat shit. And you don't have to walk her this morning, I already did that."

"I… what?"

"I already walked her this morning."

"No, I mean… about the cat…"

"Oh. She likes eating cat shit. Don't let her do that."

"Why?"

"Because eating cat shit isn't healthy," he clarifies.

"No, I mean… why does she like to eat… what the cat does?"

"I really can't say. I think she finds it tasty. Anyway, thanks for helping me. I really appreciate it. I'll only be a week, maybe ten days."

"Ten… days?"

"Two weeks tops. Thanks again, Amy. Goodbye!" He smiles charmingly and walks away, leaving me staring after him in shock.

"Who was that?" Mom asks, descending from upstairs.

"It was Alex, the neighbor," I say dumbly.

"What did he want?"

"He wants me to take care of his dog while he's away."

"Oh, my. Does he know that you're not exactly the best person for the job?"

"Well, I told him… Hang on. You think I can't take care of a dog for a couple of days?"

"Well, when you had to water the plants when I was in Mexico, they all died."

"Not all of them!"

"All but the cactus."

"There you go," I say triumphantly.

"Well, good luck with that," she replies. "Now go on, you're gonna be late for school."

I nod. Two weeks. Heavens help me.

Chapter Eleven

"Hey," Shane says as he joins me and Coral in the cafeteria. "What's up?"

I look at him. He doesn't look angry anymore, and I feel relieved.

"Shane, I'm really sorry about—" I start saying.

"Forget it," he interrupts me, then adds in a softer tone. "It's okay. Let's just not do this again, okay?"

"Do what?" Coral asks and immediately adds, "Oh, you went there yesterday, didn't you?" She sounds as if she's asking if we've jumped into a pool of snot by any chance.

"Yeah, it was terrible," Shane says. We tell her about last night, and as is customary, interrupt and contradict each other as much as possible, to ensure that Coral's idea of what happened is as convoluted as possible.

"Amy, that's really scary," she says when we finally sum it up. "Promise me you're dropping this."

"I promise," I say.

"How's math study going?" Shane asks Coral.

"I don't know," she says, shrugging. "When I go to sleep at night I dream that I'm solving algebra exercises."

"Ugh," Shane says, frowning. "Maybe you should ease up a bit."

I brace myself for the imminent angry answer, but Coral just sighs. "I don't think I can," she mumbles, her hands flat on the table. "When I stop studying I become really stressed out."

Shane lays his hand on hers. She smiles at him. "I know I'm weird," she says. "I can't help it."

"We're all weird," I say.

"Yeah," Shane says. "I mean... look at Amy and her murder hobby. Doesn't get weirder than that."

"You make it sound like I like to murder people," I say. Coral giggles.

"Oh, that reminds me," Shane says, leaning back in his chair. "Did you hear? They finally mentioned the dead woman from Lake Street on the news last night."

"Really?" I ask, my heart suddenly beating fast. "Did they say what had happened to her?"

"No." He shrugs. "They didn't even say she was murdered. They simply reported that an old woman named Alice Hendrix was found dead at her home in Narrowdale."

"They didn't say anything else?" I ask, surprised.

"Nope."

"I don't get it." I shake my head. "Why would they hide the fact that she was murdered?"

"I don't care why," Shane interrupts me. "Let the police handle this."

"Maybe the police are hiding the fact that it was a murder to confuse the killer," Coral suggests. "Or to avoid any panic."

We all think about it for a second.

"Or maybe it was hushed up," I finally suggest. "Like they hush up all the weird stories here."

"Right!" Coral says. "Maybe it was hushed up by the same government agency that faked the moon landing. Or better yet, it was hushed up by the Illuminati to prevent us from realizing their world domination scheme."

"Oh, you're a total riot," I tell her. "You should really have your own show. Fine, whatever. The police didn't release the story to avoid any panic. Alice Hendrix, huh? Did they say anything about her?"

"I think they said she was elderly," Shane answers. "I'm pretty sure they said she was a retired something or other."

"Who do we know by the name of Hendrix?" I ask. "It sounds familiar."

"Jimi Hendrix," Shane and Coral reply together.

"Okay, other than him," I say.

"It's probably a pretty common surname," Coral says. "I mean… our Spanish teacher is named Vivian Hendrix."

"Right! Vivian," I say. "Hang on! She was missing yesterday. Maybe she wasn't sick. Maybe she was missing because her relative just died!"

"And maybe she was sick," Coral suggests.

"We should check it out," I say.

"We really shouldn't," says Shane. "Because it doesn't concern us."

"Aren't you worried that your Spanish teacher's mother might have died?" I ask Coral.

"Now it's her mother?"

"I mean… if it's true she might be gone for a while. And there's a test coming up, isn't there?" I gamble. There's always a test.

"You're right." Coral nods. "There is a test. And she hasn't told us what's on the test yet… Oh, fine." She's clearly irked. "Let's go check it out. Just to make sure that everything's fine."

"You two do what you want," Shane says. "I'm not coming."

"That's exactly what's happening," I tell him.

He ignores me with disgust, fiddling with his camera.

We walk over to the main office to talk to the school's secretary. I have to admit, I'm not even sure where the main office is, nor do I know what the secretary's name is. Coral, however, approaches her as if she's approaching a dear friend.

"Hey, Rozanne." She smiles at her. "How are you today?"

Rozanne's face is a classic makeup catastrophe. Too much lipstick, ugly topaz-colored eye shadow, shiny forehead… ugh. Why doesn't anyone ever take her aside and help her with all that? Her face lights up as she sees Coral. You'd think it was her own daughter who was asking about her well-being. "Oh, you know," she says, sighing. "Can't complain."

Her tone indicates that, in fact, she can complain. It hints that if she started complaining, it'd be a while before she'd stop. If Rozanne wrote her complaints down in a book, it'd become a trilogy.

"I was wondering, when is Miss Hendrix coming back?" Coral asks.

"Oh, honey, you haven't heard? Her mother just passed away," Rozanne says, shaking her head sadly. "It'll be a while before she returns."

Me and Coral exchange glances. Two points for Amy.

"It's really very sad," Rozanne carries on. "After the business with Ron Hammond."

"Ron Hammond, the social studies teacher?" I say, surprised. "What has he got to do with it?"

She looks at me coldly, and I recall that I'm not really a part of this conversation. I'm just a random student. Coral is her bosom friend.

"Ron and Vivian were a couple," she finally says, addressing Coral. "It wasn't a secret or anything. They lived together. Until he decided to take off."

"You mean until he disappeared," Coral corrects her.

"Oh, no. He definitely took off. He took his dog with him."

"Ron had a dog?"

"Yes, a large one. I saw him take it for walks many times." Rozanne says. "And, well, if he simply disappeared, his dog would still be here, wouldn't it?"

"Not necessarily," Coral says, irritated. The girl simply can't stand people who jump to conclusions. Makes me wonder how she can bear being my friend. "The dog could have run away. It may have disappeared as well. I can think of a dozen reasons why the dog wouldn't stay."

"You're very sweet," Rozanne says in a condescending tone.

"Why did Mr. Hammond leave?" I ask. "Didn't they get along?"

She looks at me, and I can practically feel the hatred blossoming. Good one, Amy. Get on the school's secretary's bad side.

They got along just fine," she says curtly. Something in her tone makes me believe that they did not get along fine at all. "I'm surprised that you would gossip about your Spanish teacher on a day like this."

"What happened to Miss Hendrix's mother?" Coral asks. "Was she ill?"

"Didn't you hear? She was killed!" Rozanne says, clearly excited to find someone who hasn't heard. "They found her body two days ago! It was even in the news!"

"Really?" Coral asks, her voice full of awe. "In the news?" The girl once again amazes me with her acting skills.

"Yes." Rozanne nods emphatically. "It's so terrible." She says 'terrible' so cheerfully one might think she's talking about a party.

"What happened to her?"

"Oh, no one knows. But I've heard from my cousin, who knows a cop"—her voice lowers to a conspiratorial tone—"that all the mirrors and the windows in her house were shattered. Don't tell anyone I told you about it. I really shouldn't talk about it."

Of course she shouldn't. Coral thanks her just as the bell rings.

"So it looks like there won't be any Spanish lessons this week," I tell Coral as we are walking to class.

"It does look that way," she agrees. "Now please, do me a favor and stop poking your nose into this, okay?"

"Hey, I promised," I say.

I can see that she still doesn't believe me.

Chapter Twelve

Half an hour before dinner I walk to Alex's house. I realize that I've never actually crossed the threshold to his yard. We always talked on the street, or above his fence. I feel strangely anxious as I open the gate to his front yard and walk inside. It is well kept, though a bit dull. There's mostly lawn, with a few flowers planted in various corners. Moka jumps happily at me when I close the gate.

"Hey, girl." I smile, petting her, and she licks my hand. "You're a good dog. And I'm pretty sure that you've saved my life once, right?"

She licks my hand some more. I suddenly recall what Alex said about the cat poop. I quickly snatch my hand back. "Tell you what," I say. "Let's try to avoid licking, okay?" Moka opens her mouth widely and lolls her tongue out. She looks as if she's laughing at me.

"Did you eat today?" I ask. She looks at me hopefully, wagging her tail, her ears alert. Probably not. I walk over to the large food container and open it. There's a measuring cup inside. I fill it with food and pour it into her bowl. She charges at the bowl as if she hasn't seen food for months. I fill her water bowl with the hose, and then I notice a small post-it stuck on the door. It says, *Amy, thanks for doing this. I've already fed her today, so there's no need to do it again.* I turn to look at Moka, who's licking her lips. "You liar," I say. She wags her tail.

I locate her leash, and she starts jumping around me excitedly, barking short, loud barks.

"Okay, okay, quiet. Sit down. Sit. Sit! Hang on, I can't tie this leash like this... I told you, no licking! Sit! How am I supposed to... Oh, come on... Sit! Bad dog! Moka, please sit. Sit!!!"

Finally I manage to tie the leash to her collar, and we leave the front yard. We walk ten feet and she urinates on our fence.

"That's not nice," I say. "What if I peed on your fence? Would you like it if I did that?"

She stares at me. I sigh and try to banish the disturbing image that my last sentence conjured up. This dog is turning me into a moron.

We walk down the street slowly, Moka sniffing each fence, lamppost and tree. She stops completely next to a mound of sand, sniffing at it in concentration. Suddenly her head snaps down and she grabs something in her mouth.

Cat poop.

"Oh, yuck!" I yell. "I... what's wrong with you, why would you even... No, get that tongue away from me, crazy dog. You are never ever licking me again, you got that?" She wags her tail, looking very pleased.

We keep walking. Now, every time she stops, I suspiciously check to make sure there's no cat poop potential. We have three more close calls, but I manage to pull her back each time. I have become an expert in cat toilets. This will go straight onto my resume.

I quickly realize something about walking dogs. Half the time you are walking the dog, but the other half, it is walking you. Sure, as long as there is nothing interesting, Moka happily matches my pace, the leash feeling loose in my hand. But when something alluring appears, like a cat, or a mound of sand, or a snack wrapper discarded on the street, the leash is suddenly stretched tight, and I metamorphose from a fourteen-year-old girl into a sled. Moka simply drags me with her in whichever direction she fancies, and if I decide to fight back, she just pulls harder, making strange choking noises.

"Seriously, this can't go on like this," I tell her when she drags me to an incredibly interesting tree. "I should be the one to decide where we're going." Moka ignores me, sniffing the tree. She then proceeds to pee on it, and I wonder what message that conveys to the rest of the dogs in the neighborhood. Is this a territorial marking, or is it a simple message, like, "Good night :-)" Do dogs even have emoticons in their pee?

Several joggers go by, and while some of them simply run onward, others make a huge half circuit to avoid me. This is new to me. I always knew that some people were afraid of dogs, but now that I'm walking one, I find this strangely annoying. One of the joggers mutters a complaint, something about me taking up the entire sidewalk. That's entirely untrue, and I grit my teeth in irritation.

It takes twenty minutes, but finally Moka and I find the right pace and the right frame of mind to walk in harmony. I do my best to walk near things that would interest her, and she notices this, and stops pulling me everywhere. We have a silent agreement that when a cat crosses our path, she growls and pulls at the leash, but not too hard. I'm surprised to find that I'm enjoying this experience. There's a feeling of friendship between us, and I don't recall ever feeling like this towards any animal, not even Fluffers, the bunny I had when I was six.

We're walking past Lake Street on the way back home when suddenly I feel the leash tighten again. I turn to Moka and see that she's standing with one foot in the air, looking towards the dark street, her ears perked up, alert.

"Moka, come on," I say, pulling her a bit. She doesn't budge, simply keeps staring into the darkness.

"Moka, we have to go."

She growls, but she isn't growling at me. She's growling into the shadows, towards something I can't see. Is there something there? I squint, trying to see what she's looking at. Was there movement? A small sound, perhaps, like a dry leaf crackling? Moka growls again, and we both keep still. I don't dare to turn my back to the street. I feel as if a strange, dark presence is standing there, watching us, poised to strike.

Eventually, Moka wags her tail once and begins walking again. I follow her, glancing backwards every few steps, but there's nothing

there. I shiver.
　　Tomorrow I'll take her on a different route.

Chapter Thirteen

On Friday, my birthday, Mom wakes me up instead of the alarm clock.

"Amy, sweetie, get up!" she says cheerfully. "It's your birthday!"

"Grrrrmphhh," I moan. "Ten more minutes."

"You've asked for ten more minutes twice already," Mom says. "If you don't get up now, I'll pour a glass of water on your head."

I sit up, tossing the blanket away. "There, I'm up," I grumble. "Happy now?"

"My baby is fifteen years old," Mom says. "Of course I'm happy."

"I'm cold," I complain, but Mom's already gone, closing the door behind her. I consider going back to bed… but no. Mom's threat about the glass of water is far from idle. It has been implemented before, on a particularly tough morning. I get out of bed, shivering slightly from the cold. What's with Dad and the thermostat? I have a suspicion that he cranks it down one degree every day. We'll be popsicles by the end of winter. I open the wardrobe and rummage around in it. I actually know what I'm about to wear. I've planned my birthday outfit for several days now. My favorite black leggings are folded neatly on the shelf. I've avoided wearing them all week so that I would be able to wear them today. A blue dress Mom bought me last year, and I fasten a black belt on top, the one I got on sale at the end of last winter. I comb my hair in front of the mirror, examining the way I look. Is it possible that this dress makes me look like a box? I like its cut, but…

Mom knocks on the door, then opens it. "Well? Are you coming for breakfast?"

"Mom, does this dress make me look like a box?"

"No, sweetie, it looks lovely."

"Are you trying to tell me that I am a box?"

"Amy, come on, we're waiting." She goes back downstairs.

I put on some mascara and blink. Not bad, not bad at all. I follow Mom downstairs.

Mom and Dad begin singing "Happy birthday to you" the moment I step in the kitchen. They're standing next to the table, on which lies a beautiful birthday cake and a box. A mystery box, whose contents are not mysterious at all.

"Is that what I think it is?" I ask excitedly.

"First blow out the candles," Dad says.

I take a deep breath and blow them all. As my parents are clapping, I snatch the box. I want to tear open the wrapping paper, but Mom gets offended when I don't read the card. I open it, and a panda bear smiles at me, holding some candy. It looks kinda creepy, but I don't really care. The card says, *Sweetie, you're fifteen! We can't believe it! Sometimes we feel like we were changing your diapers just a week ago.* (Eyes rolling) *We hope you have a lovely birthday and a lovely year. You can open the box now, you don't have to pretend like the card is all you cared about. Love, Mom and Dad.* I put down the card, smiling, and greedily open the box. There they are, the loves of my life. For a moment I simply stare at them, the most perfect boots in the universe. Knee high, sharp heels, a silver buckle. When I first saw them, at the mall with Mom, I knew instantly that we were meant to be together. Mom agreed to buy them for my birthday despite their outrageous, probably illegal, price. I sit down and try them on, knowing they'll fit. I made sure on the day we saw them.

"Aren't they beautiful?" I say, beaming with joy.

"They're very beautiful, sweetie," Mom agrees.

"Aren't they beautiful, Dad?"

"They're very… are they even comfortable? That heel looks really high."

"Oh, they're incredibly comfortable," I say, spinning. What a marvelous gift!

"That's great, sweetie, I'm glad you're happy." Mom smiles. "Now, go on and take Moka for a walk. Today I'm giving you a ride to school."

"Okay, thanks, I…" I pause. "Hang on, wasn't Anthony supposed to be back for my birthday?"

"He is, but he got in really late last night, so we let him…" I don't wait to hear the rest. I run up the stairs and burst through Anthony's door.

"Happy birthday to me!" I yell. "Thanks for getting up for me! That's so sweet!"

"Happy birthday," he mumbles into his pillow. "Go away."

"Well, aren't you going to sing for me?" I ask with a hurt voice.

"Sure. Happy birthday to you. Happy birthday to you. Happy birthday dear"—he turns, grabs a shoe and throws it at me—"Amy, happy birthday to you."

I look at the dark smudge on his wall where the shoe hit. "God, you're the worst shot in the world. If it weren't for gravity, you'd have missed the ground."

"Go away!" he begs.

"Amy." Mom walks in, pulling me out and closing the door. "Anthony's really tired. Now go on and take that dog for a walk."

I shrug and go over to Alex's. Moka is waiting for me there, wagging her tail. I give her some food and water, then take her for a walk, avoiding Lake Street completely. When I get back home, Mom's doing her "I can't find my keys" dance. It involves a lot of rummaging and raising her hands in frustration.

It's not a very good dance.

"I think I saw them on the bathroom floor," Dad says, reading the paper.

"Well, why didn't you say something? Amy's going to be late!" Mom snaps and walks up to their bathroom.

"I'm not going to be late," I say.

Dad sips from his cup of coffee, completely unfazed. "I know you're not."

"Okay," Mom says, coming back down and shaking her keys. "Let's go."

On the way to school my phone rings.

"Honey!!!" My eardrum is ripped to shreds. "Happy birthday!!! You're so cool!"

"Thanks, Nicole." I smile. "Why am I cool?"

"Because you're fifteen! That's a cool age to be!"

"Really? Okay. You're coming today, right?"

"Sure," Nicole says. "We'll be leaving at about four, so I guess we'll be at your place at about six…ish? Maybe a bit before? Hang on… what?" Nicole starts talking to someone else. "Yeah, okay. My mom wants to know the address. She can't get anywhere without her navigation app."

"Thirteen Maple Street, Narrowdale," I answer.

"Yeah, okay. Say, honey, what's that thing you wrote in your last post?"

"Let's talk about it later, okay?" I say, glancing at my mom. If she finds out about what happened to me and Shane two days ago, I'm dead.

"Sure. Ooooh! Do you know what happened yesterday?" She starts rambling about something that the bus driver told her, I can't really follow the details. We reach school and it takes two more minutes until I can interrupt Nicole and tell her that I have to go. I get out of the car, Mom grumbling that she feels like a cab driver, the way I talked on the phone the entire ride.

As I'm walking towards class I run into Roxanne from my homeroom. I don't care for her much. She always has something nasty to say—

"Hey, Amy… Wow, those boots are gorgeous!"

She's actually not that bad, she can be really sweet when she—

"I usually don't really get your weird taste in clothing, but those boots are fantastic. And they make you seem kind of tall… Well, taller, anyway."

Bitch.

Once I get to class, two girls compliment my boots as well, their compliments more positive. I practically hover to my seat in bliss.

Then Coral enters the classroom, holding a big red helium balloon.

"Happy birthday!" she yells and hugs me, forgetting the balloon, which quickly floats to the ceiling. Both of us are way too short to get it back (even with my new boots). Chris, a boy who sits two rows behind us, quickly climbs onto the table and gets the balloon.

"Here," he says, handing it to me.

"Thanks," I answer, my eyes drawn to the muddy footprint he left on my desk. I hold out my hand and he gives me the balloon, but his fingers don't release the string for a few seconds. I raise an eyebrow, and the fingers loosen.

"I... uh... Happy birthday, Amy."

"Thanks, Chris." I look at him. I guess Nicole would think he's cute. He's got that messy musician vibe going on, with curly hair that's way too long, and torn pants. I'm pretty sure that he plays the guitar, though I can't recall where I got that tidbit of information.

"So... what are your plans for today?"

"Uh... school?" I say. "Then some friends from LA are coming over."

"Oh."

The silence stretches. He turns to Coral. "You should have gotten a longer balloon string," he tells her.

"Why, thank you, *Doctor Balloon*," she says.

For some reason I think that *Doctor Balloon* is the funniest thing I've ever heard and I burst out laughing. Chris shrugs as if *Doctor Balloon* is something he hears every day and walks back to his seat.

Coral sits down next to me and hands me a wipe to clean my desk. She always has wipes in her bag.

"When are you coming over today?" I ask.

"About eight thirty, after dinner."

"Can't you be at my place sooner?"

"Well, my mom really wants us to eat Friday dinner together." She squirms. "It's like... really important to her."

"Come on," I say. "It would mean a lot."

"Well... my mom's really offended if I don't eat everything, or if I leave the table too soon. I guess, maybe we could start dinner a bit earlier. I could make salad, and then Mom wouldn't need to make salad. She always complains that she hates making salad, so I guess she'd be happy if I did it..."

I let her keep on with her monologue, waving my boots in front of her face. When will she notice?

"...I could probably be at your place at around a quarter past eight, maybe even a bit sooner..."

"Coral, never mind, what do you think?"

"What do I think about what?"

I wave my boots again.

"Amy, cut that out, you almost kicked me. Maybe I should call Mom now, before class starts..."

"Coral, what do you think of my boots?"

She looks at them, and I wait, holding my breath.

"Are they new?" she finally asks.

The teacher walks in, and our conversation is interrupted.

During lunch, Coral, Shane and I sit together, and I happily open my lunch bag. Mom made me a special birthday sandwich, with omelet, lettuce, tomato and mayonnaise. It's my favorite. I take a big bite.

"The present from me and Coral is not ready yet, so we'll give it to you tomorrow, okay?"

"'Kay," I say, mouth full. A small piece of tomato drops from my mouth on my leggings, leaving a stain. I groan in horror. My perfect outfit!

"Hang on, I'll get the wipes," Coral says and starts searching in her bag.

"These are the leggings I've been saving all week," I moan. "This can't be happening!"

"Oh, I'm sure it'll come out," Coral tries to reassure me.

"You think so?" I ask, trying to smile. "Yeah, you're right. It's just mayonnaise. It could be worse. It could be machinery grease."

"How could it be machinery grease?" Shane asks.

"I'm just saying it could," I say, trying to maintain a bright outlook on life.

"So? What are you girls doing today?" Shane asks in apparent disinterest. I look at him, a bit worried. He didn't seem to mind when I told him we were doing a girls' night out, but sometimes it's hard to know with Shane. I wonder if he really thinks we will all wear shortie pajamas. It sounds absurd.

"We're going to see a movie," I say.

"That's nice."

"And tomorrow you're coming over, right?"

"Yeah, I told you, we're bringing you your birthday present."

"Oh, right."

We both sit in silence, and Coral finally pulls her wipes from her bag with a victorious "Aha!"

"You're a life saver," I tell her and rub the stain. "It's not coming out."

"I can hardly see it," Coral says.

"You didn't even notice that I have new boots on," I mention.

"I noticed the boots, I just didn't realize they were new," she says, irritated. "Fine, then wear a different pair of leggings this evening. This isn't the end of the world."

"It is the end of the world," I say. "They're the only leggings I have that match my boots so nicely."

"Then don't wear the boots."

I look at her, horrified. "Why would I ever do that?"

"Because you said... never mind."

The bell rings and we all go to class as I mourn the demise of my perfect outfit.

Chapter Fourteen

I check the time. It's a quarter to six. Nicole said they'd leave at around four, so they should be here soon. I look out the window at the empty street. No cars on the horizon. I check the time once more. Fourteen minutes to six. I decide to go and take Moka for a walk.

When I return I begin actively keeping myself busy. I search for information about Alice Hendrix. I find a short news article which reports that Alice Hendrix, age seventy-six, was found dead in her home by her neighbor. The police are investigating her death. There isn't any additional information. The article has two comments. One says that the elderly should be taken care of, and that it is a shame that a woman died like that, with no care. The second comment is by someone who complains about Republicans. What has that got to do with anything? I get up, disgusted, and turn on the TV. I locate a movie with Steven Seagal. The plot is… Well, I'm not sure there is one. There's a respectable amount of punching and kicking, and a lot of Steven Seagal walking around with a determined glare. I bet that even when he eats pancakes he's got a determined glare. Poor pancakes.

By six thirty, I'm pretty sure that my brain has melted into porridge. When ice melts, it becomes water. When brains melt, they become porridge. Just like in the book, *Frankenstein*:

"Igor, fetch the brain!"

"I forgot to put it in the freezer, Master. It is now porridge."

"Igor, fetch the cinnamon!"

My phone rings, startling me out of my daydream. "Hello?" I answer

"Honey, I think we're here," Nicole says. "Which house is yours?"

"Thirteen. Next to the house with the ugly veranda."

"I can't even see any house numbers."

"Hang on, I'm coming out to meet you." I get up and walk outside. It's really cold today, and I walk out without my coat. By the time their car stops next to me, I feel like the cold has invaded my body and is now here to stay.

"Hi, Amy!" Nicole's mom, Mabel, smiles at me. "Happy birthday."

"Thanks," I say, hopping from foot to foot. Nicole and the Jennifers get out of the car. Jennifer Scott hugs me. Her long, smooth auburn hair is swept by the wind, tickling my face. She takes a step back and smiles, her blue eyes lighting up. Jennifer Scott. The ultimate beauty.

"Girls, don't forget your bags," Mabel says. Nicole is now hugging me as the Jennifers both get their bags from the trunk. As always, Nicole's positively brimming with energy. Though her black hair is tied in a haphazard ponytail, two strands have escaped and are dangling charmingly on her cheeks. It seems completely random. It absolutely isn't. This hairstyle is designed to make her seem sexy and carefree. It does it marvelously.

The three of them, I notice, are wearing thick, warm coats. What was I thinking, walking outside like this?

Well, they saw where I live, so I can walk inside now. I turn towards the house when Mabel says, "How's your mom?"

"Oh, she's great. Really great," I say, desperately edging towards the front door.

"What is she doing these days?"

"She's working in Narrowdale's library."

"Really? Doing what?"

Doing what? Practicing dentistry. "She's a clerk."

Nicole and the Jennifers are standing by me, their bags in their hands. My teeth are chattering. I'm pretty sure the wind has gotten even colder.

"Amy, we're going inside," Nicole says. "It's kinda chilly out here."

I nod. The three of them walk inside and close the door, so the heat won't escape.

"And how's your dad?" Mabel asks with rapt attention.

Oh, we have a marvelous conversation, about Dad, and Anthony, and how I'm doing at school, and all I can think of are my limbs, which will probably fall off soon. Finally, she drives away and I stumble inside.

"Hey, Amy," Nicole says. "Lovely house you have here." She and Jennifer Scott are smiling. Jennifer Williams seems a bit anxious and fidgety.

"Hey, Williams," I say, smiling at her faintly. "What's up?"

"Bathroom?" she squeaks. Nicole and Scott burst out laughing as I point over my shoulder towards the bathroom.

"We stopped at McDonald's on the way," Nicole says. "She drank a big Coke but refused to go to the bathroom. You know how she gets with public toilets."

I nod, and there's a sudden shriek behind me. I turn and quickly walk over to the storage room. I pull Jennifer out and close the door.

"So… that's the storage room. Mom gets upset when I pee there," I tell her. "The bathroom is behind that door, over there."

"Do you have a dog?" Williams asks, looking shaken. "I didn't know you had a dog!"

"That's because I don't," I say, looking at her in amusement.

"That's so weird… I could have sworn I heard… Never mind." She shakes her head and walks off to the bathroom.

I make tea for all of us. By the time we finish drinking it I can feel all my limbs once more, and none of them is falling off anytime soon.

I take the girls on a tour around the house. Though they've practically seen all of it on my blog, they still nod and pay nice compliments, because that's how things are done. We walk to Anthony's room, and he even does his best to be civil. Then we locate a bag of potato chips and go to my room. Nicole tells a story about some teacher they ran into in the lingerie store, and Jennifer Scott can't stop laughing, though apparently she's been there herself. Williams keeps staring outside the window.

"Jen, are you okay?" Scott asks.

"Yeah, I... it's hot in here. Isn't it hot in here?" We stare at her in surprise. We're all wearing sweaters, and I suddenly notice that she took hers off and is wearing only a thin long-sleeved t-shirt. Her green eyes seem jittery, troubled somehow, and her dark hair is even more all over the place than usual. The single purple braid she has droops sadly by her left ear.

"Not really," Nicole says. "It's actually kind of chilly in here."

"Do you want a glass of water?" I ask. She nods. I get her one, and she drinks it in one long gulp.

"Do you want another one?" I ask, a bit concerned. She shakes her head.

"Oh, what about the gift?" Scott asks.

Nicole claps. "Right!" She rummages in her bag and pulls out a small package, which she hands me. "Happy birthday!"

No card. Do these girls know me, or what? I tear off the wrap. Within the package there's a beautiful red long sleeved t-shirt.

"Wow, that's fantastic," I say happily, and they all insist that I try it on right now. I do, it fits, and I look hot.

"Hey, where's Coral?" asks Nicole. "Shouldn't she be here?"

"She'll be here later," I say. "She's eating with her family."

"Oh, she's got some sort of special family event?"

"No, I think it's a simple family dinner," I say.

"Then why isn't she here?" Nicole insists. I shrug.

Nicole starts questioning me about the evening we broke into Alice Hendrix's house. What exactly did we see there? What did the policeman tell us? What was it that chased me in the darkness? Am I sure it was real? I try to answer coherently, but the memory of that evening is hazy and jumbled, and my answers are vague and seem to frustrate Nicole. When the doorbell rings, I leave with a measure of relief to open it for Coral.

It's Coral... sort of. I look at her in amazement. She's discarded her usual frayed jeans for tight black pants. She's wearing a green, long sweater which looks fantastic on her, and her neck is adorned with a delicate silver necklace. She's even wearing makeup - a mauve eyeliner which brings out her warm brown eyes, and a delicate lipstick.

"Wow, Coral," I breathe out in admiration. "You look amazing! Lipstick?"

"I, uh… borrowed it from my mom," she says shyly. "Do you like it?"

"I love it!" I lead her to my room and introduce her to Nicole and the Jennifers.

"Nice to meet you," Coral says. And they all nod and agree that it is indeed nice to meet them. They show her the shirt they bought me, and she oohs and aahs accordingly.

"I'll give you my present tomorrow, with Shane," she says.

"Cool," I say distractedly, staring into my wardrobe.

"What's up, honey?" asks Nicole.

"Well, my favorite leggings are stained, and they were perfect for my new boots. Now I have nothing to wear."

"What about your red skirt?" asks Nicole. "It'd fit your lovely boots nicely."

"Are you insane?" I ask. "Do you want me to freeze to death?"

"Don't worry about it, honey, I brought warm tights which would be great with that skirt. They have this nice pattern… red and black… hang on." She begins rummaging in her bag once more.

"Do you know where I saw those tights for the first time?" Nicole says, her face deep inside her bag. "On Deirdre. Would you believe it? She came to school wearing them with this ugly gray skirt, and a shirt two sizes too big. There was a test or something, I don't remember what it was exactly, but she was so stressed out! I asked her where she got the tights, and she thought it was something she had to know for the test. She nearly burst into tears!" Nicole laughs, handing me the tights. "There you go, try them on. I don't get that girl. What's her thing with grades? I've never met anyone so uptight…"

"Maybe she just wants to do well," Coral says. I desperately try to signal Nicole to shut the hell up, but she's to busy rummaging in her bag.

"Nah, Coral, you have no idea, you've never seen anything like it. She's so stressed out, she's like a real life Charlie Brown. And she dresses and acts like my aunt... Hang on, honey, it's twisted in the back, let me get that for you... There. Now put on your skirt... I mean... I get that she wants to succeed, but we're only fourteen once, right? She should live a little! Amy, you know Deirdre, tell her."

"Uh..." I stutter, trying to fit into my skirt. "She's really not that bad."

"Give me a break. Did she ever say anything to you that wasn't school-related? Now put on your boots... I have to borrow them sometime... don't look at me like that, I didn't mean right now." She finally becomes quiet for a second, simply watching me and smiling. "Honey, you're the sexiest of them all. If the evil stepmom was here with her magic mirror, she'd drown you with poisoned apples."

"Okay," I agree, grinning. "But what will you wear?"

"I'll borrow the pants that you wore to the concert last year. Do you still have them?"

As she's trying them on, I notice that Coral is staring at the floor, silent. Williams is still looking out the window, her fingers tapping irritably on the windowsill. Nicole and Scott chat with each other, laughing.

"Uh... how was dinner?" I ask Coral, trying to catch her eye.

"Fine," she says. "It was fine."

"I'm really glad you came," I say desperately. "And it's cool that you finally met my LA friends, right?"

She raises her head and I look at her. I know Coral well, and I can see the hurt and insecurity in her eyes. I wish I had silenced Nicole earlier, but it's too late now.

"You really look amazing," I say softly.

"Thanks," she says, trying to smile.

I smile at her for a second longer, and then I go down to check on Mom.

Tragically, the closest movie theater is half an hour away by car. Mom refuses to drive with the five of us, since the car is supposedly too small. I claim that Nicole can sit on top of Jennifer Scott, but this does not please my Mom, nor does it make Nicole and Jennifer Scott happy. Mom considers calling a taxi, when Anthony volunteers to drive two of us.

"But just two," he emphasizes. "That's the maximum amount of loud teenage girls I can stand."

I hug him, crowning him best brother ever. Nicole and Scott go with him, and Williams, Coral and I go with my mother. The moment we begin driving, Anthony hits the gas pedal, leaving us far behind.

"The way your brother drives..." Mom hisses.

"He's actually a very careful driver," I defend him, full of love towards my brother at the moment.

We leave Narrowdale and begin driving towards the highway. Initially there's a strained silence in the car, but in five minutes Coral and Williams are joking with each other and Mom and I argue about the radio station. Williams is probably relieved to be doing something. She likes action, and hates being stuck anywhere for long. The drive to the cinema is quite pleasant. The film is kind of long and complicated, but I really enjoy myself. Watching a movie with my friends is something I haven't done for a long time.

"So hang on," Nicole says as we are leaving. "Who saved them?"

"The rebels," explains Williams. "It turned out the rebels were planning to get them out the entire time."

"What rebels?"

"The ones that guy organized, what's his name."

"So where did they fly to?"

"I don't... Nicole, are you being difficult on purpose?"

"I didn't understand anything in that stupid movie," Nicole says, annoyed. "It was way too complicated."

"I'm not surprised," mutters Coral.

"What did you say?" Nicole turns towards her, her eyes blazing.

"Nothing," Coral answers innocently. There's a worrying spark of anger in her eyes as well.

"I think there's a cab over there," I say quickly, trying to change the subject. They both stare at each other for another second, then Nicole turns to me. "Good," she says.

On the way back home, no one talks.

Chapter Fifteen

I slowly wake up to the sound of quiet, intense whispering. I fumble for the night lamp's switch and turn the light on. It's the middle of the night, and Nicole is sleeping by my side on the bed, oblivious. The two Jennifers are lying on a mattress on the floor. Scott is awake as well and our eyes meet. She motions with her head to Jennifer Williams, who's talking in her sleep.

"You shouldn't have done it," Williams says. "If you'd felt what I feel for you, this wouldn't have happened."

Scott raises her eyebrows, amused. She reaches for her phone. This is too much of a good opportunity to miss.

"I don't believe you," Williams mumbles. "These things don't happen by accident."

I giggle silently as Scott aims the camera at Williams. We're going to have crazy fun with this clip tomorrow.

"You hurt me. It was a mistake."

Me and Scott have a hard time containing our laughter. She'll never hear the end of this.

"Don't tell me you love me!" she nearly shouts. "Not after you went to Rome with her!" She begins coughing.

"Jen, wake up," I say, beginning to feel uncomfortable. This dream sounds incredibly... personal.

She coughs again. No, it's not a cough. It sounds more like a...

growl. A deep, rumbling growl fills the room, and she starts rolling from side to side, her hands jerking around, her face twisted in an angry expression. "Jen, wake up, you're dreaming," Scott says, putting down her phone. Williams snarls, exposing her teeth, spit spraying from her open mouth. She then emits a bloodcurdling, inhuman howl.

"Jennifer! Wake up!" I shout.

Nicole sits up in the bed. "What's going on?" she asks, confused.

Williams is snarling and hissing. Her entire body spasms as she half screams, half roars, her fingers clawing at nothing. One of her hands knocks against my bed, banging loudly. Scott rolls away as one of Williams's hands hit her arm.

"Jen, please, wake up," she cries, half sobbing. "It's just a dream!"

"Jennifer!!!" I yell at the top of my voice. She keeps on growling and snarling, her hands and feet flailing. I can hear loud knocking from somewhere. I leap from my bed and shake her roughly. "Wake up!!!"

She hisses at me, and her hand swings, clawing at my face. I shake her harder, and suddenly her eyes open wide. They roll back, unnervingly white. Her entire body clenches, as if in pain. "So much blood," she moans silently. "There's so much blood." Her body slumps in my hands, the weight dragging me down with her. Her eyes suddenly focus, glancing around. She curls into a fetal position, hugging her knees as my hands let go.

I can now hear the knocking even louder than before.

"Amy, open the door!" I hear Anthony shout. I quickly scramble to the door, unlocking and opening it. Both Dad and Anthony are standing in the doorway, looking concerned.

"What's going on? I nearly broke your door!" Anthony says.

"Everything's okay," I say, breathing hard. "Jennifer just had a bad dream."

"You're bleeding," Dad says, his voice worried. I raise my hand to my cheek, where Jennifer clawed me. I can feel a light throbbing. When I look at my fingers, there's a bit of blood on them. "Yeah, I scratched myself when I got out of bed."

"Are you sure you're okay?" Dad asks. "Perhaps you need

some..." His sentence is left hanging. Dad has no idea how to help.

"We're fine," I say forcefully. "Thanks. Go back to bed."

They go away, and I close the door, locking it again. Williams is sitting on the mattress, still hugging her feet, as Jennifer Scott is caressing her hair slowly, whispering something in her ear.

"Are you okay?" I ask.

Her head jerks, a quick nod. "Yes. I just had a bad dream, I think," she says.

"It sure sounded like it," I say. "Do you want me to get you anything?"

"Can I have something to drink?" she asks. "It's so hot in here."

I glance at Nicole and Scott. Both are hugging their blankets to their bodies. I'm shivering a bit, my bare feet on the freezing floor. I feel Williams's forehead, but it's cold. I walk downstairs and get her a glass of water, which she drinks gratefully. Then I walk to the bathroom. I have a small scratch on my cheek, red and slightly bleeding. I wash my face and dab at it with some tissue paper before walking back to the room. Nicole is already lying on the bed, trying to sleep. I sit down next to the Jennifers.

"I'm sorry," Williams says, tears in her eyes. "I didn't know I screamed. It was just a bad dream."

"It's okay," I say softly, taking her hand and squeezing it. "What did you—"

"I don't know," she interrupts me quickly. "I can't remember." She lies back on the mattress. Scott and I exchange looks. Then she shrugs and lies down next to Williams. I go back to my bed, thankfully covering myself in the warm blanket. I hesitate before turning off the light.

It takes ages before I manage to go back to sleep.

In the morning I wake up first. I put on my slippers and quietly sneak out and walk downstairs. I heat some water, deciding to make hot cocoa for myself. Then Williams joins me downstairs, looking red-eyed, tired and upset. I try to smile at her encouragingly, and I make a cup for her as well.

"How are you feeling?" I ask.

"Fine, I don't know," she answers tensely.

"Do you remember—"

"I don't remember anything," she says, a bit forcefully. I drop the subject, though I don't believe her.

"Do you feel like pancakes?" I ask.

"Sure." She shrugs, though it looks as if the concept of eating is almost foreign to her. I spend the next five minutes trying to figure out where Mom hides the flour (in the fridge. Who puts flour in the fridge?). Nicole joins us as well, and her eyes lighten as I mention pancakes. She immediately begins to help me (which means spilling milk on the floor, dropping several egg shells into the mixture, and nearly burning the frying pan). She doesn't talk about last night's episode, and I wonder if she even remembers it. She seems unreasonably chirpy, in contrast to the morose and glum Jennifer. When Nicole flips one of the pancakes to the floor, I send her to wake up Scott, hoping to prevent her from causing additional damage. She returns with a sleepy Scott in tow, and they both get some plates from the cupboard. Nicole tries to help again, but I deftly fight her off with the spatula. Finally, we sit down and begin to eat.

"Mmmm. Pancakes," Anthony says as he walks into the kitchen. Still full of love, I serve him a plate with three pancakes, which he quickly wolfs down.

"Any more?" he asks hopefully.

"The rest are for my guests," I answer.

"Oh, absolutely," he says. "Hey, Nicole. Did you sleep well last night?"

Nicole hands him one of her pancakes. Williams, who has no appetite, gives him two.

"By the way," Nicole says with her mouth full, "you shouldn't leave your laptop out without any password protection like that. Anyone could access it."

"Why would anyone try to use my laptop?" I ask, pouring a large dollop of maple syrup on my pancake.

"Well, for example," she says, waving her fork, "since you save all your passwords on your laptop, someone might use it to access your blog."

I stare at her, still holding the syrup bottle in my hand. Then I slowly lower it to the table. Nicole flutters her eyelashes innocently.

I run up to my room. My laptop's open, the browser window live with my blog. I groan.

"You have to read it, it's hilarious," Nicole says behind me.

"I really doubt it," I say.

"I was really witty when I wrote it."

"Nicole, you're never witty."

I make a mental note to remember to delete Nicole's idiotic blog post.

After breakfast we turn on the TV. A medium-sized war over the remote control begins immediately. Scott tries as always to get us to watch cartoons. Nicole motions for a horrendous romantic comedy, which she has already seen twice. I try to explain my rationale for watching reruns of *How I Met Your Mother*, though the crowd is not convinced. We end up watching a terrible action movie. Second time this has happened this weekend. I should probably stop before it becomes a filthy habit, like biting nails, or answering trolls in YouTube comments.

"This is so corny," complains Scott. "How come she suddenly knows martial arts? And why is she walking around with an electric stun gun in her purse?"

"I walk around with pepper spray," says Nicole.

"That's not the same thing... Hang on, seriously?" Scott looks at her in surprise.

"Yeah. My mom doesn't let me leave home without it."

"Your mom's crazy," Scott says.

"Well, my mom lets me walk two blocks without an escort," Nicole says dryly, and Scott shuts up. Jennifer Scott's mother doesn't allow her to walk anywhere on her own, which sometimes can make life a bit complicated.

"Still. What if it sprays in your pocket by mistake?" I ask.

"Why would it—"

My phone rings and I glance at it. It's a number I don't recognize. I answer the call.

"Hello?"

"Hi, Amy?" It's an unfamiliar male voice.

"Yes... who're you?"

"It's Chris."

The silence stretches as I try to figure out who the hell Chris is. "What, Chris from school?" I ask eventually.

"Well... yeah." He sounds disheartened. Did he expect me to identify his voice? We've only talked two or three times.

"What's up, Chris?"

"Uh... How was your birthday party?"

"It was okay..." I let the silence hang, intentionally this time.

"So, listen... I was wondering. Do you maybe want to grab a milkshake sometime?"

Milkshake grabbing. I try to understand what he's talking about. I occasionally drink milkshakes, though I don't recall enjoying grabbing them... I then realize the obvious. He wants to grab milkshakes together. Which is not some sort of weird beverage-kidnapping activity, but a date. I can feel my face warming up. Nicole, ever sensitive to my reactions, loses interest in the television screen and watches me like a hawk.

"I don't know, I... you mean together? Yeah, I..." My brain has lost control over my mouth. I have to let him down gently, but I have no idea how to do that. I've never been in this position before!

"Hang on," I finally say, and mute the phone.

"A guy from class is trying to invite me on a date," I hiss at Nicole. "How do I let him down gently?"

"Is he cute?" she asks, her eyes sparkling.

"I don't know. A bit, maybe."

"Okay, so here is how you do it. You say, 'Sure, when do you want to meet?'"

"I... what? I don't want to date him!"

"Sure, you do."

I unmute the call. "Chris, could you hang on just a bit more? There's something... I'm frying something, and it's burning, hang on..." I mute the call again. By this time all three are looking at me. The TV has been turned off.

"Smooth," Scott remarks.

"Why don't you want to date him?" Nicole asks. "You said he's cute."

"I don't know..." Because I'm in love with Peter, but I can't say that...

Moth to a Flame

"It's that guy, Peter, isn't it?" Nicole says. Evil mind-reading witch!

"Amy," Williams says, looking at me intently. "Say yes. You can't go chasing a security guy who doesn't know you exist!"

"He knows I—"

"Do it now!" Nicole says, grinning madly.

Panicking, I unmute the call once more. First I'll tell him no, then I'll handle my crazy friends. "Hey, Chris? Okay, I turned off the frying pan. I mean the gas. So, it's okay. When do you want to meet?" Hang on. What just happened? I was supposed to say something else! Who's on the phone? Shut her up right now!

"I thought we could meet tomorrow at noon, at the mall. There's a place there."

"Yeah, sure," says the other Amy, the one who is dumb and stupid, and shouldn't be allowed to talk ever.

"Great!" he says. "Well, see you tomorrow!"

"Sure, see you," I say, and quickly hang up before stupid Amy says something else.

"Yay!" Nicole claps. "We get to choose clothes for Amy's hot date!"

"I hate you all," I mutter, my face feeling like an overripe tomato. This merely makes them even more cheerful, and even Williams cracks a smile. Fine. It's just a milkshake, and in the middle of the day. And at no point did either of us say it's a date, so this could be just a friendly milkshake, right? Which is something that should probably be clarified to Nicole, who's running upstairs, intent on tossing the entire contents of my closet in search for an outfit. I stand up, about to run after her, when the doorbell rings. It takes me a moment to realize that it's probably Coral and Shane, who said they'd be dropping by today.

"Hang on!" I call, running to the front door. I open it and smile at Shane and Coral. Shane is holding a bag in his hand.

"Hey, Amy," he says. "Happy—" He stops, looking behind my shoulder. I turn and see Nicole walking down the stairs, holding two of my skirts. "Amy, which one of those... Oh," she says, noticing Shane and Coral. "Hi."

There's a certain effect Nicole has on boys. We all know it well.

Wherever she walks (the beach, the mall, school) there's always a group of boys following her, quick to agree to whatever she says, laughing at her every joke, helping her carry anything that needs carrying. Nicole assumes that the world is like that—full of men who are always happy to help, who are always so incredibly nice. Any attempt by me or the Jennifers to explain that the world is not exactly as she sees it has so far ended in failure. A quick glance at Shane's face demonstrates that he is no different. The slack mouth, the widening eyes, the way his entire body faces her, ignoring the rest of the beings around him—it all make things incredibly clear. Me and Scott exchange glances. Another zombie is born.

"Shane, right?" Nicole says, descending the rest of the steps. "I've heard a lot about you."

"Me too," he says dumbly. "Uh… Heard. About you. About all of you."

"Shane?" Coral says. "The gift?"

"Huh? Oh, yeah, right. Um…" I swear he is about to hand the bag over to Nicole, but then he realizes what he's doing and hands it to me. "Happy birthday, Amy."

I look inside. There's a wrapped rectangular object within. I quickly unwrap it.

"Oh… Wow," I say happily. "This is so awesome!"

It's a large photograph of the three of us, printed on canvas. I quickly recognize it. Shane took it with his camera about a month ago in a small park, not far from my house. He drove us insane, endlessly fiddling with the thing, positioning it and repositioning it while I was begging him to just let me take a selfie with my phone. And it is a beautiful photograph. The three of us look much prettier than we do in real life.

"We thought it would look nice on the wall in your room," Coral says.

I choke up a bit, overwhelmed by the love around me. What did I ever do to deserve such wonderful friends? "It will, thanks!" I say, hugging both of them. I show the picture to the girls, and they agree it's wonderful.

"You have a real talent," Nicole tells Shane, and he looks as if he was just informed that he won the Nobel Prize. "I hope you'll take a picture of me," she continues. His hands immediately start fiddling with his camera. Coral looks at him, then at Nicole, then back at him, her mouth twisted in a strange expression.

"Anyway, I have to go," she says.

"But you just got here," I say.

"Yeah, but you know, the test. I really have to study."

"Oh, stay for a bit," Williams says suddenly, looking disappointed. Coral squirms uncomfortably. I take her hand and smile.

"Come on," I say. "Stay for half an hour."

"Fine," she mumbles. "But then I really have to go."

We sit down in the living room. I fetch some snacks and Cokes.

"So, Shane," Nicole says, crunching a potato chip, "tell us about that night when you and Amy broke into that house."

"It was a stupid thing to do," he says uncomfortably, staring at his glass of Coke. "We shouldn't have done it."

"Oh, but it sounded so cool!" Nicole says. "The growling animal Amy thinks she saw? And the room with the blood? I nearly peed my pants when she told me about it on the phone."

"It was really scary being there," Shane says.

"I know! Your life is like a television show! I wish things like that would happen in LA. Nothing ever happens to us!"

"I don't think that—"

"I can help you in your investigation!" Nicole says excitedly. "I'm really awesome with those things. We can go together to that house and do a stakeout, see if the murderer returns to the scene of the crime."

"Maybe the cops would let you sit in their car when you're doing your stakeout," Coral suggests.

Nicole ignores her. "What do you think, Shane? We could solve this before the police do. Wouldn't that be awesome?"

"I really don't know…"

"I have an idea who could be the killer. It could be a relative of that crazy killer, Tom Ellis! We could break into his house, check to see if we can find some clues."

"That's an even better idea," Coral says. "It's absolutely brilliant."

"Or… Hang on. The blood… Amy, are you sure it was real blood? Maybe someone only wanted it to look like the scene of a crime to hide… uh…"

"You're rambling, Nicole," Scott says.

"Shane, you have to get some additional photographs of that house," Nicole says. "Like evidence. We can make a board, like in all those police shows, with a timeline, and pictures of the suspects…"

Coral looks as if she's about to smash one of the snack bowls on Nicole's head. Nicole carries on, oblivious.

"It'll be so awesome," she says. "You'll take those pictures tomorrow, right? Post them on Instagram or something?"

The thought of Nicole following him on Instagram pushes Shane into action. "Sure," he says. "I'll do it tomorrow."

Coral stands up, a disgusted look on her face. "Sorry, Amy, I really have to go. I need to study for the test."

http://amy.strangerealm.com/NicoleIsBest.html

Chapter Sixteen

The mall in Narrowdale has only one cafe, called Alfred's. As I walk inside I feel incredibly nervous. Trying to convince myself that this is merely a friendly meeting isn't working out so well. First of all, we aren't friends. And second, well… Nicole repeatedly singing her "Amy's got a date" jingle in my ears didn't help at all. I am dressed in a skirt chosen by Nicole, with the same stockings that she loaned me for my birthday, a low-cut black shirt, and my new boots (because all other footwear in the universe has ceased to exist). Nicole claimed that I was smashing and sexy. I was aiming for a more "let's be best buds" kind of look, but I don't think I did so great. I wish Nicole and the Jennifers hadn't gone back home this morning. They could have helped me pick the right clothes for the job.

Chris is already waiting for me, sitting next to one of the tables. I have to admit, he is kinda cute. He has big brown eyes, a fact that I've never noticed before, and they match his curly black hair well. He even dressed nicely, discarding his usual worn-out black t-shirt and torn jeans for… well, for a newer black t-shirt, and some slightly less torn jeans. I wonder if he has some sort of jeans-ripping moth in his closet.

He smiles at me and waves, in case I haven't noticed him. There are four tables in Alfred's, so the chance I'd somehow miss him is nonexistent, but I smile and wave back, which makes me feel a bit silly, as I'm standing ten feet from him.

I sit down by the table.

"Hey," I say.

"Hey," he answers. "What's up?"

"Oh, you know." I shrug. "Nothing much. What about you?"

"Nothing much," he says. We are the nothing much duo—is this conversation flowing like a river, or what?

"So…" I begin to play with my napkin. Make me feel uncomfortable, and my fingers start clutching and messing around with anything. The napkin changes its shape to a triangle. "What did you do this weekend?" I don't know what he does any other day of the week, but I'm asking about his weekend. Well, you have to start somewhere.

"I had band practice. And I met with some friends."

"You play the guitar, right?"

"Yeah."

"So… what's your band called?"

"Tripping Gators of the Subtle Coma."

This makes me start a bit. "Seriously?"

"Yeah. Do you think it's too long?"

"Maybe. A bit."

"I wanted us to make it shorter. Like Subtle Coma. Or Tripping Gators. But Jamey, that's our drummer, he insists that the full name is better."

It's definitely not. "Okay," I say.

The waitress approaches us. "Do you want to order?"

"I'll have a vanilla milkshake," he says.

"Hot chocolate for me, please," I say.

For a moment Chris looks a bit disappointed. I remember that he wanted to grab a milkshake. Perhaps he thought that the milkshake was a must.

"I don't like drinking milkshakes when it's cold," I say.

"Okay." The waitress walks away.

"I got you something for your birthday," he suddenly says. He takes something from his pocket and hands it to me. It's a small bottle. Inside it there appears to be a bracelet.

"Thanks," I say, embarrassed. I uncork the bottle and try to get the bracelet out. It's stuck.

"Maybe we can fish it out with a fork," Chris says.

Further attempts to extract the bracelet are met with failure.

"I'll fish it out when I get home," I finally say. "It looks lovely."

"The woman at the store said that it'd look nice inside a bottle."

Bottles contain liquid. Jewelry comes in cases or boxes. If people start messing with the natural order of things, they shouldn't be surprised when everything goes to hell. "Oh, it does. It's very nice."

"Happy birthday."

"Thanks."

The waitress returns with a large milkshake and a nice mug of hot cocoa.

"So... how was your birthday party?" he asks, sipping from his shake.

I explain that it wasn't really a party, it was more of a get-together. I tell him about the movie. He nods, then tells me about a movie he saw. There is more small talk. An abundance of small talk. If small talk had value, I could have afforded a yacht by the time we finish drinking our drinks. I notice random things. His fingers are surprisingly delicate, and long. When he smiles, I notice that one of his front teeth is a bit chipped. He asks me about the scratch on my face, and I say I accidentally scratched myself in my sleep. Then he tells me that he shared a bunk bed with his brother as a child, and that he once fell from the top bunk and broke his shoulder. I ask him about sleeping in the same room with his brother, and this starts a chain of stories about pranks and tricks that his brother and him played on each other.

Time flows strangely. The first fifteen minutes drag on for hours. Then, the next hour speeds by in what feels like seconds. I am thoroughly surprised when I check the time and realize we've been talking for an hour and a half.

"I have to go," I finally say. "I... I have to study for a test." I've turned into Coral.

"Yeah, sure." He nods. "It was nice to see you... um."

I play with the napkin again. It does not look like a triangle anymore. It looks like a napkin that has been folded and refolded too many times.

"So…" I say, wondering how I managed to kill the conversation so effectively. Amy Parker—conversation assassin. "I'll ask for the check?"

"Oh, no, I got this," he says and quickly jumps from his seat. He walks over to the cashier, and before I can stop him, he pays for both of us.

"How much do I owe you?" I ask.

"Nothing," he says. "It's a birthday treat."

"Okay," I say. "So… I'm going home…"

"Me too." He nods.

"It was really nice of you to uh…" I struggle with defining the last hour and a half. "To buy me a drink."

"It was nice talking with you, Amy." He smiles. Chipped tooth. And very white, I notice. His teeth are all exceptionally white.

And then I realize that we obviously have to leave through the same door. And walk together to the mall's exit. Which makes all this farewell dance horribly awkward. I consider telling him I have to go to the bathroom, but that would mean going to the bathroom, and I'm unsure where the bathroom is, and I really don't want to walk through the wrong door and enter the kitchen (this has actually happened to me before). Eventually I say, "Let's go."

We walk outside in a strained silence, or maybe it's only me that's straining. Chris doesn't seem very tense. Perhaps he knows something that I don't. Once we leave the mall, I say, "I'm going that way." I point down the road.

He nods. "My house is in the opposite direction. Do you want me to walk you home?"

"No," I say quickly. "It's really okay. So have a nice—"

At which point he leans forward and kisses me. I think he is aiming for the mouth, but he does it slowly, seeming a bit confused and unsure, and I move my head in surprise, so his lips touches my cheek softly. They linger on for one long second, my head frozen in place, not daring to move, and then he draws back.

"Bye, Amy," he says, blushing, and quickly walks away.

I walk home dazed, completely oblivious to my surroundings. So apparently grabbing milkshakes might end up with kisses. Whoever would have guessed? Milkshakes always seemed like such innocent things. And that kiss, well... I was not entirely sure how I felt about it. Should I have turned my head? If I hadn't, he would have kissed me on the lips. And that would be... different. Maybe I shouldn't have turned my head. No, I definitely should have, I mean... right? What would Nicole say? She'd say I should have kissed him back, no doubt there. Nicole is all for kisses. She thinks that kisses are the best thing in the world... except maybe for designer clothes. Nicole has an impressive kissing history. There's a long list of names of boys who kissed her, and one girl as well. I compare Chris's kiss to my other kissing experiences.

Experience number one: a kiss during a game of spin the bottle in LA. Kyle spun the bottle, and it pointed at me. He kissed me on the lips, eyes closed, lips clenched—it was more of a lip accident than a kiss. Our lips exchanged insurance information and went on their respective lives, never to meet again. That was my first kiss. Today's kiss was better.

Experience number two: when me and Peter went on a walk on the beach together. The wind toyed with my hair as Peter took me in his hands, tilted his head and kissed me passionately, his lips feeling soft and warm, his hands caressing my back, with me grabbing his arm, feeling the muscles underneath, my other hand on the back of his neck, pulling him towards me, reluctant to ever let go. One problem—this never actually happened. This was a dream I had about three weeks ago. Then again, it was an awesome kiss, so... apples and oranges, I guess.

Experiences number three to infinity: kisses from Mom. Well, seriously, I'm not going to compare Chris's kiss to them.

I should have kissed him back.

I shouldn't have. I'm in love with Peter.

Peter doesn't even know I exist.

Yes, he does, and he said he was glad to see me.

He once called me a little girl.

He's always smiling when he meets me.

I once saw him smile at a bird. That doesn't mean he's about to kiss the bird.

Images of Peter kissing birds are very disturbing.

When I finally get home, I'm thoroughly exhausted by my brain. I go upstairs to my room and try to study math. Which is as effective right now as trying to learn to play the trombone using only a manual written in Japanese. Nothing makes sense. Nothing. Math used to make sense once, long ago. You take some numbers, add them up, and this results in larger numbers. You can also subtract them—lo and behold, this results in smaller numbers. There are practical ways to use this knowledge as well—you multiply your allowance by six weeks, you get enough to buy a shirt. Add two weeks more, and you can also buy a bra. It's all crystal clear and helpful and nice. Also, and this is awesome, if you're unsure about the result, you can use a calculator to verify it!

Everything went awry when the unknowns were introduced. Seriously, they even sound creepy. They are the unknowns.

I think I liked that kiss. I could do it again.

He has really big eyes.

I shake my head, forcing myself to focus. I open my notebook. I prepare two pens, and some markers. I list all the material for the test. I browse the Internet and watch a video of a screaming frog. I check my blog for comments. I… hang on! I'm supposed to be studying for the test. Study, right now! I'm hungry. I should get something to eat.

I go downstairs, fix myself a sandwich. I notice there are some plates in the sink. Mom's working so hard these days; wouldn't she be happy if I did the dishes? I put the dishes in the dishwasher. I diligently clean the sink. Go back to my room.

What would it feel like if Peter kissed me?

No, no time for that. Test on Tuesday, important test. Very important for college. Maybe I got a new e-mail? Instagram? Facebook? Twitter? Twenty minutes pass. Fine, now I'm really doing this. I'll study even if it kills me. First exercise. Hmmm… no idea. Let's skip to the second one. Oh god, it's even worse.

Fine. Reality can't be avoided. Only one person can make me study for the damn test. I call Coral.

"Hello?"

"Hey," I say. "What are you doing?" Just polite. I know exactly what she's doing.

"Studying."

"Cool. Hey, listen, I'm having some difficulties. Would you mind if we study together?"

"Will you constantly interrupt me, ask for a break, talk about things that are totally unrelated to math and ruin my academic future?" she asks.

That sounds about right, but I suspect it's a trick question. "No, I'll be good," I lie.

She sighs. "Then come over."

Yay! Group study!

Chapter Seventeen

"Hang on, Coral," I beg. "You're losing me."
"What's so complicated? Minus b plus minus—"
"Hang on... b is... six... plus..."
"Plus minus."
"Right. Plus minus the square root of six to the power of two minus four times c..."
"Why four?"
"Because that's the formula," I say, my head pounding.
"The formula is four times a times c," she says, poking at the page.
"Right! But a is always equal to one, right?"
"Not here. Come on, Amy, concentrate!"
I'm pretty sure that the concussion from five months ago is making a comeback. "I'm concentrating, I swear."
"Okay. So what's the result?"
"Hang on..." I calculate it in my head. "What's the square root of minus eight?"
"What? There's no such thing as a square root of negative numbers. That means there's no result... let me see your notes." She snatches the notebook from me. I am very familiar with her horrified face.
"Why did you write six here? It's b to the power of two. It's

supposed to be thirty-six! And even if it was six, I have no idea how you got to minus eight…" She shuts her eyes and takes a deep breath.

"I just get confused," I say in despair. "It's all mixed up in my head."

"Because it's mixed up in your notebook! Copy the exercise to scrap paper and do it all over again patiently."

"Hey, listen. You know Chris, from class? Well, he called me yesterday, and guess what…?"

"Amy, I'm trying to concentrate," she says, frowning. Fine. Maybe not the perfect time for girl talk. She's definitely not in the mood. I glance over her shoulder at the exercise she's solving, and my eyes tear up. Coral solves exercises that I'm not sure I'm able to read. I copy my own exercise to scrap paper and solve it again, calm and patient. I get the square root of two. I think the number I get most is the square root of two. I put down my pen, and consider crying.

"Coral," a tiny voice calls behind us.

"Mia, not now," Coral says.

"But Coral, he wants to eat me!" Coral's sister Mia says in an urgent voice. I glance at Mia, smiling at her serious face, her big green eyes wide as she frowns, lost in her own story. Her curly blond hair is combed backwards and held with a pink headband. She's dressed in an orange shirt with a gator on it, and gray pants. Coral told me that Mia's wardrobe is full of dresses… which she never wears. She always insists on shirts with animal pictures and simple pants, to her mother's ever-growing exasperation.

"Who wants to eat you?"

"The fish! I'm just a little worm who went for a walk, but the fisherman found me and put me on a hook and he threw me into the water and then a big fish came after a little fish came and said he won't eat me and he'll be my friend if I give him my favorite green crayon, and the big fish is the chief of all the fish…"

"Mia!"

"What?"

"I'm really busy!"

"If I had my favorite green crayon I could give it to the big fish, but I gave it to the little fish, who is now my best friend and..."

Coral looks as if she's about to have a heart attack.

"Maybe you can tell the big fish that if he eats you, the fisherman will catch him," I suggest.

She thinks about it for a moment. "Amy?"

"Yes, Mia?"

"Where does lightning come from?"

"I don't know."

"Maybe it's constructed in the clouds."

"Maybe."

"I don't want to be a worm anymore."

"Then why don't you be something else?"

"Okay," she says and leaves the room.

"I can't believe I'm stuck with her here," Coral mutters.

"Where are your parents?" I ask.

"Well, my dad is on one of his endless business trips, and my mom went shopping with her friends. Shopping! Never mind that I have this really important test to study for, I still have to watch over Mia. Couldn't they watch Mia for once, and give me two days to study in silence?"

I remain quiet. Experience has taught me that replying to Coral's rhetorical monologues about her parents results in bitterness and anger for all sides involved.

"Do you want a drink?" I try to get her to chill out a bit.

"I have to solve those exercises."

"I'll get you a drink. You don't need to get up."

She nods distractedly, and I walk over to the kitchen.

"I've made something for you," Mia tells me as I fill a glass with water.

"What is it?" I ask.

"It's a friendship bracelet. You're my friend."

I look at her in surprise. She's handing me a small friendship bracelet, made of intertwining green, white and black threads. I take it from her. "Wow! Thanks, Mia! That's so sweet of you!"

"I've also made one for Coral, but she never wears it. And one for Mommy and one for Daddy. And one for Ginny, but she lost it."

"Yeah? Who's Ginny?"

"My friend. I want to go to Ginny's," she says.

"You can't go right now. You have to stay here with Coral."

"But you're busy, and Ginny always wants to play chairs with me."

I wonder what playing chairs involves, but decide to let it remain a mystery. "You can ask Coral. Maybe she'll agree, but—"

"I'll go ask her!"

"No, wait one minute. Let her cool off a bit."

"Okay."

I walk back to Coral's room and hand her the glass. "I think there's a mistake in the exercise," she says. "I should write them an e-mail about it."

"Maybe you have a mistake in your calculations..." My voice dwindles to nothing under Coral's threatening gaze.

"Amy?" Mia shouts from the kitchen.

"What?"

"Is she cool yet?"

"No, just wait... a bit longer." I try to copy my exercise once more.

"Amy!" Another shout from the kitchen. I try to ignore her.

"Amy!" A third shout. Coral thumps the table in anger. I've never seen her so tense. I quickly walk over to the kitchen.

"Is she cool now?" Mia asks me.

I sigh. "Hang on," I say. "I'll ask her." It'll be better if Coral murders me and not her sister. Her sister might still amount to something. I walk back to Coral and gently lay a hand on her shoulder. "Coral?"

"What?"

"Mia wants to go to her friend's. Someone called Ginny?"

"Well, I can't take her right now."

"I can take her," I suggest. "And then we'll be able to study in silence."

She looks at me for a moment, then nods. "Okay," she says. "They live down the street. Mia knows the way."

"Don't we need to call her mom first?"

"Nah. They drop by each other's houses all the time."

"Okay." I walk to the kitchen. "Come on, I'll take you to

Ginny's."

"Wait!" Coral calls from her room. "Mia, wear your coat!"

"It isn't cold outside!" Mia calls back.

"Wear it, or you're not going."

Mia walks over to her room, grumbling. She returns wearing a red coat. She has her hood on, her face hidden almost completely within.

"I'm an Eskino," she tells me.

"You mean Eskimo," I say.

"Okay," she agrees, and we leave the house.

"It's over there." She points and we start walking.

"I'm a mouse," she says.

"I thought you're an Eskimo."

"I'm an Eskimo mouse. I just got here from the North Pole, looking for cheese."

"I see."

"The North Pole has only cream cheese."

"Okay."

"Because snow is white, just like cream cheese."

"Fine." I begin to feel quite tired.

"You're the evil cat who wants to catch me."

"Sure, whatever."

"Yay!" She suddenly leaps and starts sprinting down the street.

"Wait, Mia!" I shout, but she doesn't stop. I mutter a curse and begin running after her. She turns right onto a small street, disappearing from sight. I turn right after her, and stop.

Mia is gone.

Chapter Eighteen

"Mia! Mia!!! Get back here, this isn't funny!"

I look around me at the empty street. There's no sign of Mia anywhere. How could she have disappeared so quickly? There's a bitter taste in my mouth, and I can feel beads of sweat on my forehead. The air feels still, suffocating. I've lost my friend's sister, a six-year-old child. A little girl who might get run over by a car, or get hurt while climbing something, or follow a stranger into his house or car... My mind is filled with terrifying images. I have to find her. I look around me. It's a small street, not a lot of places to hide. I start walking slowly, examining every detail around me. Where would Mia go? Most of the houses are simple, no front yards, the doors closed. Would she have knocked on one of the doors in an attempt to hide from me? Not likely, though it's impossible to tell with Mia. I pass by a house with a front yard, but the gate's locked. Would she have climbed the fence? She couldn't have; she's too small.

"Mia? Mia!"

I notice a small shrubbery adjacent to the fence and walk over to check if she's hiding within. She isn't. I can feel the tears coming, and I force them away. I'll panic later. There's no time for that right now. What about that house? Its gate might be open... I approach it and lay a hand on the gate, when a huge black dog appears in the crack between the fence and the gate, barking viciously, making me jump back, my heart thudding. Mia would never have entered this place. The street is coming to an end and…

There's a small, shabby house, looking old and unkempt. One of its windows is broken, the paint is peeling off the walls, and the entire yard is barren.

The gate is open, swinging slowly in the wind.

"Mia!"

I push the gate, walking inside anxiously. The house looks creepy, and I suddenly know that she entered it, that I'll have to follow her inside. I can see only darkness through the windows. I try to control my breathing, walking closer to the door… then pause.

To the side of the house, there's a path to the backyard, and I can see all the way through. The backyard looks long abandoned as well, and the fence around it is falling apart. Bordering the backyard, beyond the fence, there's an untended field, running wild with weeds and bushes, waist high. And within the overgrown plants I notice something red. As I walk down the path to the backyard, I can see the red shape more clearly. It's Mia, and she's lying down, hiding. My entire body is filled with relief as I half walk, half run through the backyard. I locate a place where the fence has completely fallen apart and cross through it into the field. I walk towards Mia, pushing aside the weeds, scratching my hands in several places by sharp thorns.

"Mia!" I say when I'm nearby. "You can't run away like that! What were you thinking?"

She turns her head, and I can see that her face is full of tears.

"Are you okay?" I ask in concern. "Did you hurt yourself?"

"Amy," she whispers, crying. "The bad animal wants to kill me."

"We're done with this game," I tell her. "Get up and I'll take you to Ginny's."

"No," she says. "It'll hear us. It was eating something, but it heard me and now it wants to hurt me."

"Come on," I say, grabbing her hand, trying to drag her up. "Let's go to Ginny's."

"I want to go home."

"Don't you want to go to Ginny's house and play chairs?"

"No, I want to go home."

"But Mia…"

"I want to go home." She starts sobbing.

I take a deep breath. No wonder Coral is driven insane by this kid. "Okay, okay, I'll take you…"

A branch snaps somewhere. And another. I can almost hear something within the field. Something… breathing heavily. I slowly lower myself, crouching near Mia.

"It's here," she whispers. "It's coming nearer."

I lay a finger on my lips, motioning for her to be quiet. Is there something there, or is Mia simply infecting me with her fear? For a moment, we both stay silent, hearing nothing but the wind, and the sound of a car driving down a nearby street.

"There's nothing…" I begin to say, but then I hear something and I instantly stop talking. It's that breathing again, deep and heavy. More like panting. And then something else. Amidst the breaths, I can hear a growling sound. I freeze, feeling a cold sense of fear. There is something here with us. Maybe it's nothing, just a runaway dog. But somehow I can almost feel something else. There's a sense of… of…

Anger. Hate. Blood thirst.

Time seems to slow down, every sound intensified. I lick my dry lips, breathing fast through my nose.

"Come on, we have to get out of here," I whisper. Mia shakes her head in terror, refusing to move. I try to take her hand, force her to start moving, but it's hard to do without alerting whatever it is that's in the field with us.

"Mia," I hiss desperately. "Come on! We have to move."

She just shuts her eyes, clenching her entire body. Suddenly the breathing stops. Then I can hear sniffing, more branches cracking as the animal walks closer. And then a clear, low growl.

"It's here!" Mia suddenly screams. "The animal!" She bolts up and starts running. I stand quickly, going after her, stumbling, not daring to look back, knowing that the animal is behind us, getting closer fast. I can hear the branches snapping around us, behind us, feel the thorns scratching at my hands, my feet, ripping my shirt. Mia stumbles, falls down. I run towards her, full of terror. Glancing behind I spot a black shape, not more than fifteen feet behind us. I grab Mia, help her stand and drag her after me. We reach the backyard and cross it, reaching the street, and I look back once more.

There's nothing there.

The black shape that I saw is just a big rock. There's no animal, no sound at all except for Mia's sobbing and my heavy breathing.

Is it possible that there was nothing there all along? That I simply convinced myself that Mia was right?

"Mia," I say hollowly. "There was nothing there. It was just a rock. Look."

"I want to go home," she wails.

"Sure," I say. "I'll take you home now." I half hug her all the way home. It was just a rock. There was no animal there.

But I keep remembering the heavy panting and growling that we heard, and I know I didn't imagine it.

Chapter Nineteen

"So what happened after you got your friend's sister back home?" Doctor Greenshpein asks.

I shrug. "Coral took her in, calmed her down, and gave her a bath. We were both a bit scratched... There were a lot of thorns in that field, so Coral cleaned Mia's scratches. Then she put her to bed, and I went home."

"I see."

He sees. That's why he's being paid, after all. I shift in my chair. I've been tense since the moment I got in.

"It was weird. When we were running in the field, I was almost certain that... something was chasing us. She was so scared that she managed to infect me with her fear as well."

"And you were scared as it was," Doctor Greenshpein says, leaning forward in his chair, "because you lost her for a few minutes."

"Yeah. You think that's the reason why this happened? Because I was already really stressed?"

"It sounds likely. It's definitely a common occurrence. Fear is very infectious, and we hear and see what we expect to."

I let out a long breath. Nothing chased me, and I'm not insane. That's nice to hear. But I can't seem to relax.

"How did your friend react when you returned with her sister?"

I shuffle uncomfortably, recalling last night. Coral was really alarmed when she saw Mia's state. She kept hugging her and kissing her long after Mia calmed down.

"I think she felt guilty, because she sent her sister with me, and things got so… screwed."

"Do you think that she blamed you?"

"No," I answer truthfully. "I really think she blamed only herself."

"And what do you think?"

"Why does it have to be anyone's fault?" I ask defensively.

"Fair enough."

"I was on a date yesterday," I say, suddenly desperate to change the subject.

"Really?"

"Don't sound so surprised."

"I'm not surprised," he says, and I suspect he's lying.

"There's this guy from school. Chris. He called me on my birthday, asked me out."

"That's nice. So how was your date, if you don't mind me asking?"

Since when does he care if I mind him asking? "It was good, I think," I say. "It started kinda slow, but then we got talking, and… he's an interesting guy."

"Really?" he asks.

"I don't know if I'll date him again," I add.

"But it went well," he says, raising his eyebrows.

"Yeah, but…" I can suddenly recall Chris's lips on my cheek. My heart thumps a little faster, and my face feels warm. Can Doctor Greenshpein see that I'm blushing? "I don't know if I am into him."

"Well, it was only one date," he remarks.

"I can't really focus on that right now," I say. "I have a really important math test tomorrow."

"I see. And do you think you'll do well?"

"No, I think I'll definitely fail."

"That sounds… defeatist."

"Well, it's true. When I solve an exercise, no matter what, something gets messed up in my head, I replace plus with minus, and then I always get the square root of two."

"And that's bad?"

"Do you know what the square root of two is?" I ask.

He gets up and walks to his desk. He picks up a calculator and sits back down. Then he presses some buttons. "Well, it's one point four one four two one three..."

"See?" I say morosely. "That's not a number, that's an abomination. When a number misbehaves, its mother says that if it goes on like that, it'll be the square root of two when it grows up. Trust me, the square root of two is never the correct answer."

"Okay, did you try working more tidily?"

"What?" I ask, feeling irritated.

"You know, writing all the steps on scrap paper, going over them carefully to make sure you didn't miss anything..."

Great, another one. He can form a small club with Coral. He can be treasurer, and they can invite my mom. I'm sure she'll be thrilled.

"Of course I did!" I lie. I tried several times. But my mind kept wandering, filled with thoughts about Coral and Mia, about Chris, about Alice Hendrix... "I'm just not built for it. I'll never get into a good college."

"What has college got to do with it?" he asks, sounding confused.

"This is a very important test," I say.

"You're in the ninth grade..."

"That's what they check, these colleges. Your ninth grade scores. And then they ask you if you've ever been contacted by the square root of two."

"I doubt it's so dramatic," he says.

"Coral thinks it is."

"She's afraid of failing?" He asks. His questions are starting to irritate me.

"I think she's afraid she won't get a perfect score," I say. "Failing is not really something that ever happens to her."

"I see."

I stare at the floor. I have no idea why Mom insists on these sessions. They don't accomplish anything except for annoying me.

"Did you think about what I asked you last time?" Doctor

Greenshpein asks.

I try to remember what he's talking about. No idea. But if I tell him that, he'll be offended, or worse, think I'm repressing it, so I gamble.

"I thought about it, and it isn't true," I say.

"What isn't true?" He raises his eyebrow and I suspect I'm heading in the wrong direction.

"The... thing."

"I asked you why it is that you're so interested in a woman's murder that possibly never even happened."

"Well, it did happen, you know."

"Are you talking about Alice Hendrix?"

"Yes, she was murdered," I say.

"As far as I know she was found dead in her home and the police are investigating."

"Bullshit." I say, gritting my teeth.

"I don't understand..."

I lose my temper. "You have no idea what happens in this place! The things I see here, the stories I hear! Alice Hendrix was murdered, I know that for a fact, but that's just a fraction of what goes on in this town! I can't walk alone at night without feeling that some predator is out to get me! I had a conversation with a woman who had died years before! I saw Tom Ellis kidnap Kimberly even before I knew they existed! I was possessed once! Do you have any idea what it's like to live here?"

Silence. Doctor Greenshpein removes his glasses and thoughtfully cleans them with his shirt. I've screwed it all up. He'll have me committed to an asylum, or drug me, or...

"Why do you think I don't know what goes on in here?" he suddenly asks.

"I... what?"

"Why do you think I'm blind to what goes on in Narrowdale? Most of my patients live here. Don't you think I hear my share of crazy stories?"

I feel like I've somehow forgotten how to talk. I stare at him, dumbfounded.

"Teenagers play a game here, right? Only in Narrowdale?" He

smiles at me.

"I... I don't..."

"Strange things happen here all the time, that's true." He nods. "But most people can handle it. We ignore things, we repress them, we avoid dangers. When we meet people who don't live here, *we never talk about it*. The residents of Narrowdale are the masters of concealment."

He puts the glasses back on. I suddenly feel like his eyes are burrowing into my mind.

"Most of us don't even know we're doing it. We just let things fade naturally. It's easy to find rational explanations when you need them."

"Then... why do you keep asking me those questions?" I ask, my throat dry.

"Because you don't do what everyone else does," he says. "You broke into a murderer's home. Now I'm guessing you're trying to find another woman's killer. If I didn't know you as well as I do, I'd think you liked toying with death."

"I don't like toying with death," I say, swallowing hard.

"Well, then," he says. "Why do you do it?"

"I don't know," I whisper.

"Okay, Amy," he says. "Then I suggest you find out. Because it's a dangerous game you're playing here." He glances at his watch. "I think our time is up," he says.

Chapter Twenty

"So... how do you think you did?" Shane asks.

We're sitting in the cafeteria, eating our lunch. I just finished the math test. Coral hasn't joined us yet; she probably cornered the teacher with some questions and clarifications.

"Terribly," I answer. "I couldn't concentrate, I got weird answers, some of the exercises I didn't even know how to solve... If I somehow manage to avoid failing this test, it'll be due to divine intervention. I'm just not built for math. It's like I'm allergic to numbers or something."

"Bummer," Shane says. He doesn't seem upset at all. "Say, did Nicole talk to you?"

"About what?"

"About the pictures. You know, the ones of Alice Hendrix's house. I sent them to all of you yesterday."

"No, I didn't talk to her. I have no idea if she saw them," I say.

"She probably did. She checks her messages a hundred times a day."

"Oh," he says. Now he does look a bit upset. Welcome to Nicole's broken-hearted men's club. Each member gets his own badge and a manual titled *So You Thought You Were the One*. The yearly membership dues can be deposited straight to Nicole in the form of bouquets of flowers or fuzzy teddy bears.

Coral sits down next to us, looking distracted.

"So how did it go?" I ask.
"I think it was fine," she says, opening her lunch bag.
"Yeah? Did you solve everything?"
"Sure. How did you do?"
"Terrible," I answer.
"Bummer," she says.

Shane and I exchange worried glances. When Coral finishes a test, everything is the test. She compares answers. She talks about the way she approached each question, about what she felt when she saw the question. She fondly recalls how just three weeks ago the teacher taught her how to answer the question. She commemorates other tests and analyzes how they compare to the last test.

"Do you want to compare answers?" I ask.
"I don't think there's any need," she says.
"Coral, is everything okay?"
"No," she answers miserably. "It's not. Mia won't go to school. She keeps saying that the bad animal wants to eat her. She's been staying home for two days now. My parents are going crazy. It's all my fault."
"That's nonsense," I say. "If anything, it's my fault. But it isn't. It's no one's fault. Your sister just has an overactive imagination."
"If I had taken her to Ginny's—"
"She would have run away from you," I say. "Just like she ran away from me. Mia is really fast, you know."
"Who's really fast?" Chris asks, and joins our table.

We all have our habits and routine. When that routine breaks, it unnerves us. If it were up to most of us, nothing would change. Ever. Coral and Shane stare confusedly at Chris as he lays his cafeteria tray on the table casually, as if he does it every day. Chris doesn't know them, so he doesn't notice the small changes, but I can see it all. The way Coral shrinks a bit, suddenly becoming much quieter. The way Shane's hand immediately flies to his camera case, as it always does when he feels uncomfortable or stressed for any reason.

"Coral's sister, Mia," I answer, trying to appear nonchalant. Primary objective: do not blush. "I was taking her to a friend's yesterday, and she ran away."

"Oh," he says, examining the unappetizing horrors on his tray.

"Was she okay?"

"Yes," Coral says before I can reply. "She's fine."

"Cool." Chris nods and starts sticking his fork into random things on his plate.

"How did the test go?" I ask him.

He shrugs. It seems he isn't entirely aware there even was a test. "Whatever," he says. He locates some miraculously unburnt tater tots on his plate and eats them. I suddenly realize that the three of us are staring at him in fascination. It's almost like some sort of wildlife documentary show. Behold the musician as he roams his territory, choosing his food without care. Usually, he stands with his herd, but today he has chosen for some reason to wander away and stand by the three weirdos. Truly, nature is full of mysteries.

"So," he says. "Did you manage to get the bracelet out of the bottle?"

"What bracelet?" Shane asks.

"Oh, I got Amy a bracelet for her birthday," Chris says.

Objective failed—blushing imminent. Time for extraction.

"Coral's sister was a bit freaked out, because she thought she saw an animal that was going to eat her," I say quickly, feeling my face heating up. "So we were talking about that."

Coral's eyes slay me on the spot, leaving a smoking pile of ash. Or, at least, that's what would've happened if looks could kill. "It's no big deal," she says.

"My little brother gets scared sometimes," Chris says. "I think it's like a phase or something. He sneaks into my bed at night."

"Mia has been sleeping with me for the past two nights," Coral admits, looking relieved that someone understands. "I don't know what to do."

"Well." Chris waves his fork a bit. "I guess there isn't a lot to do. It can help to show her there's nothing to be afraid of. Like with my brother, I show him that there's nothing in the sock drawer. We get all the socks out, and he sees it's empty."

"The sock drawer?" Shane asks.

"He thinks there are goblins in the sock drawer. Don't ask me why. I don't even think he knows what goblins are."

"Well, I can't show her there's no animal," Coral says. "She thinks it's hiding in a field nearby our house."

"A field?" Chris asks. "What kind of field?"

Coral shrugs. "Just an untended field. I think the farmer who owned it died or something. My mom told me the story once, but I don't remember the details."

"Maybe we can go to the field, let Shane take some pictures," I suggest. "We can show Mia that there aren't any footprints. Take a picture of that rock."

"Why are you dragging me into this?" Shane asks. "Can't you take some pictures with your phone?"

I hold my temper. He's still upset because Nicole didn't call swooning to talk about his photos. "Well, it'll be more convincing if we used a real camera. Besides, Mia looks up to you."

"That's true," Coral says, perking up. "Ever since she met you, she's like 'Shane said this' and 'Shane did that.' She thinks you're practically the president of the United States."

"Fine, fine," Shane grumbles. "Today?"

"Yeah," Coral says. "After school."

"I can't make it," Chris says. "I have band practice."

We all stare at him in wonder. How can someone have so much self-esteem that he simply assumes he's wanted? I was once like that, I suddenly recall. What happened to me?

"Maybe next time," I suggest hesitantly.

"Cool." He smiles at me. There are butterflies somewhere. They are not necessarily good butterflies. They might be the bad kind of butterflies. I don't really know which kind, but they're there, flapping their wings.

The bell rings. Chris stands up. "See you later, Amy," he says and walks away.

"What just happened?" Shane asks me.

"I had a date with him two days ago," I say.

"You what?" Coral stares at me in amazement. "And you didn't tell me?"

"You were a bit hard to talk to," I say. "I tried, but you were all math math math, mathy math math."

"Well, you should have tried harder," she says, a bit hurt.

"Fine, sorry," I say wearily. "I'll do better in the future."

Chapter Twenty-One

We decide to get off the school bus next to Coral's house. From there we can easily walk to the field. During the ride I try to talk to Coral and Shane, but they're both glum and silent, each thinking about his own problems. Finally we reach the bus stop and get off.

"You want to go to my place and get something to drink before going over to the field?" asks Coral.

"Your place," Shane says, just as I say, "To the field."

"Let's go to the field first," I say. "We'll be done in five minutes, then go to Coral's."

"But I'm thirsty," Shane complains.

"Come on, it'll just take a moment," I tell him.

"Dehydration also takes only a moment," he mutters, but he follows as I lead them to the street where Mia disappeared.

We walk past the house with the large dog, which barks at us in rage.

"Perhaps that's the animal from the field," suggests Shane.

"There was no animal," I say, and wonder if he could be right. We reach the abandoned house, and I lead them inside. Shane hesitates for a moment, and I can almost see his thoughts as he recalls our encounter at Alice Hendrix's house. He eventually enters the yard.

"We keep trespassing on other people's property, did you

notice?" he says. Coral and I ignore him.

We walk together through the backyard and into the field. "This is it," I say. "I mistook that rock over there to be the animal chasing us."

"You mean that's the rock that Mia mistook for an animal," Coral says, looking at the rock.

"Uh... right."

"And this is where you found her?" Coral asks, motioning to a place where the plants are trodden to the ground.

"Yeah, I guess so."

"Shane, are you taking photos of this?" she asks.

"Yeah, I am," he says, pointing his camera at the ground.

I walk over to the rock. It's uncommonly dark. I lay my hand on it. Rough, and cold. I wonder how I could have ever mistaken it for an actual animal.

"Take photos of the ground all around," Coral says. "There are no footprints."

"Coral, that's what I'm doing."

I shoo away a random fly that lands on my cheek. It flies away and lands on my nose. I shoo it away again. Another fly lands on my arm.

"Take pictures of the rock as well."

"Damn it, Coral, that's what I'm doing. Stop giving me instructions!"

I walk slowly away from them. Another fly starts flying around me. In fact, once I'm far enough from Shane and Coral I can suddenly hear a loud buzzing noise. There's a swarm of flies here.

"Hey, Amy? Let's go, I'm done," Shane says.

"Hang on," I call back. Where are all those flies coming from? I edge forward, then almost stumble over something. I look down. It's a dead cat, its mouth wide open, exposing sharp yellow teeth, its fur rotting away. I moan in disgust, raising my head, and my gaze encounters something horrid. There are more dead animals here. Birds, rats, cats, all discarded together. Some are half-eaten. Some are only bones. The buzzing is so loud I can practically feel it. There's strange movement on the bodies, and suddenly I realize what it is. Maggots. Hundreds... thousands of maggots crawling over the dead animals. The rotting flesh smell invades my nostrils and my mouth as the horror of what I'm watching sinks in. I stumble backwards, coughing, then turn away and throw up.

"Amy? Are you okay?" Coral asks.

"Dead animals," I spit. "Over there." I can't say anything else. I wish this hadn't happened. It's a moment I'll never be able to forget. Shane walks past me and groans in disgust.

"Wow," he says. "She's right. There are dozens of dead animals here. God… the stench…" He takes a few photos. I have no idea how he can stand so close to these things. All I can think of is getting as far away as possible from this field. Coral approaches me, pulling back my hair as I retch once more.

"Thanks," I mumble. "Let's go. Please."

We walk away, Coral half leading me gently. We get back to the street and start walking towards Coral's house.

"It's the animal that Mia saw," I say, breathing heavily. "It ate them. She was right. There was something here."

"Maybe," Shane says.

"Not maybe. Definitely," I say angrily. "I saw it too. I thought I had imagined it but… it was real."

"But what is it?" Coral asks. "A wolf? A hyena?"

"I don't know."

"Well, don't tell Mia about this, okay?" Coral says.

"Of course," Shane answers.

We walk in silence for a while.

"God, I hate this place," I say.

Chapter Twenty-Two

Coral's mom is in the process of making a sandwich for Mia as we walk inside, and she cheerfully begins to make sandwiches for us as well. Coral's mom always makes sandwiches the same way. Bread with cream cheese, cucumber and salt. I have no idea what the point of the salt is. I don't like cream cheese with salt. Coral and Mia think it's the best meal in the world. Mia, in fact, is munching happily, and does not seem to be struggling with trauma at all. I suspect that by now she's completely gotten over it, and today's whole trip was for nothing.

In Coral's house there are so many rules regarding food that they probably have an actual rule book somewhere. Most of the rules specify where food cannot be eaten. It cannot be eaten in Coral's room. It cannot be eaten in the living room, on the couch. It cannot be eaten while standing up, because it isn't polite. There are more; I can't remember them all. Collect all these rules together, and you quickly realize that there's only one rule. Food is eaten while sitting down at the dining table.

We all sit around the dining table, chewing salty sandwiches.

I feel nauseous and can't eat more than two bites. The memory of the dead animals keeps invading my mind. The real horror was not the blood, or the bones, or the strangely immobile bodies. It wasn't even the maggots. It was the stench. That's something you don't see in the movies. You see the murder investigators looking at bodies, you see the blood. Sometimes they discuss the stench. But you can't smell it. It's the worst smell in the world. It consumes everything in its path. It coats your nose and your mouth, and it feels like it gets into your clothes, your hair.

I put down my sandwich.

After the meal we go to Coral's room. Coral locks the door to stop Mia from barging in. My mom hates it when I lock the door to my room, but here it's standard practice to lock the doors. I suppose it's literally the only way to keep her sister away.

"Okay, now what?" Coral asks.

"Nothing," I answer. "What do you mean?"

Both Coral and Shane stare at me in surprise.

"There really was an animal in that field," Shane says. "Mia was right. Don't you want to go all Sherlock Holmes on it? Investigate it, follow clues, find suspects, break into houses?"

I shrug. "So there's some sort of wolf or something loose in the field. So what? We should probably report it to the city council."

"A wolf that carries all of its prey to one place?" Coral sounds skeptical.

"Maybe if it was its den," says Shane. "But it didn't look like a den."

"Oh, I forgot both of you were such experts on wild animals," I say, irritated.

"I don't claim to be an expert, but you have to agree it's extraordinary," says Coral. "I mean, so many dead animals in one place. Some of them weren't eaten at all. It's almost like it killed for sport."

"Coral, please," I beg. "I'm trying to get that image out of my mind. You're not helping."

Both Coral and Shane quiet down.

"Let's get out of here," I say. "Get some fresh air, maybe go to the mall. I could really use a change of scenery to distract me right now. We can talk about this there, okay?"

Coral agrees, mostly because she's afraid that Mia might be listening through the door. She has her usual discussion with her mother (I'm off to the mall. Yes, I know you're making chicken. I won't lose my appetite. I'll be home by seven thirty. Fine, seven. No, I can't take Mia. I know, the chicken is very tasty when you get it out of the oven, and it isn't when you heat it up later). Shane and I roll our eyes. Finally we leave.

As we walk and I slowly loosen up, the sight of the dead animals gets hazier. I even begin to develop an appetite, and the image of a warm, sweet cinnamon roll takes shape in my mind. The air, though chilly, is clean, and I breathe in deeply, trying to banish any trace of that sickly rotting smell.

When we get near the mall, I notice Edgar, the town's homeless guy, walking towards us. He's wearing an old coat, which hangs on him as if he was a scarecrow. He seems grumpier than usual.

"What took you so long? I've been waiting for you three to get here for more than an hour," he says. "No, no, take your time. It's not like I didn't have any lunch today. It's not like I was waiting just for you. You have all the time in the world." He looks at me and adds, "What, you think you're the only one who wants a cinnamon roll?"

"Hello, Edgar," I say weakly, pulling out my wallet. I hand him one dollar.

"Nice." He nods. "Alfred's cook gives me a small meal for a dollar if I come through the back door. As long as I don't bother the customers. And I don't. Well, unless the man who the trees hate dines there. When that happens... I bother the customers."

"Okay," I say. "Enjoy your meal."

He smiles. "You're a nice lady. It really is too bad that you're marked."

"I'm... marked?" I look at him in confusion. "What do you mean?"

He cocks his head slightly. "You know what I'm talking about. No predator likes to lose its prey. It gets even worse when it loses it twice."

"What... what predator?"

"Don't act dumb," he says gruffly. "I should ask them for a cup of water. They have paper cups that they keep just for me." He suddenly grabs my hand tightly. I try to pull it back, but he doesn't let go. His eyes stare into mine, and I suddenly realize that underneath his rambling, there's a sane man who simply… gave up one day. But he's still there, and he's looking at me right now.

"It'll find you eventually," he tells me. "You should be prepared. Think carefully—why are her eyes so big?" He lets go, and starts walking briskly away towards the mall.

"Edgar, hang on!" I call. I consider running after him, but I already know there's no point. Once Edgar says what he had to say, he refuses to add anything useful. I turn to face Shane and Coral, both of them looking pale and afraid.

"What the hell was he talking about?" I ask.

"Isn't it obvious?" Coral asks with a tight voice. "No predator likes to lose its prey. Just yesterday you got away from an animal, and you're marked. And that means that Mia is marked too!" She bursts into tears. I look at her dumbly as Shane tries to comfort her. Edgar's words keep ringing in my ears: *It'll find you eventually. You should be prepared.*

Chapter Twenty-Three

"What do you think Edgar meant when he talked about the big eyes?" Shane asks.

"Who knows?" I say. "It's Edgar. Half the things he says don't make any sense."

We're sitting in Shane's room. After our meeting with Edgar, we've lost our desire for hot chocolate and cinnamon rolls. We decided to crawl somewhere safe. Shane's place was closest. His parents aren't home, as usual. I think I've seen his mother only once, and I've never seen his father.

"I have to go home," Coral says for the seventh time. "I have to look after Mia."

"Coral, Mia is fine," I say testily. "The predator won't pounce on her in her own home."

"What if she goes to a friend's?"

"Then she'll be with your mother. Besides, we don't even know that she is marked. Whatever that means."

"Yes, we do! You two were together!" She seems on the verge of bursting into tears once more.

"Okay, okay." Shane tries to calm her down. He gives her one of the glasses of water he got from the kitchen earlier. "Let's think about our next step."

Our next step. Should we call the cops? As always, there's

nothing to tell them. Homeless people's ramblings are not considered evidence. Maybe this one time I should talk to my parents? Just thinking about it makes me shudder. My parents are already freaking out about my safety, ever since the Tom Ellis thing. If they thought I was in danger, I would never be allowed to leave home again.

"Why did he say you got away twice?" Shane asks.

"What?"

"Edgar. He said that the prey got away twice. Assuming the prey is you, and that you got away once when you were with Mia, why did he say you got away twice?"

"Maybe he meant that Amy got away and Mia got away as well. So the prey got away twice," Coral suggests.

"It didn't sound like that," Shane says.

"Well… The night we went to Alice Hendrix's house, I felt something following me down the street afterward," I say hesitantly. "And I think I saw a pair of eyes looking at me from the bushes. Something was stalking me, but then my neighbor turned up, and whatever it was disappeared."

"And inside the house," Shane says. "You saw something inside the house as well."

I nod.

"You think it's the same predator?" Coral asks, terrified. "What was it doing there?"

"Well… The cop said Alice's body was covered with scratches," I say. "That's something that a predator would do, isn't it? Maybe the same predator killed Alice Hendrix." I recall the shape in the darkness, the strange cage.

"I was there with you," Shane says. "Perhaps I'm marked as well."

"Well, you got out before me. You weren't there when it appeared. And only I got away twice."

"Three times," corrects Coral. "If you saw it in the house and on the street as well, you got away three times."

"Maybe." I consider this. "No. In the house… it almost felt like it was toying with me. Trying to scare me away. I don't think it really tried to get me there. No, the street and the field, that's twice…" I instantly regret saying that.

"So you do think it was trying to get you and Mia in the field," Coral says in a hoarse voice.

"I don't know. Maybe."

I think about the pile of dead animals we saw. I recall the dried blood in the room where Alice was killed. This predator is deadly. I shudder. Why did I even start messing with all this?

If I didn't know you as well as I do, I'd think you liked toying with death.

Maybe, for some reason, I do like toying with death? It doesn't feel like it right now. Right now I only wish for death to go somewhere else.

My phone blips. I pull it out of my pocket. It's a message from Chris: *How did it go?* Well, you know, a pile of dead animals, creepy warnings from a homeless maniac, complete meltdown by friend, salty sandwiches. Pretty much what you'd expect. I hesitate for a second, then type, *Not good. Ran into some trouble.* Sent. I instantly regret the message. I should have written that it went well. Could have added a smiley face.

"We need help," Shane says. "We need to tell someone about this."

"Who?" I ask impatiently. "Who would you—" Another message. *Are you okay? I'll come over. You at home?* I frantically reply, *I'm okay, not at home right now. Thanks.* This time I add a smiley face.

"I don't know, Amy," Shane says. "But just telling no one is stupid. Even if you aren't in danger, there's still something killing animals in the fields. We can't just ignore that."

"I can tell Peter," I say. "That's his job, right?"

Shane shrugs. I call Peter.

"Hello?"

"Peter? It's Amy."

"Hi, Amy, how are you? Is everything okay?"

"I don't know," I say. "Listen, Peter, we found a few dozen corpses of animals near Coral's house. Some of them looked as if they were partially eaten."

"Really?" He sounds concerned. "Maybe it's a hyena or

something."

"No, listen, we have a different idea. Maybe it's the animal that killed Alice Hendrix?"

"What?" Now he sounds less concerned and more angry. "Who told you an animal killed Alice Hendrix? The police are still investigating the case, and—"

"I know the body was covered with scratches. The cop at the crime scene told me. And I saw an animal near Coral's house, and—" I notice Shane motioning at me to shut up. "—and that's it."

"Amy, I don't know what made you figure out this weird connection. The cops think that whoever killed Alice Hendrix just made it look like an animal, because… Well, never mind why. They're handling it. Now can you please give me directions to the place where you saw the dead animals?"

I give him the directions.

"Okay. Listen, Amy, if I haven't made it clear by now, leave the murder of Alice Hendrix alone, okay? Leave it to the cops. Can you promise me you'll do that?"

I hesitate. "Okay."

"Promise me."

"I promise I'll leave the murder of Alice Hendrix alone."

"Good," he says. "I'll check out that thing with the dead animals. Have a nice day, okay?"

"Okay."

He hangs up. I look at Shane and Coral. "He didn't believe me."

"Well, duh," says Shane. "You didn't tell him about Edgar, and even if you did, he wouldn't really pay any attention."

"He said that the police think that a person killed Alice and made it seem as if an animal had killed her."

"Really?" Shane frowns. "Why would the police think that?"

"Maybe there were fingerprints at the crime scene," I say.

"But in that case, the thing you saw that night in Alice's house probably wasn't the same predator."

"Maybe it's someone who trained his dog to attack people," I suggest. "Maybe when Edgar was talking about a predator, he was actually talking about a man."

"Then what did you see in Alice's house?" Coral asks. "You saw something there, right?"

"I don't know," I say. "Maybe I saw the dog"

"The dog turned off the lights?"

"The man turned off the... look, I don't really know," I say, frustrated.

"And why did he follow you and try to get you, then?" Shane asks.

"I don't know, Shane," I repeat. "Maybe he thought I saw something and decided to kill me." I shudder at the thought.

"But... is Peter going to report this to the police?" Coral asks, biting her lip.

"He didn't sound like it," I answer. "He'll maybe go and check it out himself, I don't know."

"Well... if the police and the town's fantastic security force won't do anything, someone else should." Coral says. She stands up and paces around the room. "Maybe they just need a push. If they took it more seriously..."

"Why would they?" Shane asks her.

She shook her head, her eyes distant. "I'm going home," she says. "I have to look after Mia."

"I'm going as well," I say. "I need to think about all this."

"You can't walk home alone in the dark," Shane says, horrified. "The predator might be out there, looking for you!"

Walking home right now does sound terrifying. I call Mom.

"Mom, can you pick me up from Shane's?"

"I'm making dinner, Amy. Get back home by yourself."

"But, Mom, I think my head hurts a bit," I say, playing the concussion card.

There's a moment of silence. "Fine, I'm on my way." She sighs and hangs up.

"My mom is on her way," I tell Coral. "We can drop you off as well."

Coral nods, frowning at the floor.

Shane tries to change the subject, to talk about school, about the test, about Chris. Me and Coral ignore him, and after a minute he gives up. Trying to keep busy, I grab one of Shane's albums and flip the pages distractedly. Coral glances at her phone every minute.

Finally Mom calls me and tells me she's waiting in the car outside. We say goodbye and descend to the street. During the ride to Coral's house, Mom asks Coral some polite questions, and Coral tries to answer them all, but as soon as we get to her house, she nearly bolts out of the car.

"So?" Mom asks, driving home. "How was your day?"

"It was great, Mom," I say glumly, staring outside at the passing streetlights. It occurs to me that while I was happy to call Peter for help, I was just as quick to evade Chris's offer of assistance. Chris is sweet, and cute. But let's face it, he's not Peter, right? I take out my phone, thinking of writing him something, though I don't really know what, when I notice I have an unread message from him: *Glad you're okay. I'll see you tomorrow.*

I put the phone back in my pocket without replying.

Chapter Twenty-Four

"Thanks for coming," I tell Peter. "We thought someone should see this."

"Sure," he answers. "No problem."

We're marching through the field, the weeds and plants whispering in the wind. I stay close to Peter, his proximity reassuring. With him, I know, I have nothing to fear.

"Where is the thing, anyway?" Coral asks.

I look around. It all looks the same; it's hard to pinpoint the exact location. Then I notice the buzzing of the flies.

"Over there." I point. We all walk towards the sound. I notice the corpse of the cat first. "There," I tell Peter. "See?"

"I see," he says, sounding far away. I look back and notice they hadn't followed me at all. All three of them are standing at the edge of the field, looking at me.

"Well, are you coming?" I ask, irritated.

"We can't," Peter says, his voice sounding hollow, bored. "We can't come near you. You're marked."

"What? Peter, what are you—" I turn towards the cat's corpse, but it's gone. "Where did it go?" I glance back at Peter, Coral and Shane. They are still standing at the edge of the field, but it is somehow further away now.

"Guys, the cat is gone!" I say. "Come on! I think—" I hear a rustle. I turn and notice something moving between the shrubs, moaning softly.

"It's still alive," I mutter, horrified, as the cat drags itself with its front legs. It moves slowly forward, towards me. Behind it I can see other shapes moving. Other animals, limping, crawling, hopping, all getting closer.

"Peter," I whimper, but he's gone, I know that he's gone. I'm marked, and I'm alone. The cat is almost at my feet when I turn around and flee.

I run through the high shrubs, the thorns cutting at my shirt, tearing it up. I can hear the slithering sounds behind me, accompanied by moans and groans of the injured animals. If they touch me, it'll all be over. I stumble, slip, fall into a puddle. Getting up, I see that it's a puddle of blood. The blood is on my clothes, on my hands. I can smell it, a coppery sickly smell. And the animals can smell it as well. Their moans become louder, angrier, hungrier… And above them all I can hear a growl. It's low, and menacing and vicious. It's the predator. It can smell me and see me, and I'm marked… I sob as I start running again, and the growl behind me becomes a roar as it pounces after me, getting closer, and everything is ringing, ringing, ringing…

My phone is ringing as my eyes fly open, my hands clutching at the bedsheets. I fumble for the light switch, desperate to dispel the suffocating darkness and the memory of that roar…

There. I turn on the light, nearly blinding myself. I pick up the phone, somehow managing to answer it…

"H—Hello? What? What?"

"Amy?" It's Coral. "Are you awake?"

"I am now…" I say, my heart still thudding. "Why? What time is it?"

"I don't know, about three thirty. Listen to this. One Narrowdale resident reported that a large animal was wandering in his backyard. The local security was sent to investigate, but by the time they got there, the animal was gone. Sound familiar?"

"I don't know. What is that? What do you want?"

"It's a report in *Narrowdale Gazette*."

"Don't they have something a bit more interesting to write

about?" I try to sit up in my bed. It turns out to be a difficult maneuver.

"It's Narrowdale's local newspaper. What do you want them to write about, exactly? Now listen to this. A resident of Oak Street complained about strange growling outside her window. That's from the newspaper published three weeks ago."

"Okay. Sounds like a really boring article. Is that all it says?" I take a deep breath. My hands are shaking. What a horrifying dream.

"No, of course not. There's the response of the security company, and another response from Narrowdale's city council, and a section about rabies that if you ask me is just ridiculous. I mean, come on, do your research. If I had written this report—"

"Coral, can I go to sleep now?"

"No, listen. I've done some digging in the newspaper's archive. There were a lot of pets that disappeared. There's a picture of a cute cat which went missing a month ago, and here's a picture of a puppy—"

"Yeah, it's just that I'm really tired, and—"

"This has to be connected to the predator! Maybe it ate Kitty, or maybe it was the murderer's dog..."

"Uh... Who's Kitty?"

"A cat that disappeared."

"They called their cat... Kitty?"

"Yes, and—"

"Maybe it just ran away because it was upset with its owners," I suggest. "And then went looking for a better name."

"Amy, this is serious."

"Yes, it's very serious, and we can talk about it tomorrow. I need sleep."

"Okay, okay," she says and hangs up. She doesn't sound as if she's about to sleep anytime soon. Then again, neither am I. I lie in bed, my eyes open. What a horrid dream. I'm lucky that Coral woke me up. On the other hand, now I'm wide awake, and morning is still hours away.

I get up and get myself a drink of water. On the way back I manage to hit the bedpost with my pinkie toe. I sit down on the floor, grasping my throbbing toe, trying not to scream. Why did God create bedposts? Why did God create toes? Why can't I look where I'm going? Eventually I get back to bed.

The mixture of a bruised toe, a terrible nightmare, and a nightly talk about missing pets does not help when you want to fall asleep. My thoughts keep spiraling round and round in my head. What does it mean that I'm marked? Was Alice marked before she died? Peter said that the police think that whoever killed Alice was a man. How do they know? According to TV police shows, they have all sorts of ways to find DNA and fingerprints. Does that mean that they know who did it? If they do, why haven't they arrested him yet? I'm marked—why isn't the murderer behind bars?

Eventually I fall asleep. The alarm wakes me up after what feels like several seconds.

Chapter Twenty-Five

Crossing the cafeteria, I notice Chris sitting with his friends. He is listening as his friend is talking animatedly, waving his hands around to illustrate something. Windmills, perhaps. One of them is drumming with his fork and spoon on the table, half a smile on his face. Another one, Donna, if I'm not mistaken, sits next to the cutlery drummer, her head leaning on his shoulder. They seem so engaged, so familiar with each other. I spot Coral already sitting by herself, and I walk towards her. Chris notices me and smiles. He motions towards an empty seat next to him. For a moment I'm almost tempted. They all seem so normal. Would one lunch without a discussion about lethal animals be such a bad idea? But I shake my head and give him an embarrassed smile, motioning with my head towards Coral. He seems disappointed. Am I missing my chance to get to know this guy better? As I sit in front of Coral, I feel torn. Maybe I can suggest that we join their table. I can't see Shane, and it's entirely possible that he decided to skip lunch.

"Hey, listen," I say. "Do you want to… maybe… join that…"

"I've been researching some more," she says. "I found out some really amazing things."

I sigh and look at her. She looks terrible. Her eyes are bloodshot, her hair looks like an abandoned bird's nest, and I'm pretty sure she's wearing the exact same outfit as yesterday.

"Do tell," I say, opening my lunch bag.

"First of all, I found some additional things in the *Narrowdale Gazette*. People complaining about strange animal sounds, or about missing pets. Then I did some additional searching on Facebook and found some more info. There's a group called 'Narrowdale's Residents.' It's mostly just messages from the mayor, or pictures of the town, but some residents did post in the group about their missing pets. I found two additional missing pet posts in 'Narrowdale's Moms'—"

"In what?" I interrupt her.

"'Narrowdale's Moms.' It's a group of mothers in Narrowdale."

"Why would there be a group for that?"

"Well, they share info about kindergartens and parks, recommendations about nannies—"

"Being a mom sounds like so much fun!"

"Anyway…" she says, displeased with my attempt at derailing the conversation. "Another mom complained there about her missing cat. So I cross-referenced all the data…"

She cross-referenced things. That's something they do in cop shows. I'm not even sure what that means.

"…and a half. Amy, are you listening?"

"Sure, sure." I try to focus. "So… cross-referenced, huh?"

"Right. I took all the reports, put them in an Excel chart…"

"You put them in an Excel chart?" I ask weakly.

"That's right, and I made some graphs. Check this out. Doesn't this look very indicative?" She thrusts some pages at me. I look at them. There are numbers, and pie charts, and a weird graph with many lines… Heavens help me.

"Why do you hate me? What did I ever do to you?" I whine.

"Never mind the graphs," she says, and plucks the pages from my hand. "What I found out is—"

"Hey, Amy. Hey, Coral." Chris sits down in front of us. Coral barely seems to notice him. She thumbs her pages, frowning.

"Hey, Chris," I say, feeling my face heating. What's wrong with me? Why can't I talk to him without blushing?

"What are you two doing?" He takes a peek at Coral's pages. "Math homework?"

"Not exactly..." I say. "Coral's done a bit of research about missing animals."

"Really? Is that like a school project or something?"

"No," Coral says distractedly. "I'm trying to figure out what killed all those animals in the field. It might have killed Alice Hendrix as well."

Chris blinks a few times. "Why do you think it killed Alice—"

"Because Amy thinks she saw an animal when she broke into Alice's house."

"Amy broke into..." Chris tries to digest this new and interesting information as I kick Coral under the table. She doesn't even say "ow."

"Why did you break into Alice Hendrix's house?" he asks me.

"I don't know," I say. "It was stupid..."

"And now we think that Amy might have been marked by the predator. Along with my sister."

Well, it was bound to happen. The moment when Chris realizes that me and my friends are a bunch of escaped lunatics, and walks away, taking his big eyes and cute curly hair with him. But surprisingly, he doesn't yet.

"Why do you think..."

Coral raises her face from her graphs, and I can see the impatience in her eyes. She can't be bothered right now with explaining things, and if Chris won't get on with telepathically extracting the information from our brains, she might snap.

"Let me fill you in," I quickly say before she hits him with her research paper. I tell him briefly about the night Shane and I entered Alice's house, about our findings yesterday and about Edgar. I explain that though Edgar is just a homeless guy, he seems to have good instincts and can usually tell when something's going on. Then I silently wait for him to run away screaming back to his friends. He will tell them all about it, and they will tell their friends. Everyone in school will soon know about our mental problems. We will be shunned, possibly rolled in tar and feathers, and I'll have to move to Mexico, changing my name to Esperanza.

"Only in Narrowdale, huh?" Chris says.

"Yeah." I nod, relieved. "Only in Narrowdale."

"So what did you find?" Chris asks Coral.

Pleased that someone is taking a real interest, she lays a page on the table. It's a map.

"This is a map of Narrowdale," she says. "The blue spots are where people complained about missing pets. The red spots are where people reported animal noises. The square here is the field where we found the animal corpses, and the star is Alice Hendrix's house. Do you see something interesting?"

Chris and I both lean forward, examining the map. I realize that I like his smell. I hadn't noticed his smell before, but now that we're close, I wonder how I hadn't noticed it sooner.

"All the incidents seem to happen in the same area," Chris says. I realize that I'm staring at him, and I force myself to look at the map.

"Hang on," I say. "That blue spot over there is all the way on the other side of Narrowdale. What about that one?"

"Some pets just go missing." Coral shrugs. "It happens."

"I live here." Chris points at the map.

"How very interesting and relevant," Coral says sharply.

"She hasn't slept tonight," I explain to Chris.

"I slept a bit," she says, annoyed. "Now, do you want to hear another interesting fact?"

Chris and I nod.

"All the reports started forty-two days ago. Before that, nothing."

"What happened forty-two days ago?" I ask.

"I don't know," she admits. "But I think it's—"

The bell rings.

"Well, lunch break's over," I say. "Let's go back to class."

"Never mind class right now," Coral says. "I'm telling you—"

"Hang on, what?" I say, feeling as if my world is collapsing.

"I'm telling you that—"

"You don't want to go to class?"

"—forty-two days ago this animal started prowling around in Narrowdale—"

"They might teach something important," I mumble.

"Amy! This animal is loose for six weeks, killing animals, probably your old woman as well—"

"She's not my old woman... listen, we're late for—"

"It wants to kill Mia!" Coral half screams. "Amy, this animal wants to kill my sister, and no one has done anything for the past six weeks!"

"Okay, calm down," Chris says, raising his hands. "From what you told me, there's no reason to think that this animal is after your sister, right? I mean... that homeless guy was talking about Amy, wasn't he?"

"Well, I don't want Amy to be killed as well." Coral thumps the table.

"Neither do I," Chris says, sounding as if he's trying to calm a wild bull. "Just... chill, okay?"

"Let's get out of here, at least," I say. "Before someone kicks us out."

We leave the cafeteria and sit down on a bench in the hallway.

"So what do you want to do?" I ask Coral.

"Well, I found out something else," she says, laying the map in her lap. "Three of the people who reported their pets missing blamed a guy called Alan Billings. They said on Facebook that he has a vicious dog that escapes from his yard all the time and attacks passersby."

"Okay," I nod. "What do we know about this Alan Billings?"

"Well, Alan Billings lives here," Coral says, pointing at the map.

"That's the exact center of all the incidents," Chris says.

I suddenly feel cold as I raise my eyes from the map. Coral looks at me and our eyes meet.

"You know what I think?" Coral says. "I think we found our predator."

Chapter Twenty-Six

"I don't know," Shane says. Coral and I stare at him in disappointment. Chris chews a donut contentedly and doesn't seem to mind what Shane knows or doesn't know.

Once school was over, the four of us met outside at the gate and went to Barbar Koffee to discuss Coral's findings. Coral told Shane about her research, and we waited expectantly for his enthusiastic response. It appears we're about to keep on waiting.

"What's there to know?" Coral asks. "It's clear-cut. Look. See here? This is the printout of the first report of a pet missing. Just a few hundred feet from Alan Billings's house. Now look at what Tiffany seven wrote in this forum—"

"Tiffany seven?" Shane interrupts.

"That's her nickname on the forum. Look, she writes that her cat went missing—"

"There were six Tiffanys before her? Or maybe she's royalty, and you should read it as Tiffany the seventh."

"She says she lives on Lake Street, which is the one running parallel to Allan Billings's street—"

"Who's just some guy who has a dog," Shane points out.

"A vicious, deadly dog," I remind him.

"So says a random woman on Facebook. I saw a post on Facebook the other day in which a woman claimed that aliens were trying to communicate with her through TV commercials. Despite that, I'm not about to tell my TV that we come in peace."

"Careful, Coral has graphs," I warn him.

"You don't scare me with your graphs," he says. "Show me that map again." He looks at the map. "Yeah, fine, whatever. Don't you think you're in a bit of a hurry to accuse a random man of murder? I'm sure that there are other people living next to him. Maybe they have dogs too."

"Maybe it wasn't murder," Chris suggests. "Maybe the dog ran away and killed some animals by mistake. Maybe that dead woman has nothing to do with this."

"Maybe," says Shane. "But I don't know—"

My phone rings, and I answer.

"Honey!!!" Nicole screams. My ear is ringing, and I quickly turn down the volume and switch to the other ear.

"Hey, Nicole," I say. "What's up?"

"What's up with me? What's up with you?"

"I don't know." I sigh and look at my friends. Coral is reorganizing her papers, muttering. Chris is holding the map in his hand, examining it. Shane is watching me as if I'm holding the Holy Grail to my ear. "We're trying to find the animal that Mia saw in the field a couple of days ago."

"Who cares about that? What about the murder?"

"Well, we think the murderer might have sent the same animal to kill Alice Hendrix."

"What???" she shouts. My other ear starts ringing as well. I decrease the volume a bit more.

"Yeah," I say and give her a short version of what Edgar said and the connections that Coral made with her research.

"That's sounds troubling," Nicole says, concerned. "Honey, you have to be careful. Don't go out alone at night. In fact, don't go out alone at all."

"Yes, Mommy."

"And what are you about to do with that Alan guy?"

"We haven't decided yet. Shane thinks we're jumping to conclusions."

"But didn't you say that you have evidence pointing to him?"

"Well, yeah, but…" I suddenly have an idea. "Nicole, hang on, I'm putting you on speaker."

"What? Why are you—" I put the phone on speaker and place it on the table.

"Nicole, I want to involve you in the discussion," I say aloud. "Just… you know, so everyone here can hear what you have to say."

Coral doesn't seem as if she is even remotely interested in anything Nicole has to say, and Chris seems to take it all in stride, but Shane is looking at my phone as if it suddenly grew legs and began tap dancing across the table.

"Okay, honey," she says, her voice a bit metallic through the phone's speaker. "I was just saying that from what I hear, Coral said that about a million people complained about that Alan guy, right?"

"Three people," Coral says dryly.

"Right, and that sounds like a good reason to check it out, doesn't it?"

"Yeah, but I thought we shouldn't jump to any conclusions…" Shane says weakly.

"Shane, Amy's life might be in danger," Nicole says. "We should do whatever we can to find this predator. You should definitely check out this Alan."

Shane looks as if the fact that Nicole called him by his name just destroyed half his brain cells. "But he's just some guy who—"

"There's no reason to ignore any lead," Nicole points out. "No matter who suggested it."

Coral seems as if she's contemplating smashing my phone to pieces, but Shane is beaten. "Sure, I mean, I guess we can check it out…"

"We can all go together," says Chris. "Safety in numbers, right?"

"Hang on, who's that?" Nicole says.

"My name's Chris," he says. "Hi, Nicole, nice to talk to you."

"Chris?" Nicole says, her voice changing completely. "Nice to talk to you, Chris. Amy, you didn't tell me that there was someone named Chris over there. Now, Chris, I wonder why that name sounds familiar…"

"It's really hard to hear you when you're on speaker," I quickly say and lift the phone, removing her from speaker.

"Honey…" she whispers to my ear. "You little vixen. So that's how you date boys these days? Drag them to investigate murders? That's so—"

"It was nice talking to you, Nicole—"

"Don't you dare hang up. Why didn't you tell me about this? I want every dirty detail—"

I hang up.

"So?" Coral says venomously. "Are we going to check Alan Billings out?"

"Yeah, sure," says Shane. "I was about to say that, even though it's probably nothing, we should check it out, right?"

We all sit in silence for a moment.

"So… when is Nicole coming over to visit again?" asks Shane.

Chapter Twenty-Seven

Coral has Alan Billings's address, which she found online the night before. It turns out he even has a small website for professional dog training. We decide not to call, but to check his house out first.

"It's really… fenced," Coral says, looking at the house.

Fenced is an accurate description. An eight-foot-high metal fence surrounds the entire house and its yard. I can't spot any hole in the fence that would substantiate the reports about a dog which escaped from this house. Any such dog would either have to escape through the gate while it was open, or fly. The gate is heavy, ugly and imposing. It has a small intercom on it.

"Okay," I say, trying to sound confident. "Shall we ring?"

"Maybe we should call first," says Shane.

I ignore him and ring the intercom. There's no answer.

"Try again," says Chris, and I press once more.

"Coral, what's his phone number?" Shane asks.

I press the gate handle. The gate opens with a squeak. I start walking across the yard, looking around me. The yard is barren, except for a few brave sunflowers growing in one of the corners. I can see several small pits around me, and I wonder what they're used for. There's an unpleasant smell that I can't quite place. My footsteps make a sharp crunching sound as I walk along a pebbled path. I can hear Shane and Chris saying something, their voices sounding strange, fearful, but I'm already at the front door, knocking three times.

At first, I hear nothing. Then I start hearing a strange, low hum. The sound makes me feel a bit anxious, and then I realize why. It's coming from behind me. Reality shifts into focus as my breath halts in fear. The pits, I realize, were dug by an animal, and the unpleasant smell was the smell of its feces. I turn around.

In the middle of the path, between the gate and me, stands a huge dog. On all fours it's almost as high as me. If it stood on two legs, it would tower high over my head.

You're marked.

Its mouth is slightly open, exposing two rows of sharp yellow teeth, and its eyes stare at me, angry and thirsting for blood.

Blue eyes, gazing at me malevolently in the darkness, knowing that I'm trapped.

Its fur is in various shades of brown and gray, except for its back, where there's one wide black stripe. As it paces closer, I can see the black stripe bristling.

I can feel its jaws snapping at my throat.

A drop of drool drops from its mouth, and I watch it splash on the ground, transfixed. I can hear Shane talking to someone hysterically, but it's hard to hear what he's saying, to concentrate on anything beyond what's in front of me.

Marked.

Only two things exist in this world right now: me and this dog.

When it's less than six feet from me I make a small movement, tiny, really. It's a mistake. It lunges at me, half barking, half roaring, as I flatten myself to the wall. It closes in, growling, and I can see every tooth, knowing that they can easily snap every bone in my body like a flimsy branch…

"Pepsi, sit!" an unfamiliar voice intrudes. The dog stops snarling and sits immediately, though its eyes still glare at me threateningly, waiting for any movement. They're not blue at all, I suddenly notice. They're brown.

"She won't hurt you," says the voice. "Not now, anyway."

I stand still, refusing to even open my mouth.

"Pepsi, go home. Go, girl," the man says. The monster—

Pepsi?—gets up and walks by me, wagging its tail. I turn aside to watch it walk inside the house, through the open door. By the door stands a bald man wearing only pants, no shirt, looking at me with a hostile frown, his arms crossed.

"You're lucky that your friend caught me on the phone," he tells me. "I was in the shower."

"Okay," I say, my voice squeaky and trembling. Now that the dog's gone, I can feel my body once more. My heart is racing, my hands are trembling and my cheeks are wet from something. Tears.

"You can come in now," he calls over my shoulder. I can hear the gate opening, and then Shane, Chris and Coral walk inside. Coral hugs me, and I notice she has been crying as well. Her hands feel sweaty. Shane and Chris stand back, embarrassed.

"Didn't you see the sign?" the man says, his voice sharp. "There's a big damn sign saying 'Beware of Dog' on the fence, didn't you notice it?"

"No," I say just as Shane says, "Yes, but…"

"There's a big sign," the man points out once more.

"Are you Alan?" I ask, trying to recover.

"Yes," he answers gruffly.

"Okay…" Suddenly I have no idea what to say.

"We're here because my mom took in a dog, and we're interested in training him," Coral says.

"What kind of dog?" Alan asks.

"It's uh… black and brown… kinda big…" Coral hesitates.

"A German Shepherd?" he asks.

"Right, a German Shepherd," she says.

"How old?"

"Uh… three."

"When did you take him in?"

"We only just got him. Umm… how long does basic training take?" Coral tries to take control over the conversation.

"It depends. Usually about six weeks."

"And do you do it in our house?"

"No. You have to bring the dog over here. Part of the training is done in the yard, and part of it is done on the street, where we teach it to walk obediently next to you."

"Okay... are there ever any problems with the training?"

"Problems?" Alan narrows his eyes, his jaw clenched. "What kind of problems?"

"I don't know... can a dog suddenly attack me during training? Or... attack someone while we're on the street?"

"Why would that happen?" he asks. "I'm very careful. Sometimes dogs are more hostile, especially if they've been mistreated before, so we use a muzzle in the beginning. There are never any problems."

"It's just that we've heard some complaints..." Coral says.

"Are you talking about the idiot with the cat?" Alan says, raising his voice, his face becoming red. "Look, I told those morons from the compound, it wasn't my dog. I don't know why he'd think it was my dog. My dog never gets out without me! It's someone else's dog. Some people can't control their dogs, that's the problem. Then they act all surprised when their dogs attack someone, and the poor dogs are put to sleep! The dog that killed that cat is probably Hammond's."

"Who?" I ask.

"This guy... used to live here. He had a really wild dog. Couldn't control it at all. The thing kept getting into fights with my dogs. He even bit poor Pepsi's ear once, nearly tore it off."

Poor Pepsi. No empathy from me.

"I'm telling you, that's the dog that killed that cat. Not my dog. It couldn't have been my dog."

This guy has a tendency to repeat himself. I'm getting frustrated. Then suddenly I say, "Hang on! Are you talking about... Ron Hammond?"

"Yeah, that's the guy. Ron Hammond. Had a real vicious dog with him. It was never any of my dogs." He turns to face Coral once more. "Couldn't be."

"Okay." She raises her hands. "Just wanted to make sure. So I'll talk to my mom..."

"If you want, bring the dog over, and we'll see. I don't charge for the first visit. But call first. Don't come without calling!"

"Oh, we won't," she says.

"There's a sign on the fence."

"We saw it," she says.

He walks inside and slams the door behind him. We all quickly leave, closing the gate to make sure that Pepsi doesn't change its mind about letting us live.

"What an unpleasant man," I say.

"Yeah," Chris agrees. "Are you okay? We thought that thing was about to kill you."

"I'm okay." I smile at him.

Chris clears his throat. "I was about to come inside, but then Shane managed to get the guy on the phone." He stares at the floor.

I burst out laughing. "That's really sweet," I say. "Were you about to protect me by becoming a chew toy?"

Chris raises his eyes, his face red, and I instantly regret making fun of him. Mental note, Amy, never make fun of a guy when he's trying to sound heroic.

"Well, unpleasant or not, I don't think this is the guy," Shane says.

"I agree." Coral nods.

"Okay," I say. "But Ron Hammond's dog…"

The four of us look at each other.

"Ron and Vivian were having problems," Coral says.

"It wasn't just problems," I say. "Ron took off."

"A few months later Vivian's mom was found dead, her body looking as if it was mauled by an animal," Shane says.

"Yeah," I say. "But the police think that whoever killed Vivian's mom was a man. They must have additional evidence."

"A man, like Ron Hammond," Coral says.

"Who has a large, wild dog," I say.

"Well, it's wild according to this Alan guy," says Chris. "I'm not sure we should take everything he says seriously."

"Anyway, Alan is probably not the guy," Coral says.

We all look at Alan Billings's house. Sure enough, there is a sign on the fence with a large dog face and bold red words: 'Beware of Dog'. I should really try to pay more attention to details.

"I don't know how I missed this sign," I say.

"You're lucky you're still alive," says Shane.

I don't answer him, though I agree completely.

Chapter Twenty-Eight

"There's really no need to escort me home," I say. "It's a huge detour for you."

"Well..." Chris shrugs. "I'm not sure what to believe, but you all seem to think that you're in danger, so there's no way I'm letting you walk home alone in the dark."

"Thanks," I say, feeling a bit grateful.

We walk in silence for a bit.

"So what do you think?" I say. "Do you think Ron Hammond killed Vivian's mom?"

"No." He shook his head. "I don't."

"Why not?"

"Because it's a weird explanation for this. It's much more straightforward if it was simply a startled burglar who Vivian's mother interrupted by accident."

I look at him, frustrated. "But the corpse was mauled!"

"That's your explanation for something a random cop told you," he points out. "He could have been pulling your leg. Or maybe he thought so, but he was wrong. I feel like you're looking for really strange explanations where simple ones are enough."

"Are you about to tell me to leave this to the police?"

"Nope."

"Seriously?"

He laughs. "Amy, two weeks after you got here, you broke into a killer's home and managed to get him arrested. I just saw you nearly get eaten by a giant mutant killer dog, and you just shrugged it off, going 'meh.' If I told you that this isn't your business, would you listen to me? I don't think so. I don't know what makes you tick, Amy, but I'm not about to try and stop it."

"Oh." I feel my face growing warm again. "Thanks."

"But I would be happy if you didn't take unnecessary risks," he adds.

I nod. He's right. No point in taking unnecessary risks.

We reach my house and stop by the gate.

"Well, thanks for walking me home," I say.

He smiles and then leans forward, his mouth approaching mine. I can imagine how it would feel, the soft lips touching my own, a warm, thrilling kiss. I take a step back.

"Sorry, I…" I struggle to explain myself. "It's just that… It was such a crazy day… I don't know what I feel…"

He frowns, his lips pressed tightly. "No problem," he says. "Totally fine. I'll see you tomorrow, yeah?"

"Yeah."

He walks away. I sigh, looking at the floor. What's my problem? Nicole would decapitate me. Speaking of which… I call Nicole as I enter the house.

"Hey, Mom," I say, running up the stairs to my room.

"Amy, can you please…" she starts saying, then Nicole answers and I close the door behind me.

I can hear the frustration in her voice. She wants to be angry at me for hanging up on her, then ignoring her calls (seven missed calls from her today), but she's dying to hear about Chris. She gives up, reprimanding me just to follow protocol, then quickly asks for details. I fill her in about our date on Sunday. Then I tell her about tonight, at which point she wails and moans at the fact that she has a moron for a friend.

"Why didn't you kiss him?" she says. "I want kissing!"

"I don't know how I feel about him," I say defensively. "I mean… I'm getting to know him for the first time."

"And how do you expect to know how you feel without kissing?"

she asks, frustrated. "That's the best way to tell. You kiss a guy, maybe your hands get busy for a bit, then you figure out if it's something you want."

"I'm not sure that's the right way."

"Honey, how do you know if you like apricot ice cream?"

"I don't know."

"You taste it!"

"I don't think your comparison holds," I argue. "Chris is not ice cream. He isn't cold, he doesn't melt, and he doesn't make me fat."

"Honey, can you speak slower? I want to write down your words of wisdom."

"Nicole, did you want anything else?"

"Yes. I wanted to tell you that I'm coming over this weekend. You guys need my help, and you sound like you need some kiss coaching."

"Fine. But I'm not doing kiss drills for you."

"Oh, honey, you have no idea," she says and hangs up.

I put down my phone.

Is Nicole right? What's the matter with me? Half a year ago I'd have been thrilled to have someone like Chris interested with me. So what's wrong? Well, it's all really confusing with the predator and the—

Stop that. I can't blame predators and dead women for not being able to make up my mind. I need to face the truth, and it always comes back to the same point, right? Peter. I have a serious crush on Peter. So now what? Should I tell Peter how I feel? That's actually a great idea! And after I do that I can hide under the bed for the rest of my life because there's no way in hell I can face the humiliation of him explaining why we can only be friends.

But Chris does make me feel a bit funny. He makes me blush. And he got me a bracelet. I pick up the bottle, open it and try to fish the thing out with a pen. It quickly gets very annoying. Well, his intentions were good. I should give him a real chance, shouldn't I?

My phone starts ringing once more. It's Jennifer Williams.

"Hey, Jen, what's up?"

"I don't know," she says. "What about you?"

"Had a weird day. This dog almost attacked me and... Jen, are you okay?" She is clearly crying. She tries to answer me, but the crying intensifies, making it impossible to understand what she's saying. I try to calm her down helplessly.

"Amy!" Mom calls from downstairs. I ignore her.

"Jen, what happened?"

She takes a deep breath and says, "Amy, do you remember how when you moved to Narrowdale, you had—"

"Amy!" Mom calls once more.

"Mom, I'll be down in a minute!" I yell back.

"Did you walk Moka yet? I don't want you to walk her too late!"

"I'm going now!" I say and run downstairs. "Sorry, Jen, what were you saying?" I ask as I walk out the front door.

"Those nightmares," she says, her voice a bit more stable, but still quivering. "Do you remember the nightmares?"

"Sure."

"You kept telling us how they felt real, as if you were really there…" She takes a deep breath. "Amy, ever since that night in your house… I keep having the same nightmares."

My heart sinks. Someone else would have said, "It's just nightmares, they'll pass." But I know. They're not just nightmares.

"What do you dream of?" I ask, opening Alex's gate.

"It's a bit hard to explain. The first nightmare is the one I had in your house. There's a man there, and I keep screaming at him that he hurt me, that I loved him… and then it all becomes blurry. And then there's blood everywhere, Amy, so much blood." She takes a deep breath.

"So do you see him attack you? Or does it simply happen?"

"I… It's all so blurry. I think there is something that hits my face, but I'm not sure what it is. There's just a lot of blood afterward."

"Okay." I leave the yard with Moka on a leash. "And what's the second dream?"

"The second dream is even worse somehow. I'm walking through a strange house. I enter a room with a woman… An old woman. She looks angry, and she says something, but I can't really understand what. Then I step forward, and she suddenly looks so scared. And… and… I know she's about to die." She starts crying once more.

I feel the hair on my neck prickling. "What happens then?"

"Then I wake up," she says. "Every time this happens, I wake up. I can't sleep ever since Saturday night, Amy, I'm going crazy. What can I do?"

"Um..." I have no idea what to say. "I need to think about it. Don't worry, Jen, We'll figure it out."

"I'm so tired, Amy, but I'm afraid to go to sleep. I never felt so scared and exhausted in my life." She starts sobbing once more. Jennifer Williams, one of the strongest people I know.

"Hang in there," I say. "We'll..." I suddenly have an idea. "Jen, if I send you an e-mail with some photographs, do you think you could point out the people in your dreams?"

"I don't know. Maybe. But how could you—"

"Don't worry about it. I'll send you an e-mail in a few minutes, okay?"

"Okay."

I hang up and turn back home. Moka looks at me, upset, her tail between her legs.

"We're cutting this walk short," I tell her. "I'll compensate tomorrow, okay?"

She looks far from convinced.

A few minutes later, back in my room, I locate pictures of Ron Hammond and Vivian Hendrix on the school website. They're a bit low quality, but hopefully it'll be good enough. I find a picture of Alice Hendrix from a newspaper with an article about her death. Alan Billings doesn't have an image on his website. I struggle with this a bit, then look for "Alan Billings Dog" on Facebook and find "Alan Billings Dog Trainer." His profile page has a nice clear picture of him. I copy all four images to an e-mail and send it over to Jennifer with the subject: *There. Recognize anyone?*

I get up and pace around the room nervously. No matter how much I try, I can't put the pieces together. Is Ron the murderer? Why would he kill Vivian's mom? Maybe the cops have it wrong, and it's not a man at all, but a loose dog? (*A predator. And you're marked.*) I look out the window at Alex's house. The windows are dark, and I curse inwardly. Maybe Alex could shed some light on this. He knows more than he lets on, I'm sure… I suddenly notice a slight movement in the darkness. A dark, low shape in the shadows, moving slowly. It turns and I can see its eyes, two cold blue dots, looking at me, and I know that it sees me, it knows I'm here. I can almost feel its claws on my body, the teeth clamping on my throat. It knows that I'm trapped, I have nowhere to go, and this time it won't let me get away. I try to scream but no voice escapes my mouth as the blue eyes consume me with hatred and fury…

My phone blips, and I start. Incoming mail. I look outside, but the shape is gone, and I'm unsure it was ever there. My reflexes scream at me to get into the closet, to lock all the doors and windows, to cry for Mom and Dad to come and save me… Instead I open Jennifer's e-mail.

"Hi, Amy," it says. "The first image is the old woman from my dream. The third image as well… that's the man I'm shouting at in my dream. This is creepy. I have no idea how this could be. I've never seen these people before."

I stare at my phone, my hands shaking as I match the images Jennifer indicates in her e-mail to the people. The man that she's shouting at is Ron Hammond. The old woman is Alice Hendrix. I try to understand what this means, but all I can think of is a pair of blue eyes, and Jennifer saying, *There's blood everywhere, Amy, so much blood.*

Chapter Twenty-Nine

"It sounds like Jennifer dreamed of the moment before Alice Hendrix was murdered," says Coral.

"It does," I agree. "She said that Alice seemed scared, and that she knew that Alice was about to die. That definitely sounds like she saw the moment before Alice was killed."

"It would have been useful if she had seen the killer," Shane says.

"Yes, thank you, Shane, for pointing that out," I grumble. "It would have also been useful if today was sunny and pleasant. But it's not, is it?"

We all stare out the window. The sky is dark and cloudy, and rain is spattering on the school grounds.

"No," Shane agrees. "It's not."

"I like rain," Coral says.

"That's great," I say. "Then you must be so happy right now."

The three of us are sitting in an empty classroom. Lunch break just ended, but the next class is Spanish, and Vivian is still missing. I'm thinking about Chris. He messaged me this morning, just a friendly "What's up?" I stared at it for about ten minutes before writing back, "Nothing much." He asked if I wanted to hang out, and I wrote that we'd see. I've managed to evade him in the cafeteria. I should be nicer—or maybe I should be meaner, just tell him that I'm not interested. Instead I'm dragging this out, hoping that it'll somehow turn out well. Of course, it won't.

"What's on your mind?" asks Shane.

What's on my mind, indeed? I shake my head. I'll handle this later.

"I'm still trying to figure out the second dream, the one with the blood," I say. "So she was shouting at Ron Hammond, and then something hit her, and there was blood everywhere, right? Did Ron hit her?"

"Maybe both dreams are in fact the same thing," suggests Shane. "Maybe after Ron walks into Alice's room, they get into an argument. Alice screams at him and he loses control and attacks her. In that case, Jennifer dreams the first part from Ron's point of view, and the second part from Alice's point of view."

"But why was she screaming at Ron that he hurt her?" Coral says. "That sounds like something a lover would say, not the lover's mother."

We sit in silence for a while. It stands to reason that all of us think the same thing.

"Ew," I say. "Do you think that—"

"No," Shane quickly interrupts me. "Amy, I'm begging you, let's not go there, okay?"

I drop the subject.

"There's still one person we can go to who can shed some light on the truth," says Coral.

"Who?" I ask.

"Vivian."

"Seriously?" I look at her in horror.

"Well, she was close to Ron Hammond and Alice Hendrix, right? Relationship with one, daughter of the other. Maybe she has a piece of the puzzle that we don't hold yet."

"You want us to interrogate her while she's mourning her mother?" I ask.

"I want to go and offer my condolences while she's mourning," Coral answers. "What do you think?"

What do I think? I think it's a situation I would very much rather avoid. I have been to three funerals in my life. I cried at all of them.

And now Coral wants us to actively pursue a woman who is mourning her mother? "I don't know…" I say.

"Even if she doesn't have any information, it's the right thing to do," says Coral.

"Now why did you have to go and say something like that?" I complain. "Now I feel guilty for being a horrible person."

"I know how to fix that," she tells me. "We'll go and visit her. We can bring her a condolence letter, signed by the people in Spanish class."

"Where do you come up with those ideas?" I ask curiously. "Do they simply pop up in your brain?"

"And a casserole," she adds. "We can bring a casserole."

"I can make an omelet," I say helpfully. "I make great omelets."

"You're in charge of the card," she tells me.

"Nonononono, Coral listen, I can't do that…"

"Can you make a casserole?"

"Uh…"

"There you go. Better start working on that card."

"You are a… bad, bad person," I moan and start searching for a pen in my bag.

"Vivian isn't my teacher, so I think I won't come along," Shane says quickly. "But it sounds like a good idea."

"Fine," Coral says in a chilly voice. "We'll update you later."

"Do you know where she lives?" I ask.

"It's not a secret. I'm sure Rozanne will give us the address if we say we want to offer our condolences."

"Rozanne?" Shane asks.

"The school secretary," I explain. "Coral and her are BFFs. So when do you want to go?"

"Let's go after school," Coral says.

"Fine," I mutter. Outside, the weather looks just like my mood. I open my notebook and start drafting a condolence letter.

Chapter Thirty

"I'm really proud of you, sweetie," Mom says as she's driving me to Vivian's house. "Visiting your mourning teacher is a really kind thing to do."

"Yeah," I say, looking out the window. It's raining so hard, it almost feels like we're driving though an incredibly long car wash. The streets are completely drenched, puddles everywhere. "I guess."

"And writing a condolence letter?" she carries on. "Signing up your classmates? That teacher must be really special. I should meet her. You know what? I'll come inside with you."

"No!" I say, panicking. "No, no. There's really no need. You can meet her some other day, okay, Mom? Not now. Not today."

"Okay." She sighs, sounding disappointed. We drive in silence for a short while.

"So," she says. "What did the girls say about the boots?"

"Oh, they thought they were fabulous," I say, wiggling my feet and looking at my sneakers, suddenly sorry I didn't wear the boots. "Of course they did. Those boots are the most wonderful thing in the world."

"Even more wonderful than your mom?"

"Mom, you know I love you, and you're great, but… have you seen how those boots look on me?"

Mom smiles, and I have a moment of pleasure, treasuring this calm, nice moment of a mom-daughter conversation, no nightmares, no predators, no dead women. But then we reach Vivian's house, and I see Coral waiting outside with an umbrella, her face grim and determined, and my heart plummets back to its usual spot in my stomach.

"Why is she outside?" asks Mom. "Is she trying to catch a cold?"

"She's waiting for me," I say, grasping my own umbrella. "Bye, Mom."

"Bye, sweetie." She pecks me on the cheek, a proud mother full of love for her compassionate daughter. If she knew why I'm really here, she'd install a dungeon in our house for the sole purpose of locking me in there.

I get out of the car and quickly open the umbrella. Even though that takes only a second, I still manage to get wet. If the rain doesn't let up soon, we'll all need boats. I join Coral at the front door.

"Do you have the note?" she asks. I nod. I don't bother to ask her if she has the food. She has a bag in her hand, and anyway, when has Coral ever forgotten anything?

Coral knocks on the door. We wait for a moment and an unfamiliar man with Clark Kent glasses and a small ugly mustache opens the door.

"Uh... is this Vivian's house?" Coral asks.

"Yes..." he says, looking at us suspiciously.

"We're her students," Coral explains. "We've come to express our condolences."

"Oh." His look softens up. "I'm Clark, her cousin. Please come in."

Clark. With those glasses. This guy definitely has an S symbol under his shirt. We walk inside and he closes the door behind him. There's a stale smell of unpleasant cooking in the air. I don't know why some homes smell like that. What are they eating, and why? The living room is dim, the bare light bulb in the ceiling doing little to lift the darkness. There are several large windows, but since it's raining, hardly any light filters into the room. The upholstery of the entire living room is dark brown, radiating stiffness. No wonder Vivian is so vicious with her tests. I'd be angry as well if I had to live here.

"Vivian? Some of your students are here," Clark says.

Vivian gets up from the couch. There are several other men and women sitting around, talking and drinking. A family gathering, probably. Vivian approaches us. Her eyes, which always bulged a little, are red and swollen, as if she cried not long ago. Her nose, which earned her the nickname "The Aardvark," is slightly red as well. Despite these signs of grief, she smiles at us.

"Coral. Amy. How lovely of you to visit," she says.

"Hi, Miss Hendrix," I say. "We, uh… we brought you a card." It suddenly feels like the most pathetic attempt at making anyone feel better, but her eyes light up as I get the card out of my purse and hand it to her.

"And a casserole," Coral adds. "It's rice casserole. I wasn't sure if you liked chicken. I know how to make really good chicken casserole, but I thought you might be a vegetarian. So I made rice casserole. No onions."

Vivian nods as if Coral's weird casserole speech makes sense and takes the bag from her hand. "You two are so sweet. Please, sit down. Everyone, those are my two favorite students. Coral and Amy."

Favorite students. Ha. The way I treat Spanish, there's probably a warrant for my arrest in Spain. We sit down and she asks if we want to drink.

"Actually," says Coral, "I would love to use your bathroom."

"Second door on the right," says Vivian, pointing down a corridor. Coral gets up and walks slowly away.

"So you're Vivian's student?" says a woman whose hair looks like an unappetizing spaghetti dish. "I hear such wonderful things about her students. She loves you all so much."

News to me, but I keep my mouth shut and nod as if I agree completely. Vivian offers me a plate of cookies that look like dog treats. I take one politely and say, "I'm really sorry for your loss."

"Thanks, dear," Vivian says and smiles again.

"Your mom… her death was very sudden, wasn't it?" I ask, and wish I could bite my tongue. Her face crumples in pain, and she looks as if she's about to burst into tears. I feel like I'm about to burst into tears as well. "Yes," she says hoarsely. "She died very…

violently."

"How did it happen?" I ask. Coral, where the hell are you?

"Oh, she... well, the police aren't sure yet. But apparently she messed with some dangerous people. She thought she was in control... but..." She shuts her eyes in pain.

"I'm sorry," I say. "I'm sure she was a wonderful woman."

"She was," Vivian answers. "I think I'll go get some plates for this delicious-looking casserole." She gets up and walks away to the kitchen. I look around. Everyone else is ignoring me, talking softly with each other. I get up and walk down the corridor after Coral.

The second door on the right is open, and I can see the bathroom through it. Coral isn't there. There's a closed door on the left just opposite the bathroom, and I open it softly. It's a small room with a desk, a chair and a computer. Coral is sitting on the chair, and as I walk in, she whirls around, a terrified look on her face. When she sees it's me, she relaxes. I quickly close the door behind me.

"What the hell are you doing?" I hiss at her.

"Looking for Ron Hammond," Coral answers, her eyes fixed on the monitor.

"Why do you think—"

"This computer has an application which monitors your cell phone's location in case it gets stolen," Coral interrupts me. "Someone installed it and entered a phone number into it."

"It's obviously Vivian's phone," I say. "Because this is her home. And her computer. Which you are now poking around in."

"It's not Vivian's phone," Coral answers impatiently. "Rozanne gave me Vivian's phone number. This is not it. No, I'm betting it's Ron's phone, which he typed in when he stayed here."

"That sounds like a lot of guesswork," I say, trying to sound skeptical, though I'm secretly impressed. "So... supposing this is Ron's phone, do you know where he is?"

"Well, his phone is currently off or something, but this is a map of the last locations he visited," she says and clicks the mouse. A small map appears on screen. There's a small red line squiggling in the street, and four circles mark different locations on it.

"The circles are places he stopped for some time," says Coral.

"Hey, that's our school," I say, surprised. "He was at our

school!"

"And this is where we are right now," Coral says. "So he was here as well."

"What's this circle?" I ask, pointing. I read the name of the street and suddenly feel very cold inside. "Lake Street," I say. "This is Alice Hendrix's house."

Coral nods and points at the fourth address. "Maxwell Street. I think I know where that is. It isn't far from my house."

"That's probably his house," I say.

Coral nods, reading the address. "I think you're right," she says.

"Fine, we'll check it out," I say. "But we have to get out of here. If Vivian walks in…"

Coral shuts down the application, and we both walk to the door. I open the door silently and glance out. No one in the hallway. I open the door and we both sneak out.

"There you are!" Vivian says, walking into the corridor, smiling warmly. "I was wondering where you disappeared to."

"I… I had a bit of a stomachache," says Coral. "Amy came to check up on me."

We go back to the living room and sit there for another fifteen minutes. Then we get up, tell Vivian once more how sorry we are, and leave. Outside it's no longer pouring, more like a small drizzle. We open our umbrellas and look at each other. Coral's eyes are sparkling with determination, and I know we're both thinking the same thing.

"Well…" I say, glancing at my watch. Quarter past five. "Want to go check out that address?"

Coral nods. "Let's go to Ron's house."

Chapter Thirty-One

By the time we get to the address from the computer, it stops raining altogether. The house on Maxwell Street is a small house with a freshly painted green fence, a nice little front yard and an outdoor parking space behind an electrical gate which is currently empty.

"Looks like he's not here," I say, motioning at the empty parking space.

"Or maybe he has no car, or his car is parked on the street, or he loaned it to a friend, or—"

"Okay, okay," I interrupt Coral. "I get it."

"I just want to clarify that there will be no breaking into houses, especially not houses of possible murderers," she says. "Not again."

"Fine." I raise my hands. "I hereby solemnly swear there will be no breaking into this house."

"Thank you."

"Unless we see something really suspicious."

"Amy!"

"I was kidding."

Coral looks as if she wants to grab my hair and shake my head in frustration.

"We can knock on the door," I suggest.

"What if he opens?" Coral asks.

"Then we can ask why he's stopped coming to school. We are his students, after all."

"But, Amy, Ron Hammond disappeared. I doubt that he wants to be found. And anyway, he's supposed to have a huge vicious dog, remember?"

I shudder. "How can I forget?"

A car drives down Maxwell Street. As it reaches us it slows down. The electrical gate suddenly begins to open. Coral looks like she's about to bolt, but I grab her hand. The driver is an unfamiliar woman, not Ron. The gate opens completely and the car drives inside, the gate shutting behind it. The woman gets out of the car and looks at us for a moment with a bored expression. She seems to be about thirtyish, blond, thin, her face beautiful, but cold. She looks as if someone sculpted her out of ice. But not just any ice—really cruel, hateful ice. I know instantly that this is a woman that shatters the hearts of men and women alike. She's dressed in a business suit that makes her even more imposing.

"Can I help you?" she asks.

"Hi," says Coral, her face transformed to what I call 'innocent angel kitten' face. "We're students at the local high school, and we were wondering if you would maybe want to donate some money. We're fundraising for—"

"I don't donate," says the woman.

"Maybe your husband, or uh… friend or…"

She takes a step towards us. I could swear the temperature drops. "I said no. Goodbye." She turns around and starts walking towards the door.

"Is Ron Hammond here?" I blurt. Coral looks at me with anger, but the woman turns to look at us, and the change in her entire demeanor is incredible. Her eyes become desperate, thirsty. Her mouth slightly opens, looking hopeful and sad at the same time.

"Ron?" she asks in a quivering voice. "No. He hasn't been here for weeks. Where do you… How do you know Ron?"

"He taught us," I say. "He was our history teacher."

"And how did you know he might be… here?"

"We didn't," I shuffle uncomfortably. "But we thought—"

It starts raining again, and the sound of drops spattering on the pavement fills the air. She looks at us with the same desperate eyes and says, "Come in. I want you to explain how you got here."

Coral hesitates, and I approach the entrance to the yard, a small white gate. I lay my hand on the handle.

"Can you please make sure your dog doesn't attack us?" I ask.

"I have no dog," she says, and turns and unlocks the door.

She enters her house, and Coral and I follow her. We walk into a small, clean living room. The entire space feels loved, homely. There are two blue couches in the room, making an L shape around a low wooden table. There's a vase of flowers on it and more flowers and plants everywhere. When I move to my own house, I want to live in a place like this.

"Do you want something to drink?" she asks, her tone signifying that this is not something that she'll happily provide.

"No, thanks," Coral and I say together.

"Okay," she says, leaning on the back of one of the couches. "Please explain how you got here."

"It's a bit complicated—" I begin, when Coral interrupts. "My mom is Ron's friend," she says. "He gave her the phone number here once. We found the address online."

The woman's face falls as she realizes that we don't have any idea where Ron is. "He isn't here," she says. "You can let your mom know. He disappeared about six weeks ago."

"Was this his home?" Coral asks.

"No, it's mine," the woman says. "He sometimes slept here. We were in a relationship."

"He... slept here?" Coral asks, staring.

The woman shrugs. "Sometimes. He preferred sleeping at his own house."

I'm about to ask for his home address, but stop myself. If Coral's mom is supposedly Ron's friend, she should know his address.

"I sometimes took care of Ron's dog when he was away," Coral says. "I just wanted to know if it's fine, or if something happened to it."

"What are you talking about?" The woman looks at Coral suspiciously. "Ron didn't have a dog."

"W—what do you mean? Of course he did."

"I think I know Ron well enough to know if he had a dog or not!" the woman says, tears of anger appearing in her eyes. "I don't believe you knew Ron at all, and neither did your mom! What do you know about Ron, you little liars?" She takes two steps forward. But I'm already holding the doorknob, and as she takes another step towards us, raising her hands to clutch Coral, I swing the door open and pull Coral away, outside. We turn and run out into the rain, hearing her screeching behind us. "Get back here! Get back her right now!"

I glance backwards and I see her chasing us, her face twisted in anger. But she is wearing high-heeled shoes, and Coral and I are both wearing sneakers and we outrun her easily. We quickly leave Maxwell Street behind, running until we are out of breath.

"What the hell was that?" Coral asks, breathing hard.

"I… I think it's Ron Hammond's girlfriend. Other girlfriend," I say, bending over, holding my knees.

"Why was she so mad?"

"I don't know," I reply. "Maybe she thought we knew where he went. Or maybe she believes we're right, that he does have a dog, that he was hiding things from her."

Coral nods. "He was."

"Yeah."

"I don't think she knew about Vivian," Coral says. "She seemed to think she was the only one."

"I think there was a lot she didn't know," I answer.

There's a lot we don't know as well. The search for Ron Hammond has led us to a dead end.

Chapter Thirty-Two

Coral escorts me home. We walk only on main streets, where there's traffic. Presumably on such streets, the chance of me ending up in some predator's jaws is low. The rain has stopped once more, but my shoes are wet, and I feel cold all over.

"I'm freezing," I say, my teeth chattering.

"Me too," says Coral. "We'll get to your house soon."

"You don't have to walk me all the way," I say, knowing it's useless. "You should go home yourself, have a warm shower."

"I'll do that after I see you home," she answers. "I'm not the one who's marked."

"I hate this feeling," I mutter. "I can't go anywhere by myself."

"Once we find out where the predator is, we might be able to fix this," Coral says, trying to cheer me up.

"Or he might eat us."

"That's also a possibility."

"Anyway, I don't see it happening anytime soon."

She doesn't answer. There's nothing to say, really. We reach my house.

"Do you want to come in, take a warm shower?" I suggest. "I can give you some clothes."

"No, thanks." She smiles. "It's okay. My house isn't far."

"My mom can take you," I say, feeling guilty. "You shouldn't walk all the way home wet like that."

"I'll be fine, Amy. Good night."

"Good night."

Coral walks away and I turn towards our house. An angry bark makes me turn around. Moka is staring at me through Alex's gate, wagging her tail.

"I'm sorry," I tell her. "I can't take you for a walk today."

She whines, her tail freezing in midair.

"There's something out there that wants to kill me. I'm marked. It's too late to walk around alone."

She crouches, her belly touching the ground, and whines again.

"I can't, Moka. Tomorrow, when there are more people on the streets, okay?"

Her big unhappy eyes stare right into my heart, puncturing it. I walk inside, laden with guilt. Dad's in the kitchen.

"Hey, Amy," he says. "Do you want something to eat?"

"Not really," I mutter.

"Really? I'm making soft-boiled eggs."

"Yeah," I say, cheering up. "That actually sounds great!" It's hard not be hungry with Dad's soft-boiled eggs. Mom always overdoes them, usually because she's trying to do eleven things at once. When I make them, I always panic, certain that they've been boiling for far too long, only to discover that they're completely runny, the white of the egg wobbly to the point of nausea. Dad has somehow managed to find the secret for cooking a perfect soft-boiled egg—the white completely cooked, the yellow part runny and tasty. He also makes some toast, which he cuts into small triangles. Each egg gets a small triangle stuck in it. You can't get better service anywhere.

"I'm just going to take a quick shower, okay, Dad?"

"Sure."

I run up and take off my wet clothes. A hot shower makes me feel better. Things like predators and crazy screaming women feel far away. I begin pondering the route we saw on Vivian's computer. Four locations. School, Vivian's house, the other woman's house, and Alice's house. All of them strike me as strange. The first three don't make sense. No one has seen Ron at school for six weeks, and supposedly Vivian hasn't seen him either. The other girlfriend also said she hadn't seen him. And Alice's house... well...

I get out of the shower and dress. Moka is barking outside. I ignore her. I go downstairs and start setting the table. Moka's angry barks are heard even here.

"Isn't that Alex's dog?" Dad asks me.

"Yeah. Should I set a place for Mom?"

"Mom is out with her friends. Shouldn't you be walking her?"

"Mom? I'm pretty sure she can handle herself, Dad," I say.

"Funny. I meant Alex's dog."

"Yeah, later."

"Maybe you should walk her before dinner?"

"Later, Dad."

He doesn't argue. I make a small salad, and he finishes making the eggs, which are divine as usual. We both eat some toast with cream cheese as well. As always, Dad and I can't find anything to talk about, and after some failed attempts, we eat in silence. Four locations. I start reordering the things on my plate. The empty egg cup is school. This bit of toast is Vivian's house. This piece of carrot will be the other woman's house. And Alice's house... will be the saltshaker. I stare at the four items. If Ron went over to kill Alice...

"Amy? What are you doing?" Dad looks at my plate, raising an eyebrow.

"Nothing." I sigh. I finish eating and go up to my room, where I find a piece of paper and a pen. The first point...

Moka barks again. I open the window. She looks at me from below, giving me a half wag with her tail.

"Tomorrow, okay?" I say. She whines. I close the window.

Okay. First location—the school. Second location—the other girlfriend's house. I stretch a line between them. Third location—Vivian's house. Or was that the second location? Did I get them confused? I'm pretty sure I didn't. I stretch another line. Fourth location... Alice's house. I stretch the final line, furrowing my forehead. Was this Ron's route the day Alice Hendrix was killed? Why did the route end in Alice's house? Did his phone break while he was struggling with her?

More barking.

Did this really happen the day Alice was killed? Did Ron Hammond kill Alice? What did Vivian say? That she messed with some dangerous people…?

School, girlfriend, Vivian, Alice. School, girlfriend, Vivian, Alice. The first three locations can be explained, but the fourth? Why did he go over to Alice's house? It doesn't make any sense. There must be something that I'm missing. Something with that place…

I get up, get my sneakers, realize that they're wet, toss them aside and put on my boots. I go down the stairs, go outside and walk over to Alex's house. Moka is wagging her tail, her tongue lolling as she looks at me excitedly.

"You'll look after me, right?" I say. "Like you did the last time, with Tom Ellis?"

She barks happily.

"Okay, let's go… no licking, I know what you put in your mouth! Sit. Sit! No licking, I said!"

Finally, the leash is attached, and Moka drags me happily outside.

I lead Moka down the street, looking around me nervously. I can't really be sure this dog will be any protection against the predator if it suddenly lunges at us from behind a bush. A cat that leaps out of a trashcan nearly makes me pee in my pants, and I contemplate turning around and walking back home, but I keep thinking of those four places, and I walk on until we reach Lake Street.

We start walking slower, and I notice that Moka is also more careful and suspicious, stopping every few feet to sniff around, one leg in the air. Alice's house stands dark and foreboding, even scarier than before now that there are no cops milling about. Should I really go inside? Last time almost ended very badly, but I somehow know that the missing puzzle piece is in there. I don't know what makes me so certain, but I can almost feel an invisible thread tugging me forward. Moka and I start walking towards the door, but as we get closer, she starts pulling me sideways.

"We'll go inside just for a moment," I whisper at her. She looks at me silently, but when I try to approach the door, she pulls me aside once more.

"Come on, Moka," I whisper and tug. She doesn't budge. I tug harder, and she pulls the other way. I tug with all my strength and she yelps in pain.

"Oh, I'm sorry!" I say, my hand momentarily letting go of the leash. That was a mistake. She instantly bolts away, around the house, towards the backyard, barking excitedly. I run after her, yelling, "Moka! Come back here!" The backyard is dark. I really shouldn't go there. It's full of shadows in which anything could hide...

"Moka!"

Another bark. It doesn't sound as if she's barking at another animal. It sounds as if she's barking to get my attention. I walk slowly towards the sound of her barking, my heart beating, the darkness closing in around me... I pull out my phone, pressing the power button, and its screen lights up, illuminating my way with a ghostly pale light. I notice Moka digging a hole in the ground.

"Seriously?" I say. "More cat poo?"

She barks and digs some more, wagging her tail.

"Come on, let's go home," I say.

She barks again.

I don't want to come near that hole. I know deep inside that this is not just a hole. It's something else. Something bad. But my feet have a mind of their own, and they lead me towards it. I kneel besides Moka, holding my phone over the dark opening. There's a piece of cloth sticking out of the ground.

"What is it?" I ask Moka. "What did you find there?"

Another bark. I try pulling the cloth but it's stuck. I start digging around it, removing handfuls of wet earth with my hands, scratching myself on loose roots, on tiny pebbles. I feel one of my nails cracking, but I don't stop, can't stop as my knees feel the wetness and cold seep through my pants. No good can come of this, but still I dig, my breaths short, full of effort and fear. I can feel something inside screaming at me to stand up, walk away from there, but I can't—I don't know why, I just can't. Must get the cloth out. Must get it out. More pebbles. More roots. Moka barking, and I ignore her, horror slowly filling my gut. I already know what's in here, I want to

go home, and I dig, and dig, and uncover something long and hard. And another. And another. And another.
   Fingers.
   A human hand.

Chapter Thirty-Three

"Hello?"

"P—Peter?"

"Amy? Is everything okay?"

"No!" I yell at him, weeping. "Everything is absolutely not okay! I'm at Alice Hendrix's house. There's a human hand buried in the backyard! I think there's a whole body there!"

"What?"

"I was walking my dog… it's not my dog, it's my neighbor's dog, and… and… she dug in Alice's backyard and she found this hand…"

"Amy, don't touch anything, I'll be right there."

"Okay."

He hangs up. I start walking towards the road, then stop, turn, and take a few pictures with my phone before leaving the backyard. I sit down on the curb of the road and start sobbing.

"Why me?" I ask Moka. "Why is it that I keep looking for those horrible things? I don't want this. I don't understand why I'm doing this. Why didn't I go back home? What's wrong with me?"

Moka stares at me, her eyes full of compassion. She seems almost as if she understands every word. Then she scratches her ear. The illusion is broken, and once again she looks just like any dog.

A white car stops next to me, its brakes screeching. Peter gets out of it, wearing jeans and a white t-shirt. Civilian clothes. He wasn't on shift when I called.

"Where is it?" he asks. I sniff and motion towards the backyard. He takes a flashlight from his glove compartment and walks behind the house.

"A flashlight," I tell Moka, my voice still quivering. "I need to get me one of those."

He comes back, his face severe. "I thought I told you to stay out of this."

"I did! It was my dog! I mean, the neighbor's dog! She just ran there. You know, dogs always find bodies. I saw it in like a million TV series."

"In TV series," he emphasizes. "And anyway, did your dog decide to walk over here?"

"Uh..."

"And," he continues, glancing at my dirty fingers, "I would guess that she's not the only one that dug back there?"

"Well..."

"Damn it, Amy!"

"I just wanted to look around one more time."

"Why didn't you call the police?" he asks.

"I called you," I point out.

"It's an easy number to remember. Nine one one."

"I know the number. I just thought, with Tom Ellis and everything... You know. Maybe it's better if I'm not the one who makes the call."

"Well, they'll want to talk to you in any case," he says. "They're already on their way."

My phone rings. I answer.

"Amy?" It's Dad. "Are you okay? How long is your walk?"

"I was just turning back," I tell him, trying to sound as if I'm simply walking dogs and definitely not discovering bodies. "I'll be home in fifteen minutes."

"Okay, hurry up. It's late."

I hang up. "I have to go," I tell Peter. "My dad is worried about me."

"He should be," Peter says. "You keep getting into trouble."

"Can you tell the cops that there's no reason to interview me? Tell them I'm just some girl who ended up here by mistake."

"I'm not going to lie to the cops, Amy," Peter says, and in the silence that follows, we both think of the words left unsaid—'not again.'

"But I have to go home, and if they come over tonight—"

"I'll tell them that you're shaken up and ask if they can postpone the interview," he says. "That's the best I can do."

"Thanks."

"Amy, I'll tell you again, though obviously it's difficult for you to understand. You're messing with dangerous things. If anything ever happens to you, I could never forgive myself."

I can feel my heart skip a beat as he says that. "Okay." I blush. "I'll leave this alone."

"Yeah." He looks very skeptical. Can't blame him. "I'll call you if the cops need anything."

"Okay."

"Good night."

As I'm walking home, I look at the pictures I took. Then I send them to Coral and Shane. Coral calls instantly.

"Amy? What the hell is that?"

I tell her how Moka ran into Alice's backyard and dug up the remains.

"What were you doing there?" she asks sharply. "What are you doing, walking alone at night?"

"I was just taking Moka for a walk."

"Sure, you were."

"Coral, I really can't talk right now. Let's discuss this later, okay?"

"Amy…"

I hang up. My phone rings again almost immediately. Shane this time.

"What the hell, Amy?"

I fill him in.

"You need to call the cops."

"Peter already did."

"How did Peter find out about this?"

"I called him."

"You should have called the cops."

I reach Alex's house. "Shane, I have to go, okay?" I hang up and turn off my phone. Then I lead Moka into Alex's yard. She yawns, walks over to the front door and cuddles up next to it, as if this was just like any other walk. I take a deep breath and go home.

http://amy.strangerealm.com/body.html

Chapter Thirty-Four

I feel wound up to the point of breaking. Small noises make me start. I'm constantly gritting my teeth, to the point where my jaw begins to hurt. I don't want to talk to anyone today. I don't know what would happen once I opened my mouth. To my immense relief, both Mom and Dad are not home when I go downstairs to fix breakfast. I have a vague hope that once I eat I'll feel better. I put some cereal in a bowl, add some milk and stare at it. I force myself to eat a spoonful. Swallowing feels impossible. I spit the mouthful into the sink and throw the rest of the bowl's content into the trash. My throat feels clogged with anxiety and sadness. Can I go to school today? Will I be able to sit down in class? If I don't, they might call Mom and Dad.

I get my bag, not bothering to check if everything I need is inside. Yeah, I'll go to school, but actual learning is off the table.

My phone rings. I glance at the display. It's Nicole. I take a few deep breaths and consider ignoring the call. But she's supposed to come here today. I answer.

"Honey! I hope I didn't wake you up!"

"No."

"Good. Listen, the blog post from yesterday is really creepy. I think we should talk about this."

"Okay."

"I'll be at your place around five thirty, is that okay?"

"I…"

"It's just that my mom is… honey, are you okay?"

I realize that I am silently sobbing. When Nicole asks if I'm okay, I instantly burst into tears.

"No!" I almost shout at her. "I'm not okay!"

"Oh, honey… Come on, calm down. Everything will be fine, you'll see. We'll fix this."

I just keep on sobbing.

"I… I'll try to get to your house sooner, okay? I promise. Just keep it together for a few more hours."

"Yeah," I manage to say. Then I hang up.

I go up to my room and wash my face. I brush my teeth, trying to blank out my brain, concentrating on mechanical tasks. Combing my hair. Putting on makeup. Going outside. Locking the door.

Walking to the bus stop, my mind revolves around the same moment over and over. My hands digging in the ground, brushing against the dead fingers, thinking they're just more roots, actually pulling one of them once. Then the flesh exposed, the stench beginning to register. And the instant in which I realize that this is a human hand.

But I knew, didn't I? Once I began digging in the hole Moka made, I somehow knew this was what I'd uncover. I don't even know how I knew it, but I did.

Was this how it was for the cops when they uncovered Kimberly's body five months ago?

A cold, calculating part of me thinks—no. Kimberly was buried for almost ten years. All they found were bones. You found what seems like a fresh body.

The school bus feels like hell. Every sound, every joke, every echo of laughter feels as if it's burrowing into my brain. I stare fixedly out the window, intent on avoiding everyone. It's almost disrespectful, in a way. I just found a dead body yesterday. How can everyone here be so loud, so cheerful? I want to scream at them to be quiet. I want to hit one of them. I want to kick the back of the seat in front of me. I want to smash the window and jump out. I want to cry.

I do none of those. I simply stare until we get to school.

I walk inside, my eyes fixed on nothing, not even entirely sure what my first class is when suddenly someone touches my arm.

I twist, panicking, feeling a mixture of fear and rage at the sudden intrusion. It's Chris.

"Hey," he says, taken aback by my reaction. "What's up?"

"Nothing," I half say, half spit. "I'm just… preoccupied. You startled me."

"Yeah, I can see that. Listen, I know that we talked about it, and you were kinda confused, but I thought maybe we could meet this weekend? You could drop by my band practice. We're getting really good, and we've got this awesome new song…"

"No, I can't. My friend from LA is coming to visit."

"Oh. Well, she can come too, it's cool. We don't mind a crowd…"

"No."

He frowns. "Yeah, okay."

"I can't handle this right now," I say. "I just…"

There are no more words. Can I even explain myself? How can I make anyone understand my current state of mind? I shake my head.

He looks hurt. He nods, and turns away, leaving, his shoulders slumped. Regret floods me, and I nearly call after him, asking him to wait… but I don't. It's probably better this way. He should find a nice normal girl who'll gush over his music and cool demeanor. He really shouldn't be spending time with someone whose hobby is locating dead bodies.

I turn around and walk towards the exit. School is definitely not happening today. I'll just hurt anyone I talk to, and hurt myself in the process.

I walk home. The streets are silent. The streets know about last night. They know they shouldn't talk to me, shouldn't touch me.

Eventually I make it back. I unlock the door, walk upstairs, take off my shoes and get into bed.

When Mom gets home, I'm still in bed. When she calls me, I don't reply.

Chapter Thirty-Five

"Amy!" Mom calls me. "Nicole is here!"

I open my eyes and stand up, feeling a bit dizzy. I haven't eaten since last night, but the thought of food makes me nauseous.

I walk downstairs slowly, my feet feeling disconnected as I watch them descend stair after stair. I hear Nicole talking to my mom.

"I think she might not be feeling well," Mom says.

"Really?" Nicole says innocently. "She sounded fine when I talked to her."

I enter the kitchen. Nicole is drinking a glass of water, my mom smiling at her. As they notice me, Nicole puts the glass down.

"Honey!" she says. "I'm here!"

I smile weakly. Mom looks at me, concerned. "Amy, do you want to eat anything?"

"Later," I say.

"Well? Honey, where's that shirt you told me about?" Nicole asks. I stare at her dumbly and she quirks an eyebrow.

"Oh! The shirt! Right. It's upstairs."

"Well? What are we waiting for?" she says, slinging her bag on her shoulder. "See?" she tells my mom. "She's totally fine."

Mom frowns. Obviously 'totally fine' is not the way she'd describe how I look.

We go upstairs. Even before Nicole closes the door behind her, I'm already crying. She sits on the bed, and I lie down, my head in her lap. She slowly caresses my hair. After a few minutes I begin to calm down.

"I can't take it anymore," I say.

"Okay."

"Coral was right. I'm just putting myself and my friends in danger. It's stupid and selfish."

"Okay, honey, you're right."

"I want to go back to doing normal stuff, like… like… shopping, and partying and…" I try to recall what other normal activities the world has to offer. "I don't know. Facebook. I don't want to find any more bodies."

Nicole keeps running her fingers through my hair. "Of course, honey. Obviously."

"What is it here with burying dead bodies in backyards? First Kimberly White, then the body in Alice's yard. How many other bodies are buried in Narrowdale's backyards?"

"I'm sure it's just a coincidence, honey."

"You don't live here. This place is… weird."

"You just had some bad luck, that's all."

"That's not it," I say, recalling last night. "It's not like in the movies, you know."

"What are you talking about?"

"The body. It's not… clean. There's rot, and a terrible smell, and… it feels wrong, seeing an actual hand in the ground like that."

"I saw the pictures," Nicole says.

"That's not like being there."

"Okay," she says, and I can feel her shifting a bit. "I'm sure it was horrid. I think you're right, best to leave it for the cops."

"I thought you wanted to investigate it," I say sharply. "I thought it was cool and—"

"There's nothing cool about finding a buried body's remains," she interrupts me. "And I don't want my best friend to risk her life." She becomes silent for a second. "You know that night? When you called me and then broke into Tom Ellis's house?"

"Yeah?"

"I was so scared, you know? After I called Peter, I tried calling you, and calling him, and no one answered, and I just sat there, certain that my best friend was about to be killed or... or..." She swallows. "Anyway, he answered. An hour later. Worst night of my life."

I listen to her, recalling that night, tied in that room, certain that I was about to die. I remember how Coral got me out and we escaped, Tom Ellis running after us, screaming...

"Seeing those pictures you took made me realize that this is real. I don't want anything to happen to you, honey. I love you too much."

We sit for a while in silence.

"Why did you put that bracelet in a bottle?" she suddenly asks me, looking at my desk.

"I didn't put it there. It was like that when I got it."

"Why would anyone put a bracelet in a bottle?"

"I got it from Chris. The woman in the shop told him it would look nicer or something."

"Chris got you jewelry?" she asks, incredulous, and then adds, "In a bottle?"

"It's not exactly jewelry. I mean, it's probably glass beads on that bracelet."

"Whatever, honey. A guy buys you jewelry, that means something."

"I don't think he knows that."

"What about Chris, anyway?" She looks at me, waggling her eyebrows.

"I uh... I was kind of nasty to him today," I say.

"Why?"

"I don't know. Nicole, I don't know what I'm doing with him. I'm getting so confused, and... and..."

"Okay, honey, let me put it simply for you. Did he ask you to marry him?"

"I... What? Why would he..." My brain freezes up. "Bleh?"

"I'll take that as a no," Nicole says. "Did he by any chance threaten to kill himself if you won't elope with him?"

"Of course not."

"All right, then. What did he want?"

"He wanted to spend some time together over the weekend."

"Oh... Now I get it. You're afraid that your current boyfriend will be jealous, and will challenge him to a duel."

"Nicole, get off my back. I don't have a boyfriend."

"Then are you simply repulsed by his horrible hump? By his rotting teeth? His weird hairy wart?"

"Nicole—"

"Amy!" She suddenly raises her voice. "It's really simple! He's cute, he just wants to hang out, and you're not in a relationship! There are no more unknowns in this equation! There is no confusion here, there is only stupidity! Didn't you just say a minute ago that you want to do normal stuff? This is normal stuff!"

"I can't handle him right now, okay?" I say. "First I want to be done with the predator and dead body, then I'll handle Chris."

"Sure, honey. He'll lose interest completely by that point, but whatever you think is best. What's this?" She points at the friendship bracelet on the table. "Did Chris give you that as well?"

"No. Coral's sister Mia did."

"Why don't you wear it?"

"I don't know. I don't really like friendship bracelets."

"Everyone's giving you bracelets these days."

I shrug. "Do you want to go out tonight?" I ask.

"Why don't we stay in, watch a stupid movie on TV?" Nicole offers.

"Sounds even better."

My phone rings. It's Shane.

"Hey," I answer the phone.

"Hey," he says. There's a moment of silence, then he asks, "What's up?"

"Nothing much."

"Okay." He sounds stressed. "So... What are you doing?"

I suddenly realize the point of this call. I sigh. "Nothing much. Nicole came over. We're just chatting."

"Really?" I can practically hear his heart beating through the phone. "Hey, listen, I've noticed something in those pictures you sent. Can I come over?"

"Shane, I've decided to let this be. You and Coral were right from the get-go. It's stupid and dangerous."

"Oh, good," he says, clearly disappointed. "But, uh… We don't need to do anything. I just want to show you something. In the pictures. We won't do anything dangerous."

"Okay," I say. "Come on over."

"On my way," he says and hangs up.

If Shane thinks the way to a girl's heart is by talking to her about dead bodies, who am I to stop him?

Chapter Thirty-Six

I love my friends, I really do. And Nicole I love the most. But sometimes I have a hard time remembering why it is exactly that I love them so much. For example—right now, as Nicole, Shane and I sit in my room, and Nicole is busy telling Shane about all the embarrassing things I did when I was nine.

"So the teacher tells her, 'Miss Parker, this is totally unacceptable,' so she tells him, 'Mr. Lewis, your sweater is totally unacceptable.'" She bursts out laughing. "Shane, you should have seen his face! But you know what? She was right! That sweater was a crime against humanity. You know the tablecloths old people sometimes have?"

Shane blinks and nods, drinking up every word that comes out of Nicole's mouth. You'd think she was telling him about her adventures in the wild jungles of Africa, the way he's looking at her.

"Well—that. But in brown and hideous green. And later when he called her parents—"

"Wow, this is so much fun, talking about my ancient history," I say sharply. "Now let's move along."

"Oh, come on, honey, this is a really funny story and—"

"Hey, Shane," I say. "Want to hear what happened to Nicole during gym class in sixth grade?"

"Okay, okay, I'll shut up," Nicole quickly says. "No more

stories. Didn't you say there was something you wanted to show us?"

"Yeah." Shane gets up and sits on my chair. He turns on my laptop without asking, which is annoying, but I decide to let it go. He opens my blog and zooms in on the photo I took of the buried remains.

"There," he says. "See the cloth? It actually has a distinct pattern, see? Those thin lines? And the purple background?"

"Okay," I say. "So?"

"Uh... I thought you might find it interesting."

Sure, he did. "And couldn't you tell me on the phone?" I ask.

"Well... I thought it would be better to show you face to face. It seemed important."

Right. Face to face. Specifically Shane's face to Nicole's face. "A purple cloth seemed important to you?" I ask, deciding to torture him a bit.

"Well... yeah."

"Hang on," Nicole says. "I know what this is. It's a scarf."

"Maybe," I say. "It could be anything."

"No, no. I know what scarf this is. I've seen it in a catalog, about two years ago."

"Nicole, there is no way you can identify this as a scarf you saw in a catalog..."

"Of course I can, honey, don't insult me." She stands up and lays a hand on Shane's shoulder. "Can I sit for a second?"

Shane nearly drops from the seat in his haste to give it to Nicole. She sits down and starts browsing through various fashion sites. "I'm sure I can find it..." she mutters.

I look at her skeptically. Nicole does spend a ridiculous amount of time browsing fashion sites, flipping through catalogs and magazines, and going window shopping, but I seriously doubt that she can identify a dirty, buried scarf from an image I took in the dark with my phone.

Shane stands next to her, fidgeting, looking for something to do. He picks up the bottle from the desk.

"How did you get the bracelet into the bottle?" he asks, peering at it.

"I didn't."

"Oh. It looks nice in there."

I grit my teeth. He opens the bottle and tries to get the bracelet out. "It's stuck," he reports.

"Really? How can you tell?"

He notices my tone, screws the bottle shut and puts it on the table.

"There!" Nicole claps her hands excitedly. "See that guy? What is he wearing?"

"He is wearing a purple scarf," I answer obediently.

"Well?"

"Nicole, there is no way to know if it is the same scarf."

"Come on, honey, don't be obtuse," she says and moves around the browser windows. She positions them one next to the other—the model on the left, the buried scarf on the right.

"I think you might be right," I say slowly, not believing it myself.

"Of course I'm right."

I look at the scarf on the model's throat closely. "I've seen this scarf before," I say, frowning. "Where did I see it?"

"I think it was in a store we went shopping at last year before you moved," Nicole says. "You remember? The one where I got that black belt? And the clerk was flirting with me, and I was brushing him off and—"

"No," I say, clutching my desk in horror. "I've seen this scarf on a person."

"Who?"

"Ron Hammond," I answer. "Our history teacher."

Chapter Thirty-Seven

"I'm calling Coral," I tell Shane and Nicole. "She needs to know about this."

"Sure, honey, but when are we gonna eat?" asks Nicole. "I'm starving!"

I'm hungry as well, truth be told. "My parents went out tonight," I say. "But they left me their credit card, so we can order delivery."

"We can order Chinese!" Shane says. He always wants to order Chinese.

"I'd love to order pizza," Nicole says.

"Oh, yeah, sure," Shane says quickly. "We can order pizza, that'd be great!"

I roll my eyes and call Jerry's Pizza, the only pizza place in Narrowdale. I order one large pizza, half mushroom, half pepperoni. I like mushrooms, Nicole loves pepperoni, and I'm working under the assumption that Shane would be thrilled to eat whatever Nicole likes.

"Okay, now to call Coral… No, hang on. Damn it!" I thump my forehead. "I forgot to walk Moka."

"What's a wokmoka?" asks Nicole.

"Moka," I say. "She's the neighbor's dog. The one that dug up the body. I didn't take her for a walk this evening."

"Then let's take her now, together," Nicole suggests.

I nod and call Jerry's Pizza again. I explain that we won't be home for the next twenty minutes, and the pizza guy says no worries, they'll call before they deliver it.

We go outside. Nicole and Shane wait for me on the street as I leash Moka and lead her out. Then we start walking. I pull out my phone and dial Coral.

"Hey, Amy," Coral answers almost immediately.

"Hey! Listen, you won't believe what Shane just showed us. You should sit down, because this will—"

"Who's us?" Coral interrupts me.

"What?"

"You said Shane showed *us*. Who's us?"

"Nicole and me."

"Shane and Nicole are at your place? Why didn't you call me?" She sounds upset.

Why, indeed? Why does she care? She doesn't even like Nicole. "I don't know, it was a spontaneous thing. Nicole is here for the weekend, and Shane just dropped by."

"Oh, I'm sure he just 'dropped by.' Also, the Normandy invasion was a thing that just happened," Coral says. I seriously don't know what she's talking about.

"Whatever. So listen, you know that cloth in the pictures of the body?"

"What cloth?"

"There was a purple cloth."

"Oh, right. Yeah, I remember. What about it?"

"Well, we were looking at its pattern. And guess what? Nicole managed to identify it!"

"Of course she did, because she's just so clever."

"It's a scarf," I say, purposefully ignoring her poisonous tone. "And you know who wore that scarf two months ago? Ron Hammond."

"Ron? Are you sure?" Coral asks. The surprise takes the edge off her tone, which is a relief.

"Absolutely. I remember because he wore it that day he came in with the black jacket and the navy blue pants, and even though the scarf didn't match the rest of his clothing, he was still—"

"Okay, Amy, I get it," she says. "So you think it's Ron's body?"

"Could be," I say. "We know the last place his phone was working was at Alice Hendrix's house. Maybe… Moka! Stop that!" Moka circles around me, tying me up with her leash. I make an awkward dance, twisting around, passing the phone to my other hand. "Sorry. Maybe someone killed him there."

"Who? Alice Hendrix? Why? This is really strange. I should think about this."

"Do you want to drop by tonight?" I ask, trying to smooth things over. "We were about to see a movie."

"Shane is still at your place?"

"Yeah, we ordered pizza…" I instantly regret my last words.

"You ordered pizza?" she asks, sounding really hurt. "Why didn't you call me?"

I don't know why. I don't call Coral every time I meet Shane. I don't call Shane every time I meet Coral, either. Why the sudden tragedy? "Well… you always have a family dinner on Friday," I say.

"You could have checked," she says.

"Okay, do you want to come over, eat some pizza?"

"No, I have a family dinner," she says, her tone implying that this is somehow my fault.

"Okay, do you want to drop by later?"

"I'm busy later."

"Busy?" I ask. "It's Friday night!"

"Would it be that weird if I had plans on Friday night?" she asks. Man, how did this conversation take such an ugly turn?

"No, listen, I… Moka! No! Don't eat that!" I tug the leash, trying to pull Moka away from something horrible. "No, look, Coral, I… Hello? Coral?" She hung up. I sigh in frustration. Now I've hurt Coral's feelings. Why is everything so complicated in life? I stare at Moka, happily chewing something that looks like radioactive waste. Why can't my life be as simple as Moka's? Eating, sleeping, and looking for disgusting stuff to sniff and chew sounds wonderful.

When we get back, we spot the pizza delivery guy standing near my house, talking on the phone.

"Oh, never mind, I think she just got here," he says and hangs up. "I've been waiting here for ten minutes," he tells me angrily.

"Sorry, I called and said that we wouldn't be home," I say. "They told me they'd call before you left."

"Well, no one told me anything," he answers, clearly thinking this is all my fault. Well, me being blamed for things beyond my control is the main theme this evening.

"I'm sorry," I say. "They should have told you."

He grumbles something as I fumble with my wallet. I have enough spare change to tip him generously. This mollifies him a bit, and before he drives away he says there's sauce and spices in the pizza carton, which is practically a peace offering.

Shane takes the pizza, and he and Nicole go in the house as I walk Moka into Alex's yard. I give her her nightly portion of food, which as always she eats as if I've starved her for an entire week. Entering my house, I can already hear Nicole talking with her mouth full. I think that when she eats she actually talks more. She enjoys the feeling of food in her mouth as she's speaking. I walk into the kitchen and glance at them in anger. The two of them are munching happily on the pizza without waiting for me. Pigs.

"Honey, they make the best pizza in Narrowdale," Nicole tells me.

I shrug and grab a slice. "I think you're just hungry. The pizza in LA is better."

"You're just trying to bring me down."

I shrug once more, not answering. My mouth is full, and I don't share Nicole's joy in talking while eating. Talkeating. No, eatalking. Ha! I should write that down.

"Oh, I almost forgot to tell you," Nicole says, waving a half-eaten slice. "I got a phone number from this really hot guy. You wouldn't believe it."

From the corner of my eye I spot Shane chewing slower, the color draining from his face. I try to communicate silently that this is nothing serious—Nicole gets phone numbers from guys all the time, and most of them end up in the trash almost immediately. My silent communication does not seem to get through. I hope he doesn't choke on his pizza.

"Yeah, I met him in my yoga class. He's blond and has a body to die for. I'm pretty sure he has good taste in clothes too, but I can't be sure, since I always see him in his yoga outfit. A tight yoga outfit." She giggles.

I can see Shane making a short checklist. Blond—nope. A body to die for—nope. Good taste in clothes—nope. He looks as if the pizza is giving him indigestion.

"That's great, Nicole," I say, desperately trying to end this monologue.

She grabs another slice. Shane is still holding his first slice, and I doubt he'll take another one. "He was right behind me in class this week," she says. "And I could feel his eyes on me. And then the yoga teacher told us to do this position, where you have to bend and lift your—"

"I just remembered that I have to go," Shane says weakly. "I told my mom I'd eat dinner at home tonight. A family dinner. Can't miss it."

"Bummer," Nicole says. "It was really nice seeing you."

"Yeah," he mutters morosely. "Really nice." He gets up, lays his half-eaten slice on the counter and starts walking out.

"Shane, hang on," I say. "You forgot your camera."

"Oh, right." He comes back for his camera.

"We still need to talk about… you know. Everything."

"Yeah, sure," he mumbles. "Well… good night."

He stumbles out, and I hear the front door closing silently. It was inevitable. Nicole is a strange selective hurricane, destroying all the guys in her path. And like all weather phenomena, she has no self-awareness.

"So, honey." She smiles at me, chewing. "Let's talk about Chris."

Chapter Thirty-Eight

When I try to talk to Nicole about Ron's body, she brushes me off and says that it's the police's business, and that they'll take care of it. She reminds me that I said I wouldn't meddle with this any longer. When I try to explain that all that was before we figured out that the remains belonged to Ron, she simply ignores me.

"Stop thinking about it," she says.

But I can't stop thinking about it. We sit in front of the TV, watching a dumb romantic comedy. I can't even follow the simple plot line of girl loves boy—boy ignores girl—girl decides to move on—boy realizes what he's missing and chases after her car on foot. I keep obsessing about Ron's body, even after the movie's over, even after we go to bed. I lay awake, listening to Nicole's heavy breathing. Nicole can always fall asleep. It's her superpower.

On Saturday she tries to distract me with a Nicole beauty treatment. My dark roots are beginning to show, so she helps me color my hair. When I bought the hair color two weeks ago, I chose a darker red than usual, and I was really excited to see how it turned out. But now I couldn't care less. I keep thinking about Ron, about the last time he taught us. About how sweet he always seemed to be. The shade of hair color I chose suddenly feels so… irrelevant. As my hair is drying, Nicole does my fingernails. She has a nail polish kit the size of a small fridge. They say that Eskimos have hundreds of words to describe snow. Well, Nicole has at least two hundred different words to describe what I call "purple nail polish." She has about twenty thin, delicate brushes, and she can paint incredibly detailed images on each fingernail. Today I get a ladybug, a flower, a hot air balloon, SpongeBob, and a mouse. The nails of the other hand are all painted blue, because, according to Nicole, "asymmetry is beautiful."

"If Ron Hammond did go to Alice's house to kill her—"

"Amy, let it be, okay? Do you want me to do your feet as well?"

"Nicole, I have enough nail polish. In fact, I think my fingers now weigh two pounds more than they used to. Is my hair dry yet?"

"I think so, go have a look," she says.

I go to the bathroom to check out my hair as her phone begins to ring. My hair actually looks nice. I'm not entirely sure I can see any serious difference, but maybe in the sunlight…

"Amy, that was my mom, calling from the car," Nicole yells from my room. "My cousin is celebrating his twentieth birthday, and I totally forgot. I have to get going. She'll be here in a minute."

I walk out of the bathroom. "Okay, don't forget your nail polish."

I help her organize her immense kit. Meanwhile her mother calls twice more, and Nicole seems really stressed.

"Wow, I really have to go. Where's my bag?"

She finds it, stuffs everything in it, kisses me and bolts outside. A moment later I find her comb, her jacket, and one of her socks. I run out hoping to catch her, but she's already gone. Oh well, she'll get those back soon enough. I call Coral.

"Hey," she says, my phone practically freezing over from her tone of voice.

"Coral, I'm sorry I didn't call you, okay? Next time Shane's here I'll call, I promise."

"You don't have to call me every time you meet Shane," she says irritably. "You have a right to meet him by yourself."

"Then why…" I feel completely confused.

"But if you have a gathering of several friends, please let me know. It isn't fun to be left out."

"It wasn't a gathering, it was just two people… Hang on, you can't stand Nicole!"

"Still," she says, not trying to deny it. "Both Shane and Nicole were at your place, and Shane was probably looking at her like a lost puppy for the entire evening…"

"Sure, he has a crush on her. Like any other guy who meets Nicole. What's the big deal?"

"Shane is not like any other guy," she says. "I'd expect more from him."

"Coral…" I have a sneaking suspicion that I am missing something much bigger. "Do you… have a crush on Shane?"

"No," she says quickly. "Why would you even ask that?"

"Coral, I'm your friend, and if you—"

"Amy." She sounds as if she's about to cry. "I don't, okay?"

"Sure, whatever," I say, now completely convinced that I'm right. "Never mind."

"Okay," she says. "I was thinking about Ron Hammond. Something there doesn't add up."

"I know what you mean," I say. "If he went to kill Alice, then how did he die there as well? Maybe his dog killed him?"

"And buried him in the yard?" Coral asks skeptically. "Besides, we know he disappeared six weeks ago, right?"

"More like seven, I think."

"Right. And according to the route we saw, he started at the school, right?"

I'm beginning to see where she's going with this. "And the last time we know he was at school was seven weeks ago," I say slowly. "So…"

"So it's very probable that the entire route happened seven weeks ago."

"So he didn't kill Alice," I say, the puzzle pieces connecting. I hear the doorbell ringing and ignore it.

"No. He was murdered seven weeks ago and was buried in Alice's yard."

"And his phone was buried with him," I say.

"Right."

We both become quiet.

"So who killed him?" I ask. "Alice?"

"And who killed Alice?" Coral asks.

My door opens. Dad shoves his head inside and says, "Amy, can you come down, please?"

"In a minute," I tell him. "I'm on the phone."

"Then hang up," he says. "There's a policeman downstairs."

My heart plummets so low, it probably pays a surprise visit to my feet. "Coral, I have to go," I say and hang up.

I go downstairs after Dad. Mom is standing in the living room, her face pale, talking to a policeman.

"Hello," I say in a barely audible whisper.

The policeman turns to look at me. He has a mustache, a beard and tufts of hair sticking from his ears as well. How can someone with so much hair in his ears be a cop? Doesn't it interfere with his hearing? "Are you Amy?" he asks.

"Yeah."

"Are you the girl who called the security guy about the body she found?"

"Yeah."

"Can you please describe briefly how that happened?"

"I was walking the dog next to that house. She ran away and dug in the backyard. I followed her and saw the… remains."

"Where is the dog now?"

"It's the neighbor's dog, not ours," Mom intervenes. "Amy walks her when he's not around."

"I see." He nods. "Did you see anything else out of the ordinary? Anything at all?"

Of course, officer. A huge predator which follows me around. A crazy mind-reading homeless guy told me that I'm marked. There was a pile of dead half-eaten animal corpses in the field, not far from here. "No," I say aloud. "Nothing at all."

He nods. "Okay. We'll call if we need anything else."

He politely says goodbye and leaves. I consider chasing him, just to let him know that I need police protection, because my parents are about to kill me.

"Why didn't you say anything?" Dad asks in astonishment. "You just… kept quiet about it."

"I didn't want to worry you," I say, knowing well that this excuse won't hold.

"You didn't want to worry us?" Mom shouts. "You're saying that you kept quiet because *you didn't want to worry us?*"

"I didn't do anything, Moka just ran away—"

"And you said nothing!" Mom keeps on screaming. "My daughter finds a dead buried body and says nothing to me about it! Do you know how that makes me feel?"

"Mom, it's just that after the thing with Tom Ellis—"

"Especially after the thing with Tom Ellis!!! After we almost lost you, you find a body and say *nothing*?"

She shouts the word 'nothing' so loud, it makes me wince. I don't think Mom was ever so angry with me.

"What does it even matter?" I turn to Dad, half begging. "I didn't even do anything. I was simply in the wrong place at the wrong time!"

"For the second time in five months," Dad says quietly. When Dad is angry, he nearly whispers. "The second time. And what matters is you didn't tell us."

"And are you telling me that it was an accident?" Mom asks, her face looking as if it's about to explode. "That you went to the house of the woman who was murdered by accident?"

"Well, what do you expect?" I yell back. "I didn't want to move to this place! You know what's it like to live here? Do you think it ends with one body and one murder? Do you have any idea the stories I hear every day at school? Living here is like living in a never-ending horror movie! The weird people here, the strange things people see and hear… Do you think I'm enjoying this? You know what? I'd love to go back to my normal life in LA."

Both my parents stare at me, stunned. I decide that this is the perfect moment for my dramatic exit. "I don't know what I did wrong," I say hotly. "But I'm sure both of you know better." I run up the stairs and slam the door behind me.

This time I've gone too far, I know it. My parents will commit me to an asylum, or send me away to a boarding school. Maybe both. And we'll go back to LA, for sure. Well, at least I'll have that. Go back to LA. That's what I want most, right?

Then why do I feel like it's the most horrible thing that could happen?

Chapter Thirty-Nine

"I wanted to ask you a couple of questions," the police officer tells me. I nod, my heart beating as he pulls out his notebook. My mom looks at me, her stare severe and angry.

"One of our officers reports that a young girl and a young boy broke into Alice Hendrix's house, a murder crime scene. The description he gave us matches you. What do you know about this?"

"I... you have to understand... we didn't, I mean..." I stutter.

"Also, a woman reports that two young girls came to ask her some questions regarding the deceased Ron Hammond. Again, her description matches you."

"I didn't know he was dead when we met her. We just wanted to know—"

He shuts his notebook. "Amy, don't you think that in your position, these were not the smartest moves?"

"Well... In my position?"

"You know what I'm talking about. You're marked. It is after your blood," he says. His eyes stare into me—cold, hard, blue eyes, full of hatred and hunger. He opens his mouth, exposing two rows of sharp yellow teeth. A drop of drool trickles from his jaw and drips on the floor. Somewhere, far away, I can hear Jennifer saying, *There's blood everywhere, Amy, so much blood.* I stumble back, panicking, and turn to my mom for help, but it's not her at all. It's

Ron Hammond, covered in dirt, his eyes staring vacantly, his mouth twisted in a grimace of pain and horror. I can hear the cop growling...

I sit up in my bed, my heart beating. Another nightmare. A glance at the clock makes me realize that it's still the middle of the night. Three minutes past three. I don't think I'll be able to fall back asleep anytime soon.

I turn on the light and lie back down in my bed, my eyes open wide. Marked by the predator. Where does the predator fit in all this? We thought that the predator was Ron's dog, but Ron died long before Alice Hendrix, and his lover claimed he didn't have a dog.

I think about the cage in Alice's house. It would make sense that whatever escaped the cage killed her, and it could be the predator, but if this is the case, who killed and buried Ron? Besides, Peter said the police think that a man killed Alice, which means they have evidence.

Then there's Jennifer's dream. She dreamed that Ron killed someone. Someone he was arguing with. How does that—

No, hang on.

Jennifer never said she saw Ron kill anyone. She saw him arguing with someone, and then she saw a lot of blood. What if... it was Ron's blood? What if what she dreamed of was Ron's murder? In that case, whoever killed Ron was the woman who was arguing with him.

And maybe the same woman killed Alice Hendrix. Maybe both of Jennifer's dreams were from the point of view of the murderer.

My head is spinning. I nearly fall off the bed as I grab my phone. I dial Coral with shaking hands.

"Hello?" she mumbles tiredly.

"Coral," I say, my heart beating. "I don't think Jennifer dreamed that Ron was murdering someone. I think she dreamed that Ron was being murdered. Both her dreams could be from the point of view of the murderer."

"In the dream with Ron, she said that he was arguing with someone, right?" she asks, sounding as if she is trying to collect her thoughts.

"Right. A woman. Who said he hurt her. I heard her talking in her sleep. It sounded like an angry spouse."

"Vivian," Coral says, breathing heavily.

"So the second dream is about Vivian as well, about her murdering her own mother," I say.

"That explains everything," Coral says. "Vivian killed Ron. She buried him in her mother's backyard, since she doesn't have a backyard. She lives in an apartment."

"His phone was in his pocket, which is why we thought Ron went to Alice's house."

"She probably installed that tracking application herself," Coral says. "To find out if he was cheating on her."

"Oh my god, you're right," I say. "That's how she found out! She tracked his phone to that woman's house!"

"Then a week ago, she killed her mother," says Coral. "Maybe her mother threatened to go to the cops. It all makes sense!"

"Not all," I say. "What does this have to do with the predator? The cop said that Alice's body looked like an animal mauled her. And I'm pretty sure that the same creature I saw in Alice's house is following me around and is probably the same predator who marked me."

"Maybe. It doesn't really matter," says Coral. "We have to call the police."

"And tell them what?" I ask. "We're basing all this on a dream that Jennifer had."

"Still, this is a plausible explanation for Alice's and Ron's murder," Coral says. "Let them find the real evidence, right?"

"Well, I can call Peter in the morning," I say. "Tell him about it. He'll talk to the cops."

"Okay. Amy…" Coral says. "I have a good feeling about this."

"Yeah," I say. Maybe after this we'll move, and I won't have to deal with weird murders anymore. Why does it feel so sad? "Bye, Coral."

"Bye."

I lie down in my bed. The morning is hours away.

Chapter Forty

"Amy…" Peter sounds irritated and tired. I wonder if Sunday is his day off.

"Peter, you have to tell them. I know I don't have proof, but the body is Ron's, and Vivian is the one who killed him! There's no other explanation!"

"Amy…"

"I know you told me to stay out of it, and I swear I did. I didn't go near Alice's house again, but I had a picture I took of the remains and—"

"Amy, shut up for a minute!"

I stop talking, completely stunned.

"The police have identified the murder victim as Ron. They located both his girlfriends using his phone. They've been gathering evidence since Friday morning."

"So they believe that—"

"The cops are not a bunch of morons," he says. "They made the connection long before you called. They are on their way to arrest Vivian as we speak. I'm supposed to meet them at her house."

"They figured it all out?" I ask faintly.

"They are the police," he says slowly, as if talking to a four-year-old. "This is their job. They don't need you to help them, as I've repeatedly told you."

Tears of embarrassment and humiliation rise up my throat. "They didn't find Kimberly White," I say.

"That was a onetime thing," he replies. "This time they know who did it. She's about to be arrested, and she'll go to prison for a very long time."

"Okay," I say hoarsely.

"I appreciate your call, but seriously, there's no need, okay?"

"Okay."

"Have a great day, Amy."

"Yeah, you too."

He hangs up, and the phone drops from my fingers, a hollow feeling in my stomach. He's right. They were all right all along. What good did I do the past two weeks? I nearly got killed, got in trouble with my parents, scared my friends to death… For what? Why did I do all that? The police easily found the murderer. They would probably have found Ron without my help. It was all completely… useless.

I get dressed slowly and descend the stairs. Mom is sitting in the kitchen eating toast, her face pale, her eyes swollen and tired. I am crushed by overwhelming guilt. Mom is a morning person. She's always so cheerful and happy in the mornings. I did this.

"Dad went to get some groceries," she says. "I'm going out. I need some fresh air. I want you to stay home. Consider yourself grounded. After lunch you, me and Dad will talk about how to proceed."

"What do you mean, how to proceed?"

"After lunch, Amy."

"Yeah, okay."

She gets up, puts her plate in the sink and leaves without saying another word. I can't recall when the last time was that Mom was so angry at me. The whole thing makes me want to weep. I consider going back to bed. I don't have anything to do. But the conversation with Mom, and the previous conversation with Peter, left me on edge, and I don't think I can fall asleep. I make a quick cup of coffee, trying to shake off the tiredness after my long night. My phone rings. It's Coral.

"Hello?"

"Amy?" She's crying, sounding terrified. "Mia is gone!"

"Gone? What do you mean gone?" I ask, my fists clenching in fear.

"We were getting ready to go to church. Mom was supposed to take us both, but now Mia's disappeared! Mom is completely hysterical!" Coral sounds hysterical as well.

"Hang on," I say. "She's probably just hiding, like she did with me."

"For twenty-five minutes, while we call her repeatedly?" Coral asks. "She was waiting for us outside. She was sitting by the front door, playing with her tablet. And then she just went missing!"

"Did you check with her friend's mom?"

"What friend?"

"The girl living down the street. Ginny," I say.

"I don't know. Mom is on the phone. I think she's calling the whole world. But, Amy... her tablet. It was just by the front door. As if she left it here."

That didn't sound good at all. "Coral, I'm sure you'll find her soon."

"Can you come over? Please? Help us look?"

"Of course." I can't think of any way I can help, and Mom will probably offer me up for adoption, but Coral obviously needs me, and that's all that matters. I snatch a random piece of paper and a pen. What can I possibly write? I quickly scrawl, "Had to go—emergency, sorry," on it and pin it on the fridge. It won't make things better. It'll probably make them worse.

I grab my keys and run outside. It's freezing, and I turn back to get my coat. I spot Nicole's jacket, forgotten since yesterday, put it on and go out, locking the door behind me. I dial Peter quickly while walking towards Coral's house.

"Hello?"

"Peter?"

"Yeah, Amy, what's wrong? I'm just about to join the arrest—"

"Coral's sister is gone. No one knows where she is."

"Gone?" He sounds very worried. "How old is she?"

"Six... or seven, I'm not sure. She was playing outside, and now they can't find her."

"What's the address?"

I give him the address and he hangs up. I half walk, half run all the way to Coral's house. I finally get there, completely breathless, and barge in without knocking. Her mom is standing in the kitchen, sobbing, talking on the phone.

"… I'm telling you that she simply disappeared! Send someone over right now! No, I won't hold…"

Coral emerges, her face wet with tears, and drags me to her room. We both sit on the bed.

"My dad canceled the rest of his business trip and is trying to find a flight back home," she says. "We talked to all the neighbors, all of her friends, all the kids from school. No one saw her. Amy, what if the predator—"

"The predator didn't grab her in broad daylight," I say. "It's something else."

"Why did she leave her tablet behind?" Coral sniffs. "She'd never just forget it. Do you think she dropped it while struggling, or… or…"

I lay my hand on her shoulder, and she quiets down. She's holding the tablet with both hands. It has a pink cover with a small picture of a white cat. I gently pluck the tablet from her fingers, and she lies back, closing her eyes.

"I shouldn't have let her out of my sight," she says.

I turn on the tablet.

"If something happens to her—"

"Coral, I'm sure she's okay," I say, trying to keep the uncertainty from my voice. I open the tablet's gallery. There are hundreds of images and videos, but I can instantly see that the last video was taken outside, and I don't even need to glance at the date to know that it was taken this morning. I press the icon, and the short clip starts to play, Mia humming to herself, filming the street slowly.

"Hello," someone says. I instantly press the pause button, the hair on my neck prickling with fear. Coral sits up and stares at me.

"What was that?" she asks.

"A movie clip that Mia filmed this morning," I say, swallowing.

"But that sounded like—"

"Like Vivian," I say.

Coral snatches the tablet from my hands and resumes the clip.

"Hello," Mia says. The camera turns to film the woman's legs. Two long legs in black pants.

"You're Coral's sister, right?"

"That's right," says Mia. "You know my sister?"

"I know her very well," answers Vivian. "She's my student. She asked me to play a game with you."

"What game?"

"You and me will hide, and she'll come looking for us."

"I'm not supposed to walk with strangers."

"I'm not a stranger. I'm her Spanish teacher. My name is Vivian."

"What if she doesn't find us?"

"She'll find us." Vivian laughs, a cruel cold laugh. "She's very good at finding things. She and her friend are both very good at sniffing around and finding things."

"Okay," Mia says. "I'll just ask Mommy…"

"That'll ruin the surprise," Vivian says. "I'll call her and let her know, okay?"

"Okay."

"And you can leave this thing here."

"My tablet?" Mia sounds doubtful. "I don't want it to get lost."

"Then leave it here by the door, where your mom will find it."

"Okay."

The movie clip stops abruptly and I blink. Coral puts the tablet down on the bed, grabs her head and starts muttering to herself, whimpering. I snatch the tablet and send the video to Shane.

"Don't worry," I tell Coral. "She'll be fine."

She looks at me, her eyes empty and hopeless. "No. She won't."

I have no idea what to say to that.

Chapter Forty-One

"Amy? What the hell is this?" Shane's voice sounds confused.

"It's Vivian," I tell him. "She took Mia."

"Why would she take Mia?" he asks. "That's so weird! Do you think she maybe found out you were snooping on her computer?"

I suddenly realize that neither Coral nor I have told Shane about our conclusion. "Listen, Vivian killed Ron. She killed her mother as well."

"What? Why do you—"

"Trust me. I'm right. The police are on their way to her house to arrest her, but I bet she's not there. She took Mia as some sort of… bait or something. Maybe a hostage. I don't know."

"Bait? Bait for what? For who? If she's about to be arrested, shouldn't she be running away?"

"I don't know, Shane. I have no idea what goes on in that woman's head," I snap. "Let's figure this out after Mia's safe, okay?"

"Okay. So what do you want to do?" he asks.

"Can you get to Coral's house?"

"On my way," he says and hangs up.

"He's coming here," I tell Coral. She nods, staring at the wall, saying nothing. The doorbell rings. Coral and I both jump off the bed and walk to the living room. Peter is in the doorway, accompanied by two cops. The cops look like something from a silly comedy. One is chubby and short, the other tall and thin, his nose protruding like a carrot in a snowman's face. I'd laugh if I weren't on the verge of crying. Coral's mom is tearfully explaining the events of the morning. I march towards Peter and hand him the tablet.

"This was hers," I say. "Check out the last video. It was taken this morning."

Peter activates the video, and watches it, the cops and Coral's mom looking over his shoulder.

"I don't understand," says Coral's mom. "Why would Coral's Spanish teacher do something like that? It's so irresponsible! Didn't she realize how scared we would be?"

She sounds relieved. She thinks this has been a huge misunderstanding, Coral's teacher playing a prank on her. Peter and the two cops exchange worried glances.

"We'll ask her once we locate her, Mrs...."

"Hutchinson."

"Mrs. Hutchinson. Please stay here, and make sure your phone isn't busy."

"Of course," she says, nearly smiling. I feel sick. She has no idea. Peter motions with his head and I follow him outside. He closes the door after him.

"Do you have any idea where they went?" he asks.

"No," I say. "How would I?"

"I don't know, Amy," he says, shutting his eyes and massaging the bridge of his nose. "How did you know that Vivian killed Ron? How did you know about Tom Ellis? I suppose you have good instincts, and I was hoping you maybe had an idea..."

"I don't."

"That's too bad. Vivian is not at her house, unfortunately, but we have all the exits from Narrowdale roadblocked, so she can't get out."

"Good," I say, not feeling relieved at all.

"We'll catch her and get Mia back. You just stay here, okay?"

"Okay," I say. The subtext is clear. Keep your nose out of it, let the police do their job. Fine, I get it, the police don't need my help. He puts a reassuring hand on my shoulder. Then he opens the door and ushers me inside. He and the cops leave. Coral's mom is sitting in the living room, drinking a cup of tea, muttering angrily to herself. She's probably already planning her chat with the school principal. I walk back to Coral's room. She's sitting on the bed again, staring at her phone.

"I'm going," I tell her. "Shane's on his way. When he gets here, try and figure out where Vivian could have gone. If you have a solid lead, call me."

"Where are you going?" she asks.

"I'm going to the mall to look for Edgar," I say. "Maybe he has something to say about this."

"Good idea." She nods. "Let me know if you find out anything?"

"Sure."

"Okay. Hey, Amy?"

"Yeah?"

"Thanks."

I nod and leave the room. I hope she'll still thank me later.

Chapter Forty-Two

The mall is completely abandoned this early on Sunday morning. Most of the stores aren't even open yet. The customers are presumably still in bed, or at church, or anywhere else that's not here. The weather is uninviting as well. The wind is ruthless, sneaking through my clothes, freezing my body. I shrink into Nicole's jacket, trying to minimize the amount of exposed skin offered to the chilly air, my eyes darting around, searching for Edgar. He is nowhere to be found.

My search becomes more desperate as I glance at the time. Twenty past nine. By now, Shane must be at Coral's house. And Mia? Every minute that ticks by without finding her or Vivian is another minute in which something might happen to her, something terrible. Chilling images pass through my mind as I look between the large dumpsters at the rear of the mall, and they keep haunting me as I scan the usual spots in which Edgar likes to sleep. I'm just about to give up as someone calls from behind me.

"Um... are you looking for Edgar?"

I turn around. It's a young blond woman, dressed in black, an embarrassed look in her eyes. She seems even more underdressed for this weather than me, and keeps jumping from left foot to right, breathing on her hands, trying to keep them warm.

"Never mind," she says as I stare at her in confusion. "You just seemed... he said... forget it."

"No!" I quickly say, panicking. "You're right. I am looking for Edgar. Do you know where he is?"

She nods and motions me to follow. I follow her to a big gray metal door in the back of the mall, which she opens without hesitating. I walk with her inside, the closed space pleasantly warm, and both of us seem to grow taller, letting our body enjoy the respite from the cold. We walk through a narrow hallway into what seems to be a large kitchen. This is the kitchen of Alfred's, the cafe, I suddenly realize. Edgar is sitting on a chair, looking cleaner than usual, his face pink and flushed.

"There she is," the woman tells Edgar. "You were right, she was looking for you."

"They refuse to serve me food," Edgar tells me, his voice hurt. "That man over there is cooking, and he won't serve me anything!"

"I told you, we have to serve our paying customers first," the woman tells Edgar testily. "If you aren't happy with this arrangement, feel free to leave. I shouldn't have even let you in. The boss would kill me if he found out."

"He won't find out," Edgar tells her. "He's too busy cheating on his wife."

"Well, never mind, then. I still need to take care of my paying customers first," the woman says.

The cook lays a plate with steaming bacon and eggs on the counter.

"There, you can give me that one," says Edgar. "The man who ordered it is a bad man. Do you know what he did last night?"

She crosses her hands. "No. And I don't want to know. We've talked about this—save your stories for yourself. He ordered bacon and eggs, and I'll serve him bacon and eggs." She takes the plate and walks away into the front end of the cafe.

Edgar mutters to himself. I glance at the cook, who is clearly ignoring us both.

"I need your help," I tell Edgar without wasting any more time. "Coral's sister disappeared. Do you remember Coral? My friend?"

"Disappeared?" Edgar raises an eyebrow. "No, she didn't."

"She..." I think for a second. "Someone took her. Kidnapped

her. Someone dangerous. I need to know where she took her to."

"Why did she get off the road?" asks Edgar. "Doesn't she know she should always stay on the road?"

"What road? She—"

"He's not a good man at all," Edgar says grumpily. "And now he's eating my bacon and eggs. Do you know what he did last night?"

"Edgar, please concentrate," I beg. "My friend—"

"He threw away a plastic bottle."

"Yes, but—"

"Recycling is very important."

"I agree. Mia—"

"Also, he killed two squirrels last week with a shovel. He suspected that they knew his real name."

I find myself at a loss for words.

"Just like that, throws a plastic bottle into the trash," Edgar shakes his head. "And he gets my bacon and eggs."

"Edgar, do you know where Mia is?" I check the time. Forty-five minutes past nine.

"No. How would I know that?" he asks me, confused. "You say someone took her."

I feel the despair rising. He can't help me. This has been a waste of time...

"But the gatekeeper's hound can."

"The... gate... what?" The last sentence was even weirder than usual.

"She made me wash before coming in," he mutters.

"Who? The gatekeeper?"

"Of course not." He stares at me in disappointment. "The waitress! She wouldn't let me come inside until I washed my hands and face. And it's really cold outside! And the water was cold as well, and the soap smelled weird..."

"What is the gatekeeper's hound?" I ask, trying to refrain from grabbing him and shaking him violently.

"You should know better than me," he says. "You've been walking her for the past two weeks."

Moka! Could she help find Mia?

"But you should watch your step," he says. "The woodsman won't be able to help you. He's in the wrong place."

I'm already on my way out. I hesitate for a moment and consider asking him what he means, but I don't want to waste any more time. Mia is in danger, and Edgar pointed out the way to find her. I walk out of the kitchen and begin running home.

Chapter Forty-Three

I call Shane on the way. "Hey. Are you at Coral's house yet?"

"Yeah," he says. "Got anything?"

"I think he told me that Moka can help," I say. "I'm on my way to Alex's house to get her."

There's a moment of silence. "The dog?" he finally says, sounding disappointed. "That's your lead?"

"Well, do you have anything better?" I ask.

"We're coordinating a search party," he says.

"A search party? Who's searching?" I ask skeptically. Coordinating a search party is a pompous way of saying that Shane's mom is driving around Narrowdale in her car.

"Forty-seven people from our school," he says. "They're split into groups."

"Seriously?" I ask, breathless. "Forty-seven?"

"And counting. There's been a great response on Facebook," he says. "Some real awesome people wrote me back almost immediately, and they're making phone calls. I have Tom, Fred, Lidia, Jasmine—"

"Jasmine?" I ask, incredulous.

"Yeah. Bob, Carley—"

"Carley? You've got to be kidding me."

"Amy, people want to help."

"Well, I'm getting Moka. She can help too."

"Sure, whatever. Coral and I are staying here. We need to organize this."

"Fine," I say, feeling useless. "I'll join you and get something of Mia's for Moka to smell."

"Okay, gotta go, someone's trying to call." He hangs up.

I reach Alex's gate and open it, almost stumbling into his front yard. Moka is sitting there, looking at me. Surprisingly, she isn't hopping around, or barking, or wagging her tail. She's just sitting, attentive, her ears perked.

"We need to find Mia," I tell her. "We'll go to Coral's house, get something of Mia's and… and…"

And more time will be wasted. How long has Mia been missing? Two hours? Almost three? With a woman who killed at least two people? We can't afford to waste any more time, but there's no other way. Maybe… Maybe she can simply lead me to Mia, without a scent. Edgar said she'd lead me.

"Do you… do you know where Mia is?" I ask her.

She looks at me seriously and stands up. I hold my breath. It's true, she'll lead me. She isn't a regular dog, she's…

Moka scratches her ear, sniffs around, yawns and lies down. I feel incredibly dumb. What did I expect? For her to bark and lead the way? What's that, Lassie? Timmy fell down the well? A dog is a dog. They have a great sense of smell, and they're loyal and cute, but that's about it. I'll have to take her to Coral's house. Maybe meanwhile, Shane's search party will get lucky, who knows? In any case, Moka needs Mia's scent…

The friendship bracelet.

"I'll be right back," I tell Moka and sprint to my house. I unlock the door, run up the stairs and snatch the bracelet from the table. I haven't worn it even once. It might still have Mia's scent on it. I run back outside, return to Alex's front yard, grab the leash and tie it to Moka, who's strangely quiet. Then I let her sniff the bracelet. She sniffs it. Then she raises her head. For a moment she seems to be staring into nothing. She needs a trail, I realize. Without a trail to begin the search, she can't possibly…

A strong tug at my hand. The leash is stretched tight. Moka is pulling, straining against it, trying to run. I take a step in her direction...

She starts running, and all I can do is follow as fast as I can. As we run down the street I try to gather my thoughts and figure this out. Is Moka really leading me to Mia? Why did Vivian kidnap Mia? What are her intentions? Does she know that the police are looking for her? Could she be using Mia as a hostage? But then, why target Mia of all people? In the video clip Mia took, it was very clear that Mia was chosen as a target.

My phone vibrates. A message. I take it out of my pocket, nearly dropping it when Moka takes a right turn onto a different street, with me dragged after her like some sort of cartoon. I read the message as the screen bounces in front of my eyes.

Jasmine's group on way to Ron Hammond's lover's house. Fred and Tom checking the school. Get here with or without the dog.

I check the time again. Quarter past ten. Self-doubt fills me. Am I wasting time? Chasing a dog who for all I know might be chasing a cat's scent? I look around me. We're on a small street, which I don't seem to recognize. I haven't been paying attention to our route. It seems like a quiet, calm street. Not a place I'd go to with a kidnapped kid. I've wasted enough time. I'll take Moka to Coral's house, let her sniff some dirty laundry, take her to the front porch from which Mia was taken. I halt, but Moka doesn't; she keeps on pulling, straining against the leash, and growling.

Not a bark, intended to make me pay attention. A growl. A growl of anger. I raise my eyes and look ahead.

The street ends in a patch of dry ground. Beyond it there's an apple orchard, looking neglected and wild, its ground covered in shrubs, dead leaves and weeds. There's a small park bordering the orchard, with two swings, a slide and a rusty carousel. A few feet from the slide stands a woman, with a small child wearing a red coat, its hood almost hiding her face. But I know the coat. And when she calls my name, I know her voice as well. It's Mia. And holding her hand is Vivian.

Chapter Forty-Four

"Amy!" Mia waves at me, jumping in place, smiling happily. "You found us!"

I swallow. The situation seems so innocent, so normal. But I can hear my heart beat, feel the blood pounding, my teeth clenching. Moka growls, her body tightening, poised to leap. Vivian watches me and Moka, smiling, tight-lipped. I take several careful steps forward.

"Hey, Mia," I say, trying to sound casual. "Hi, Vivian. Mia is with you? That's such a relief. Her family is looking for her! I'm so happy you found her!" I don't sound happy. I sound scared.

"Really?" Vivian says. "Then it's a good thing she's with me. I had no idea."

"We were playing a game!" Mia says excitedly. "Hide and seek! Vivian said that if we hide really well, I'll get a prize!"

"Maybe I should call her mom," I say, my shaking hand slowly fumbling in my jacket pocket for my phone. "She's really worried." My fingers clutch my keys, then keep groping. Where's the phone? Did I put it in the other pocket?

"I don't think there's any need to call," Vivian says, her smile widening. "We can just take Mia home."

"Still," I say, looking in the other pocket, feeling the solid shape of my phone. There it is. "You know. Just to make sure she doesn't call the police."

She raises her eyebrow at my mention of the police, and I can see in her eyes that she knows. My heart sinks. A desperate runaway would do anything to get away. Even kill two girls. "There's no need for her to worry," she says, her smile widening even more. "I never wanted Mia. It was you that I was after."

"Me?" I start pulling the phone slowly from my pocket. "Why me?"

"Because you got away too many times," she says, her smile exposing her teeth. "I don't like it when people get away."

Her smile is wide. Too wide. I wonder how is it that I've never noticed how big Vivian's mouth is.

"Mia," I say. "Come here."

Mia takes a step forward, then stops. Vivian doesn't let go of her hand, holding her back.

"Let me go!" Mia cries. "You're hurting me!"

"I knew you'd come," Vivian hisses at me. "Always snooping, always shoving your nose where it doesn't belong. You and your friends. And I was right. You didn't let me down. Now this ends. You won't get away aga—" She suddenly screams, letting go of Mia.

"Amy!" Mia yells.

"Run!" I shout at her, stepping forward, grabbing her hand, pulling her away from Vivian, away from the murderer.

"You bit me!" I hear Vivian shouting after us. "You little monster, you bit my hand!"

It'll all be fine, I think, we're getting away. Vivian is much older than us. There is no way she can catch us. I glance backwards, and my hope evaporates.

Thirty feet behind us trots a huge dog. Its mouth is open, rows of yellow teeth flashing, its cold blue eyes glinting in the sunlight. This must be Vivian's dog, which she used to kill her mother. It's the predator that has been following me. I know it is. It'll get me now. Its jaws will sink into my neck, its claws will rake my back. Nowhere to run, nothing to do, no one will help us here…

Appearing from nowhere, Moka leaps at the predator, growling angrily. She'll stop it! She'll buy us enough time to…

A loud yelp. I glance backwards once more. The beast is much closer this time, Moka lying on the ground, howling in pain. She didn't even slow it down. I want to go back for her, make sure she's not badly hurt, but I can't. I'm dragging Mia forward, and she's whimpering, stumbling. We're running in the wrong direction, I suddenly realize. We should be running towards the street, where there are people who can help us. Instead, for some reason, we are running towards the orchard. Stupid, Amy. Why do I have to be so stupid? I realize that my hand is still clutching my phone. I'll call Coral. Or the police. Or throw the thing at the predator's head. I… This is not my phone at all. This is a can of deodorant. Why am I carrying deodorant in my pocket?

I let go of Mia's hand.

"Amy!"

"Go!" I shout at her. "Run!" She sobs and keeps running towards the orchard. I turn around. The predator is closing the gap, trotting, as if it's not in a hurry. Toying with its prey. It is huge. How can a dog be so huge? Our eyes meet and I freeze in fear…

You're marked.

It takes another step, knowing that it won, that its prey has nowhere to run to…

Her entire body was covered with scratches… jagged gashes. And her neck… I've never seen anything like it.

I can hear it breathing. Deep, heavy. I can almost feel its breath on my skin…

There's blood everywhere, Amy, so much blood.

Is this what Ron Hammond saw, a second before he died? What Alice saw before the jaws snapped her neck?

You're marked.

It stops, no more than six feet from me. It starts growling, a threatening, vicious growl. I can feel my knees shaking, turning into liquid. I can't move. Soon I'll fall and it'll be on top of me, its teeth ripping my neck to shreds, its claws sinking into me… Its growl becomes a roar and it leaps forward.

My hand lifts with a will of its own, holding forth the can of spray. Not deodorant. Pepper spray. The same pepper spray that Nicole's mom forces her to carry with her, left in her jacket's pocket.

My finger presses the small button, and a jet of liquid streams straight into the predator's face. It howls, shutting its eyes, stumbling as I step backwards. It misses me, rolls on the ground, sneezing and howling in pain, its front legs clawing at its snout. I can't imagine what pepper spray does to a dog, whose sense of smell is much sharper than a human's, and I don't really want to find out. I simply turn and run into the orchard.

The dry leaves crunch under my feet as I run, breathing hard. I almost slip on the muddy ground, but manage to gain my balance and keep on running, not looking back, concentrating on getting away as fast as possible. The cold air hurts my lungs, my nose, my face. Something grabs my hair and I scream in fear, then realize my hair is caught in a low branch. I disentangle it and carry on running. My lungs are bursting, I feel like I have to stop for a second. I lean against a tree, bending over, breathing hard, nearly throwing up. Did I get away? Maybe the beast is completely disabled. Maybe it isn't chasing me anymore. A loud roar fills the orchard, causing birds to fly from the trees in fright. It's still here. It is still chasing me. Time to keep on running.

I start running again, but I'm exhausted, my feet and body hurt, and I'm out of air. Another roar, much closer. What's the point? The predator is much faster than me. I'll never get away by running. I stop and look around. I spot a tree with several low branches nearby. I run over and start climbing, pulling my body upwards with my freezing fingers. A dry branch snaps under my foot, and I swing wildly, searching for something to stand on. There! Another step up, and another. Can the dog climb trees? I look downward. The tree is not nearly as high as I'd like it to be. The predator might be able to jump this high. I curse myself for not choosing a higher tree, but it's too late. I can hear it getting closer, its feet crunching on the dry leaves, its breath wheezing strangely, an aftereffect of the pepper spray. I realize that my eyes are shut, and I force myself to open them, hugging the tree trunk forcefully as I do so.

It is walking softly, just a few dozen feet from my tree, looking around, its head turning left and right. Looking! Not sniffing! For a second its eyes glance in my direction, and I'm certain that it notices me, but its head keeps on turning, searching, its eyes more blood-red than blue, and it keeps blinking. For a moment it stops, sneezes three times, then keeps on walking. The pepper spray has done its job. The huge dog can't smell, can hardly see. It gets closer to my tree and I hold my breath, shaking in fear. If it hears me, I'm as good as dead. It passes below my tree, keeps on walking. It's getting harder to keep holding my breath. My lungs feel as if they're about to burst. I open my mouth, exhale slowly and silently, then take a small breath in. The predator doesn't turn around. I begin breathing more easily as it gets further away. I might still survive this, I…

A small red shape catches my attention. She is lying on the ground, shaking, no more than twenty feet from the predator. It is bound to see her. Her red coat is like a blinding neon sign on the brown ground. Any minute now it'll turn, the red coat will catch its eyes, and I won't be able to do anything. It'll rip her to shreds. A sob catches in my throat as its head turns towards her… And it keeps on walking.

Dogs are color-blind, I suddenly recall. Color means nothing. Stay quiet, Mia, just stay quiet. Don't cry, don't cough, don't move. It's getting closer to Mia, not walking towards her, but there are fewer trees between them, less ground to cover. I can only pray that the pepper spray really messed its eyesight up, and that she doesn't make a sound. It is now walking no more than a few paces from her, and I know she's about to scream. I would. It'll grab her. She looks so helpless, a tiny girl in her red coat, lying frozen in fear, staring at the huge menacing monster walking by. She makes no sound. It keeps on walking. Getting further away. Disappearing into the trees.

I force myself to climb down slowly. I have to get to Mia. My feet land softly on the ground, a tiny leaf crackling under them. I wait for a few seconds, but the predator doesn't return. I start walking in tiny, measured paces, pushing the leaves with my feet to avoid stepping on them. I manage to reach a small path with no leaves on it, follow it towards Mia. Somewhere in the orchard, the predator howls a wild, bloodcurdling howl. Mia shrinks in fear, and I feel certain that she's about to bolt, but to my relief, she doesn't. I reach her and lay a hand on her shoulder.

She turns, her eyes wide in fear, her mouth open, a scream rising up her throat. My hand clamps on her lips, muffling the sound. Was I fast enough? Did the beast hear it? Is it coming back? We stay in silence for several moments. Nothing happens. I slowly take the hand off her mouth, and motion her to be quiet, a finger on my lips. She nods. Smart girl. Her eyes are red, her cheeks wet with tears, and her lips are quivering, but she remains quiet. I slowly help her to stand up, nudging her towards the way out, back to the street.

We walk back so slowly I feel like screaming. Small, careful steps, doing whatever we can to avoid making any noise. To my surprise, Mia does this much easier than me, her footsteps certain, her eyes scanning the ground for every dry branch, every dead leaf that might make a noise. Our progress is minuscule, step after step after step, certain that any moment the predator will leap out of the bushes, catch us for good. On and on we walk, passing by more and more trees. How many trees are there in this orchard? Did I really run so far in? Are we walking in circles? Have we been in this spot before? This tree looks familiar. I'm pretty sure we walked by it only two or three minutes ago...

And then I spot the white shape of a house. A street. Not the same one we came from; apparently we got a bit lost. But a street nonetheless. There's a low chain-link fence between the orchard and the street, sagging after years of neglect. I point towards the street, looking at Mia. She nods. We walk over, my confidence rising. We just have to get over the fence, to the street, into one of the houses. Safe inside, away from the predator's ears, I'll call the cops.

My foot steps on a dry branch, and it cracks. The noise is like a gunshot in the quiet orchard. And Mia lets out a gentle sob of fear. We freeze, and then we hear it. Something coming closer, running at a terrifying pace. We can hear the low, angry growling becoming louder and louder. No point in hiding. Only one thing left to do. Without exchanging a single word, we begin to run.

We run, stumbling, an overpowering sense of déjà vu settling over me. We've done this before, running away from a monster towards a fence, the safety of the street beyond it. But last time I didn't believe something was really after us. This time I know it's behind us, with only one desire in its mind. To catch us. Hurt us. Kill us.

Jagged gashes. And her neck... blood everywhere, Amy, so much blood.

We reach the fence, a mesh of sagging iron wires. I grab it by the bottom and lift it, exposing a gap big enough for Mia to crawl under. She does it quickly, whimpering in fright. I follow her, but my jacket and pants get entangled in the fence, and for a moment I thrash, panicking. Then small hands untangle me, grabbing the fence, lifting it. Mia didn't leave me behind. This girl is as surprising as her sister. I crawl out and get up. We resume running. Where are we? This area looks familiar. Have I been here before?

The growling is so loud it's practically inside my ears. I look back and see the dog running towards us, its mouth open wide, saliva droplets flying in its wake. How long would it take for the predator to crawl under the fence? The answer is worse than I thought. It doesn't bother. It leaps into the air and over the fence, and my heart sinks, knowing that we're doomed. Then one of its rear legs is snagged by an exposed wire and it yelps in pain, falling, rolling. We keep on going, running on the sidewalk, our footsteps loud on the pavement.

Another glance backwards. It's following us again, its rear leg in the air, limping on the other three. It's running much slower now, but still faster than us. I look around, not daring to run towards one of the houses. If the door is locked, we'll be doomed.

"Help!" I scream. "Someone!"

No one opens a door. We keep running, the predator getting closer, and then suddenly I know where we are. I know when I've last been here, and I know what I need to do. I spot the crossroad. Left or right? Which way? Left. I'm almost sure it's left. We reach the crossroad and I turn left, dragging Mia behind me, no time to make sure I'm correct. But I am. This is Vivian's street, and as I hoped, two squad cars are standing right outside her house, a couple of cops leaning on them, chatting.

"Help! Please!" I scream.

They turn towards us. Everything moves slowly. One of them tenses, his arm flying to his belt. I can hear the predator growling behind me, its jaws snapping inches from Mia. She's screaming in fear. I leap aside, throwing myself on her, both of us tumbling down. The air cracks with a sudden blasting noise. And another. And another. Then… silence. Time resumes its usual pace. Mia is weeping under me, and I quickly roll away, afraid that I hurt her.

Voices. "Are you all right?" "Isn't that the missing girl?" "Is it dead?" I look behind me.

The predator is lying next to us in a growing pool of blood, still breathing. It looks at me, and its eyes narrow in hatred and anger. I realize that there's recognition there as well. It *knows* me. Then they close and the breathing stops.

Shaking I sit up and gather Mia in my arms. "Come on," I whisper. "Let's get you home."

Chapter Forty-Five

"Okay, let's go over this one more time," says the cop.

I check the time. Mom hasn't called me yet, which probably means that she didn't get home to find me gone. But it'll happen soon, and then the police will have to open a new murder investigation.

"We've gone over it three times already," I tell him. "I think you got it. I really have to go home."

"That's no problem," says the cop. "We can take you home, continue the interview there."

Oh, good. I sigh and glance at Coral. She and her mom are sitting on the couch, both hugging Mia, talking to the other cop. I turn back to my cop, the thin one with the long nose. In a bout of childish anger I dub him Pinocchiop. Please, blue fairy, I want to turn into a real cop! One day, Pinocchiop, if you wish upon a star and fill out a lot of paperwork.

"I decided to get Moka, the dog, to help me find Mia," I say. I stop for a second, think about Moka. Is she badly hurt? She seemed alive when I last saw her, but the predator clearly hurt her and... I shut my eyes. Now is not the time to be thinking about this. I open my eyes and turn back to the cop. "I had this bracelet that Mia made for me, so I let Moka smell that and then she took me to—"

"Where did you let her sniff the bracelet?" asks the cop, jotting in the notebook.

"I told you, next to my house. And then—"

"Listen, kid, it doesn't work like that. I've been in the dog unit for three years. A dog needs a trail. He can't just pick scents from wherever."

"Well, maybe your dogs are broken," I suggest. He doesn't seem partial to the idea. "I don't know. That's how it happened." I look at Coral and her mother. They seem to wish the cops would leave as well. "Don't you have better things to do instead of harassing us?" I ask. "Shouldn't you be out there, looking for Vivian? Or did you arrest her already?"

"We have several squads looking for her, and roadblocks all around the town," he says. "We'll find her."

"Well, I really have to go, so—"

"I'm sorry, but until I get a clear picture, I can't let you–"

Someone clears his throat noisily, and we all turn our looks towards the door.

A short man is standing in the doorway. He is wearing a black suit and a brown trilby hat, and is leaning on a cane. I'm usually not bad at guessing ages, but I'm having a hard time pinpointing his. His face is quite smooth, but underneath his hat, the hair is completely gray. He slowly limps into the room, which has become completely silent. Everyone in the room is looking at the newcomer.

"Gentlemen," he says. "I think that the Hutchinson family has had a rough day. It is time that we leave them alone, don't you think?"

"Well," Pinocchiop says, "we need to follow this through sir. There are a lot of loose ends here, and a kidnapper at large–"

"Then go get her," the man interrupts him, limping forward. "I think we are all confident that you will find her in no time. Thank you officer, the police's swift handling of this matter shall not go unnoticed."

"I'm sorry sir, but–"

The short man reaches the cop and leans towards him. He whispers something quietly. Somehow, despite the fact that I am standing right next to them, I can't manage to hear what he murmurs in the cop's ear. The cop becomes deathly pale. The man draws back, smiling. "Well now, you were saying?"

Pinocchiop clears his throat and says "Mrs. Hutchinson, don't worry. We've got it all under control. And thanks, Miss Parker, for helping us find the child."

That's an interesting way of putting it. I'd say it was less "helping them find the child" and more "doing all the work while the police ran around like headless chickens." Still, they did save my life—got to give them that.

"Officer Frank," he says. "We should be on our way."

Officer Frank frowns, and Pinocchiop looks at him and shakes his head slightly.

Frank shrugs and says "Well, I'm glad we managed to find your daughter…" I roll my eyes. "We should be going."

"Excellent!" the newcomer says. "Have a good day, Mrs. Hutchinson," he adds, nodding at Coral's mom.

"Th… thank you sir," she stammers, but he is already walking towards the door, surprisingly fast for a man that's leaning on a cane. He leaves without sparing us second glance.

"Who was that?" I ask. Coral shrugs.

Coral's mom escorts the cops outside, looking completely exhausted. I approach Coral and Mia. "I have to go," I say. "My mom is going to kill me."

"Thanks, Amy," Coral says in a hoarse voice. "If you hadn't found her—"

"No problem," I quickly say, embarrassed. I wink at Mia. "What about you? Everything okay?"

"Yes," she says, nodding seriously. "Nothing to be scared of, right? The cops killed her."

"Her? You mean the dog?" I ask.

"The teacher," she says. "Vivian."

"Well… they killed Vivian's dog, and they're looking for Vivian…"

"Don't you start." She stomps on the floor. "You're just like that cop. Vivian is the dog."

I blink. "That's enough, Mia," Coral says.

"But, Coral, I swear. Amy was there too! Vivian grew hair all over her body, and her face was like Raaaawr, and then she bent over, and then she was a dog and she chased us."

"She's a bit confused," Coral says, caressing her sister's head. "It was a long day."

"Right," I say.

On my way out, I almost collide with Coral's mom, who grabs me and gives me a warm hug. "Thanks," she says.

"Yeah... no problem," I mumble, blushing. I quickly leave. On my way home I call Shane. He picks up almost immediately.

"They're done?" he asks. The cops politely asked him to leave as soon as we entered the house, to his immense disappointment.

"Yeah," I say. "It was really weird. They were digging into my story, I had no idea what to say about Edgar and Moka... and then they got a call from their boss, and they left."

"I'm not surprised," he says.

"What do you mean?"

"Well... the police will cover this up now, right? It's what they always do."

"Yeah?"

"They never tried really hard to figure out what you were doing in Tom Ellis's house, right? And they never said that Alice Hendrix was murdered either. They just let things be."

"But why?" I ask.

"Well, only in Narrowdale..."

"Shane, I'm serious."

"How should I know why?" he asks. "But that's how it is."

"Yeah," I say. "Hey, listen, before I left, Mia said something really weird. She said... Hey, girl! Oh, I'm so happy to see you're okay!"

"That's not that weird," Shane says.

"No," I say, crouching and petting Moka's head. "I just ran into Moka. She's okay! Well... she has a bite mark on her leg, but it doesn't look too bad. I'll take her to the vet."

"Yeah, listen, I'll talk to you later. I need to call the search parties off."

"Okay, you do that."

"Jasmine called to say that Ron's lover nearly tore her eyes out when she mentioned his name," Shane says.

"Really?" I cheer up considerably. "That's terrible. Is she okay?"

"Yeah, just a bit shaken."

"That's too bad."

"What?" he asks, confused.

"Nothing. Go call the search off. Tell them that Amy found Mia because she's so awesome."

"I'll be sure to pass on the message," he says sarcastically and hangs up.

"Well, time to face the firing squad." I sigh.

It's after lunchtime. Mom will already be home. And she'll be pissed.

Chapter Forty-Six

"And did she?"

"Did she what?"

"Kill you?"

"Well… I'm here," I say.

Doctor Greenshpein nods. "That doesn't surprise me. Your mother didn't strike me the type that would kill her offspring."

"Well, it got pretty close," I mutter. "And they did ground me for a whole month."

"That's not so bad…"

"And Mom said that since I can't go anywhere, I don't need any allowance, so that's off the table as well."

"It could be worse."

"I don't even need to go anywhere to buy stuff," I point out. "I can buy things online."

"I'm pretty sure that's not the point," says Greenshpein.

"Yeah." I nod glumly. "She and Dad gave me a talk about how much they believe in me, and that trust is earned by telling the truth."

"So you told the truth?" he asks. I think he would have smirked if he didn't think it was unprofessional.

"I said that I was gone helping to find Mia, who disappeared while playing hide and seek. And that it was a joint effort, and eventually she was found."

"Ah."

"Well, none of it was a lie," I say in a pathetic act of self-defense.

"You think your mom would agree to that assertion?"

"Who knows what my mom would do?" I ask, frustrated. "You know, I was absolutely sure that after Tom Ellis and after Ron Hammond's body, we'd move out. Go back to LA. But she just waved it off. Like it was a stroke of bad luck or something."

"Well, that's what people who live here do," he says.

"My mom isn't from here," I say. "She's from LA!"

"Well, she seems to be fitting in nicely," he says.

"Then why am I not fitting in?" I ask. "Why don't I act like everything is fine?"

"That's a good question, Amy."

"The police are acting that way too," I say. "They just left in the middle of interrogation. No mentioning of any kidnapping attempt in the news. It's so weird!"

"It's weird." Doctor Greenshpein nods. "But I've seen it happen before."

"Who do you think is hushing it up? The mayor?"

"I'd rather we talk about you," he says.

"Why?" I ask.

"I think that's the point of our sessions," he points out. "People don't usually go to their psychotherapist to talk about kidnappings and conspiracy theories."

"That's a shame," I say. "Your job would be so much interesting if that was the case."

"I don't think so," he answers. "If I want a good conspiracy, I grab a book. I like talking with people, trying to help them figure out how they feel and what they should do about it."

"Okay." I sigh. "Well, I guess things are back to usual. It all happened on Sunday, so… two days ago. Mom agreed to let me stay home yesterday, but today I went to school. It was just another day. No Spanish class yet, but other than that? Just like any other day."

"Good. And at night?"

"No nightmares, if that's what you're asking," I say, thinking about Jennifer. She called me yesterday to let me know that her nightmares stopped. "Slept great last night."

"Good."

"Can I ask something that's not about me?"

He sighs. "Go ahead."

"Mia said that when she looked back, she saw Vivian turn into the dog that chased us. Do you think it was her way of coping?"

"If it was, it sounds like a very unusual way," he says and glances at his wristwatch. "Well, I think our session is over. I am really pleased with the way you are handling this. I was concerned that another violent event might cause some memories from the violent incident with Tom Ellis to surface, but I'd say you are really fine."

"Well, I guess that's the real point of our sessions," I say. "To prepare me for terrifying, violent encounters."

He gets up and opens the door. "In this town?" he says. "That actually sounds like a good idea."

Chapter Forty-Seven

"Mia went to school today," Coral tells me on the phone.

"Yeah?"

"Yeah, she seemed fine. I think my mom's way more traumatized than her."

"That's unsurprising, I guess," I say, toying with the bracelet bottle on the table. I turn it upside down and shake it a bit. The bracelet stays inside, of course. "Say, does Mia still claim that Vivian turned into a dog?"

"Yeah, it's becoming the new family joke," she says. "The kid's imagination can sometimes drive me crazy."

"The thing is… There are some missing pieces to this whole thing, right? Like… Why did Vivian kill her mother? Why did she use her dog to do it? Why did she kidnap Mia? And… you know, I didn't see the dog at first. In fact, once I did see it, I don't recall seeing Vivian."

"Yeah? So?"

"What if what Mia said was true? What if Vivian did turn into a—"

"Amy! People do not turn into dogs. You know why? Because we don't live in a sequel to *Twilight*."

"Okay."

"Sometimes weird things happen. And we don't necessarily

know why."
"That's true."
"I'll talk to you later."
"Yeah, bye."
"Bye."

I put the phone on the table. It's true, people don't turn into dogs. But…

Alice Hendrix had a huge cage in her house. And Vivian said her mom messed with dangerous people, that she thought she was in control. What if Alice found out that her daughter could turn into a murderous dog, so she tried to control her, put her in a cage. And one day her daughter managed to get free…

And Rozanne told us that Ron had a dog, but his lover claimed he didn't. And Ron was in a relationship with Vivian. Maybe he knew. Maybe he went on walks with his girlfriend, and people thought he was just walking his dog…

And Vivian didn't have a real reason to kidnap Mia, but Mia did get away from the predator, and Edgar said that the predator didn't like it when its prey got away.

And Vivian told me that I got away too many times, which would make no sense, unless…

I sigh. Only in Narrowdale. I shake the stupid bottle again. God, who buys a bracelet in a bottle? What a stupid thing to do!

Who mopes after a security guy, five years her senior, while this really cute guy is trying to hit on her? Talk about stupid things to do.

I pick up the phone. Put it down. Pick it up again, scroll to Chris's number. Put the phone down. Pick it up again and force myself to dial Chris.

"Hey," he says, answering almost immediately.
"Hey."
"Heard you found Mia."
"Yup."
"That's cool."
"Yeah, it is."

A moment of silence.

"Chris, you feel like dropping by?"
"I don't know, Amy…"

"Please?" I toy with the bottle. "Pretty please with sugar on top?"

"Yeah, okay, on my way."

It takes him fifteen minutes to get to my house, a time which I use wisely by putting on makeup, removing it, putting on different makeup, removing it again, and changing my clothes three times. I take him up to my room. Mom notices, and clears her throat. I keep the door open.

"So..." I say.

"What's up?" he says, sitting on my chair. I'm sitting on the bed, facing him.

"I'm sorry," I say. "I am a bit confused. I mean... I was confused, but now... Well. I don't know."

"You sound confused," Chris notes.

"No, no."

He looks at the bottle on the desk. "Still didn't manage to get it out, huh?"

"It's a bit tricky."

"I should take it back to the store," he says. "Tell them to give me one without a bottle."

"No, I don't think—" I notice something outside my window. I get up, lean out the window. "Oh, god. Chris, that's my neighbor. I was supposed to be looking after his dog, but she got hurt, and I don't want him to find that out without an explanation. Can you wait here for a few minutes?"

"Yeah, sure, I—"

I don't wait for him to end his sentence. I bolt downstairs, fling open the front door and run outside.

"Alex!"

"Amy." He turns and smiles at me. I freeze in my place. He looks terrible. He has a long red scratch on his cheek, and something that looks like a bruise on his neck. His right arm is in a sling. His duffel bag is hanging loosely on his left shoulder.

"How did it go with Moka? Everything all right?"

"Yeah... sure, no problem at all. What happened to you?"

"Nothing. Just some problems. Nothing I couldn't handle. Can you help me with the bag?" At first I'm surprised at the request, but then he suddenly drops the duffel bag, his face twisted in pain. I quickly pick up the bag. He opens the gate and starts limping towards the front door. Moka follows him, barking and yelping in excitement.

"I see she has a bandage on her leg," he says, stopping in front of the door.

"Yeah, she…" I wonder how I should tell him that Moka helped me save a kidnapped girl and locate the remains of a dead body. Oh well. "She helped me save a kidnapped girl and locate the remains of a dead body."

"Yeah?" he says calmly, fishing for his keys. "I'm glad she was useful."

He unlocks the door and walks inside. Moka and I follow him. I drop the duffel bag once I'm inside, and it opens a bit. On top of a large pile of dirty laundry I spot a dark, ugly object. A gun.

"Alex… Where did you go?" I ask, my voice quivering.

"Had to help a friend."

"What kind of friend? What kind of help? What did you do?"

He looks at me, his eyes communicating a vast ocean of exhaustion. "Whatever it took."

"But what… What happened to you—"

"Amy." He sits heavily on a chair, taking his wallet out of his pocket. "There are other places. Places like this one. And sometimes things get out of hand. You'll learn. It'll take time, but you'll learn."

"Learn? What do you mean?"

He raises his eyebrow. "You rescued a kidnapped girl? Found a dead body?"

"I… Yes."

"Did you at any point try to talk to the police? To your parents? Get someone else to handle this?"

"Well… no. Not really."

"Couldn't get away, right? Felt like you had to keep on going? Getting closer and closer to the truth? You had to take care of it yourself?"

A shiver runs down my neck, my heart thumping. "Right," I whisper.

"Yeah." He nods. "You'll learn. I'll help." He takes some bills from his wallet and hands them to me. "Thanks. For helping with

Moka."

"Sure. Thank you," I take the money from his hand. "What do you mean—"

"Not now." He yawns. "I'm tired. I've had a really long trip. You go off, do what girls your age normally do. Buy dresses. Go dancing. We'll talk later."

"But—"

"I'm really tired, Amy."

I apologize, turn and leave. My mind is whirling. How did he know? What's going on here?

But it's true. I felt like I had to take care of it myself. And I did. And I do.

I walk inside and open the storage room. My dad's toolbox is lying on the floor. I open it, get what I need. Close the box. Climb up the stairs. Walk inside my room.

"What was that all about?" asks Chris. He notices the tool in my hand. "What—"

I grab the bottle on the table in one hand. With the other I hit it with the hammer. Not too hard. Just hard enough. It cracks into four pieces. I gingerly take the bracelet from it and put it on my wrist. It looks really nice.

"What do you think?" I ask Chris, showing him my arm.

"I…" He eyes the fragments of the bottle on the table, the hammer in my hand. "It looks… nice…?"

"I think so too," I say, twisting my wrist to look at it. "Hey, listen, you wanna go grab a milkshake?"

"Yeah," he says, looking confused. "Sure…"

"But this time," I say, smiling, "it's my treat."

Do what girls your age normally do.

Sure, whatever.

Wow, What a Finale! It Makes Me Yearn For Another!

Does it? That's great! I'm all for yearning. Subscribe to my newsletter at: www.strangerealm.com/news, and I will let you know as soon as the next book is out, and you'll be able to get it at a steep discount before anyone else!

If you liked this book, consider leaving a review at http://www.amazon.com/dp/B00ZR05W56/

If you want to let me know what you thought of the book, I urge you to contact me at: michael@strangerealm.com

About the Author

My name is Michael Omer, and I'm a writer, journalist and game designer. I wrote and published my first novel when I was sixteen, and figured I'd keep at it. Since then, I have published two more novels and wrote… who can even count how many? I'm happily married to a woman who keeps pushing me to write more, and have three kids who insist I should stop writing and come play with them. I also have two dogs.

Let's not mention the fish. I should really do something about the fish.

Acknowledgments

Like every piece of drivel I manage to write on paper, this would never have become a novel without my wife, Liora. She is my developmental editor, my cheerleader, my most avid reader, my brainstorm partner. How do other writers write books without her? I can't even imagine.

Thanks to Shahar Kober, who, once again, created the book's cover for the sheer joy of helping a friend.

Thanks to my sister, Yael Omer, who helped me with insights and thoughts about teenage girls, read my book and made me rewrite the ending. There are large parts of Amy's character which are based on her.

Thanks to Christine Mancuso for providing invaluable beta reading comments which helped shape this novel into something coherent.

Thanks to Eliza Dee for copyediting this novel. She was patient with my errant punctuation and my grammar crimes, and for that I am thankful.

Thanks to Tammi Labrecque for proofreading this novel, for laughing at my jokes, and for explaining patiently when I should use "Which", and when I should use "That".

Michael Omer

Thanks to my parents for both their invaluable advice and their endless support.

Made in the USA
Middletown, DE
15 July 2015